La sombra del águila

Biblioteca
ARTURO PÉREZ-REVERTE

La sombra del águila

DEBOLS!LLO

Papel certificado por el Forest Stewardship Council®

MIXTO
Papel procedente de
fuentes responsables
FSC
www.fsc.org FSC® C117695

Penguin
Random House
Grupo Editorial

Primera edición en Debolsillo: marzo de 2016
Novena reimpresión: junio de 2022

© 1993, Arturo Pérez-Reverte
© 2016, Penguin Random House Grupo Editorial, S.A.U.
Travessera de Gràcia, 47-49. 08021 Barcelona
Diseño de la cubierta: Penguin Random House Grupo Editorial
Imagen de la cubierta: Jan van Chelminski, *Napoleon's Troops Retreating from Moscow*, 1888-89

Printed in Spain – Impreso en España

ISBN: 978-84-663-3327-6
Depósito legal: B-757-2016

Impreso en Novoprint
Sant Andreu de la Barca (Barcelona)

P 3 3 3 2 7 C

La sombra del águila

*A Fernando Labajos, que era mi
amigo y no llegó a general.*

*Y a la memoria del cabo Belali
Uld Marahbi, muerto en combate
en Uad Ashram, 1976.*

I

El flanco derecho

Estaba allí, de pie sobre la colina, y al fondo ardía Sbodonovo. Estaba allí, pequeño y gris con su capote de cazadores de la Guardia, rodeado de plumas y entorchados, gerifaltes y edecanes, maldiciendo entre dientes con el catalejo incrustado bajo una ceja, porque el humo no le dejaba ver lo que ocurría en el flanco derecho. Estaba allí igual que en las estampas iluminadas, tranquilo y frío como la madre que lo parió, dando órdenes sin volverse, en voz baja, con el sombrero calado, mientras los mariscales, secretarios, ordenanzas y correveidiles se inclinaban respetuosamente a su alrededor. Sí, Sire. En efecto, Sire. Faltaba más, Sire. Y anotaban apresuradamente despachos en hojas de papel, y batidores a caballo con uniforme de húsar apretaban los dientes bajo el barbuquejo del colbac y se persignaban mentalmente antes de picar espuelas y salir disparados ladera abajo entre el humo y los cañonazos, llevando las órdenes, quienes llegaban vivos, a los regimientos de primera línea. La mitad de las veces los despachos estaban garabateados con tanta prisa que nadie entendía una palabra, y las órdenes se cumplían al revés, y así nos lucía el pelo aquella mañana. Pero él no se inmutaba: seguía plantado en la cima de su colina como quien está en la cima del mundo. Él arriba y nosotros abajo viéndolas venir de todos los colores y tamaños. *Le Petit Caporal*, el Pequeño Cabo, lo llamaban los veteranos de su Vieja Guardia. Nosotros lo llamábamos de otra manera. El Maldito Enano, por ejemplo. O *Le Petit Cabrón*.

Le pasó el catalejo al mariscal Lafleur, siempre sonriente y untuoso, pegado a él como su sombra, quien igual le proporcionaba un mapa, que la caja de rapé, que le mamporreaba sin empacho fulanas de lujo en los vivacs, y blasfemó en corso algo del tipo sapristi de la puttana di Dio, o quizá fuera lasaña di la merda di Milano; con el estruendo de cañonazos era imposible cogerle el punto al Ilustre.

—¿Alguien puede decirme —se había vuelto hacia sus edecanes, pálido y rechoncho, y los fulminaba con aquellos ojos suyos que parecían carbones ardiendo cuando se le atravesaba algo en el gaznate— qué diablos está pasando en el flanco derecho?

Los mariscales se hacían de nuevas o aparentaban estar muy ocupados mirando los mapas. Otros, los más avisados, se llevaban la mano a la oreja como si el cañoneo no les hubiera dejado oír la pregunta. Por fin se adelantó un coronel de cazadores a caballo, joven y patilludo, que había estado abajo: ida y vuelta y los ojos como platos, sin chacó y con el uniforme verde hecho una lástima, pero en razonable estado de salud. De vez en cuando se daba golpecitos en la cara tiznada de humo porque aún no se lo creía, lo de seguir vivo.

—La progresión se ve entorpecida, Sire.

Aquello era un descarado eufemismo. Era igual que, supongamos, decir: «Luis XVI se cortó al afeitarse,

Sire». O: «el príncipe Fernando de España es un hombre de honestidad discutible, Sire». La progresión, como sabía todo el mundo a aquellas alturas, se veía entorpecida porque la artillería rusa había machacado concienzudamente a dos regimientos de infantería de línea a primera hora de la mañana, sólo un rato antes de que la caballería cosaca hiciera filetes, literalmente, a un escuadrón del Tercero de Húsares y a otro de lanceros polacos. Sbodonovo estaba a menos de una legua, pero igual daba que estuviese en el fin del mundo. El flanco derecho era una piltrafa, y tras cuatro horas de aguantar el cañoneo se batía en retirada entre los rastrojos humeantes de los maizales arrasados por la artillería. No se puede ganar siempre, había dicho el general Le Cimbel, que mandaba la división, cinco segundos antes de que una granada rusa le arrancara la cabeza, pobre y bravo imbécil, toda la mañana llamándonos muchachos y valientes hijos de Francia, *tenez les gars*, sus y a ellos, la gloria y todo eso. Ahora Le Cimbel tenía el cuerpo tan lleno de gloria como los otros dos mil infelices tirados un poco por aquí y por allá frente a las arruinadas casitas blancas de Sbodonovo, mientras los cosacos, animados por el vodka, les registraban los bolsillos rematando a sablazos a los que aún coleaban. La progresión entorpecida. Agárreme de aquí, mi coronel.

—¿Y Ney? —el Ilustre estaba furioso. Por la mañana le había escrito a Nosequién que esperaba dormir en Sbodonovo esa misma noche, y en Moscú el viernes. Ahora se daba cuenta de que todavía iba a tardar un rato—. ¿Qué pasa con Ney?

Aquella era otra. Las tropas que mandaba Ney habían tomado tres veces a la bayoneta, y vuelto a perder

«¿Alguien puede decirme qué diantre es eso?...»

en memorable carnicería —línea y media en el boletín del Gran Ejército al día siguiente—, la granja que dominaba el vado del Vorosik. Por allí se nos estaban colando los escuadrones de caballería rusos uno tras otro, como en un desfile, todos invariablemente rumbo al flanco derecho. Que a esas horas aún se llamaba flanco derecho como podría llamarse Desastre Derecho o Gran Matadero Según Se Va A La Derecha.

Entonces, empujando una gruesa línea de nubes plomizas que negreaba en el horizonte, un viento frío y húmedo empezó a soplar desde el este, abriendo brechas en la humareda de pólvora e incendios que cubría el valle. El Ilustre extendió una mano, requiriendo el catalejo, y oteó el panorama con un movimiento semicircular —el mismo que hizo ante la rada de Abukir cuando dijo aquello de *«Nelson nos ha jodido bien»*— mientras los mariscales se preparaban lo mejor que podían para encajar la bronca que iba a caerles encima de un momento a otro. De pronto el catalejo se detuvo, fijo en un punto. El Enano apartó un instante el ojo de la lente, se lo frotó, incrédulo, y volvió a mirar.

—¿Alguien puede decirme qué diantre es eso?

Y señaló hacia el valle con un dedo imperioso e imperial, el que había utilizado para señalar las Pirámides cuando aquello de los cuarenta siglos o —en otro orden de cosas— el catre a María Valewska. Todos los mariscales se apresuraron a mirar en aquella dirección, e inmediatamente brotó un coro de mondieus, sacrebleus y nomdedieus. Porque allí, bajo el humo y el estremecedor ronquido de las bombas rusas, entre los cadáveres que el flanco derecho había dejado atrás en el desorden de la retirada, en mitad del infierno desatado frente a Sbodonovo, un solitario, patético y enternecedor batallón con las guerreras azules de la infantería francesa de línea, avanzaba en buen orden, águila al viento y erizado de bayonetas, en línea recta hacia el enemigo.

Hasta el Ilustre se había quedado sin habla. Durante unos interminables segundos mantuvo la vista fija en aquel batallón. Sus rasgos pálidos se habían endurecido, marcándole los músculos en las mandíbulas, y los ojos de águila se entornaron mientras una profunda arruga vertical le surcaba el entrecejo, bajo el sombrero, como un hachazo.

—Se han vu-vuelto lo-locos —dijo el general Labraguette, un tipo del Estado Mayor que siempre tartamudeaba bajo el fuego y en los burdeles, porque en la campaña de Italia lo había sorprendido un bombardeo austríaco en una casa de putas—. Completamente lo-locos, Si-Sire.

El Enano mantuvo la mirada fija en el solitario batallón, sin responder. Después movió lento y majestuoso la augusta cabeza, la misma —evidentemente— en la que él mismo se había ceñido la corona imperial aquel día en Notre Dame, tras arrancarla de las manos del papa Clemente VII, inútil y viejo chocho, ignorante de con quién se jugaba los cuartos. Fíate de los corsos y no corras. Que se lo preguntaran, si no, a Carlos IV, el ex rey de España. O a Godoy, aquel fulano grande y simpaticote con hechuras de semental. El macró de su legítima.

—No —dijo por fin en voz baja, en un tono admirado y reflexivo a la vez—. No son locos, Labraguette —el Petit se metió una mano entre los botones del chaleco, bajo los pliegues del capote gris, y su voz se estremeció de orgullo—. Son soldados, ¿comprende?... Soldados franceses de la Francia. Héroes oscuros, anónimos, que con sus bayonetas forjan la percha donde yo cuelgo la gloria... —sonrió, enternecido, casi con los ojos húmedos—. Mi buena, vieja y fiel infantería.

Iluminada fugazmente desde su interior por los relámpagos de las explosiones, la humareda del combate ocultó por un momento la visión del campo de batalla, y todos, en la colina, se estremecieron de inquietud. En aquel instante, la suerte del pequeño batallón, su epopeya osada y singular, la inutilidad de tan sublime sacrificio, acaparaban hasta el último de los pensamientos. Entonces el viento arrancó jirones de humo abriendo algunos claros en la humareda, y todos los pechos galoneados de oro, alamares y relucientes botonaduras, todos los estómagos bien cebados del mariscalato en pleno, exhalaron al unísono un suspiro de alivio. El batallón seguía allí, firme ante las líneas rusas, tan cerca que en poco tiempo llegaría a distancia suficiente para cargar a la bayoneta.

—Un hermoso su-suicidio —murmuró conmovido el general Labraguette, sorbiéndose con disimulo una lágrima. A su alrededor, los otros mariscales, generales y edecanes asentían graves con la cabeza. El heroísmo ajeno siempre conmueve una barbaridad.

Aquellas palabras rompieron el estado de hipnosis en que parecía sumido el Ilustre.

—¿Suicidio? —dijo sin apartar los ojos del campo de batalla, y soltó una breve risa sarcástica y resuelta, la misma del 18 Brumario, cuando sus granaderos hacían

Imitando la pose del jinete de cierto conocido cuadro de Gericault…

saltar por la ventana a los padres de la patria pinchándolos con las bayonetas en el culo—. Usted se equivoca, Labraguette. Es el honor de Francia —miró a su alrededor como si despertara de un sueño y alzó una mano—. ¡Alaix!

El coronel Alaix, que coordinaba las misiones de enlace, dio un paso al frente y se quitó el sombrero. Era un individuo de ascendencia aristocrática, relamido y pulcro, que lucía un aparatoso mostacho rizado en los extremos.

—¿Sire?

—Averígüeme quiénes son esos valientes.

—Inmediatamente, Sire.

Alaix montó a caballo y galopó ladera abajo, mientras todos en la colina se mordían los galones de impaciencia. Al poco rato estaba de vuelta, sin aliento, con un agujero en mitad de la escarapela tricolor que lucía en el emplumado sombrero. Saltó del caballo antes de que éste se detuviera encabritado entre una nube de polvo, imitando la pose del jinete de cierto conocido cuadro de Gericault. Alaix tenía fama de numerero y fantasma, y nadie lo tragaba en el Estado Mayor. A todos los mariscales les habría encantado verlo partirse una pierna al desmontar.

El Ilustre lo fulminaba con la mirada, impaciente.

—¿Y bien, Alaix?

—No se lo va a creer, Sire —el coronel escupía polvo al hablar—. No se lo va a creer.

—Lo creeré, Alaix. Desembuche.

—No se lo va a creer.

—Le aseguro que sí. Venga.

—Es que es increíble, Sire.

—Alaix —el Ilustre daba impacientes golpecitos sobre el cristal del catalejo—. Le recuerdo que al duque de Enghien lo hice fusilar por menos de eso. Y que con esa mierda de flanco derecho deben de quedar cantidad de vacantes de sargento de cocinas…

Los generales se daban con el codo y sonreían, cómplices. Ya era hora de que le metieran un paquete a aquel gilipollas. Alaix suspiró hondo, hundió la cabeza entre los entorchados de los hombros y se miró la punta del sable.

—Españoles, Sire.

El catalejo fue a caer entre las botas del Ilustre. Un par de mariscales de Francia se abalanzaron a recogerlo, con presencia de ánimo admirable pero estéril. El Enano estaba demasiado boquiabierto para reparar en el detalle.

—Repita eso, Alaix.

Alaix sacó un pañuelo para secarse la frente. Le caían gotas de sudor como puños.

—Españoles, Sire. El 326 batallón de Infantería de Línea, ¿recuerda?… Voluntarios. Aquellos tipos que se alistaron en Dinamarca.

Como obedeciendo a una señal, todos cuantos se hallaban en lo alto de la colina miraron de nuevo hacia el valle. Bajo los remolinos de humo, en filas compactas entre las que relucían sus bayonetas, haciendo caso omiso del diluvio de fuego que levantaba surtidores de tierra y metralla a su alrededor, marchando a través de los rastrojos de maizal sembrados de cadáveres, el 326 batallón de Infantería de Línea —o sea, nosotros— proseguía imperturbable su lento avance solitario hacia los cañones rusos.

II

El 326 de Línea

Hasta ese momento habíamos tenido suerte: las granadas rusas pasaban altas, roncando sobre nuestros chacós, con una especie de *raaas-zaca* parecido al rasgarse de una tela, antes de reventar con un ruido sordo, primero, y algo parecido a una pila de objetos de hojalata cayéndose después. *Cling clang.* Hacían como cling clang y eso era lo malo, porque en realidad el ruido lo levantaba la metralla saltando de acá para allá: algo muy desagradable. Y aunque aún no habíamos tenido impactos directos sobre la formación, de vez en cuando alguno de nosotros lanzaba un grito, llamaba a su madre o blasfemaba, yéndose al suelo con una esquirla en el cuerpo. Poca cosa, de todos modos; apenas seis o siete heridos que, en su mayor parte, se incorporaban cojeando a las filas. Era curioso. Otras veces, al primer rasguño que justificara el asunto, cualquiera de nosotros se quedaba tumbado, dispuesto a quitarse de en medio. Pero aquella mañana, en Sbodonovo, nadie que pudiera tenerse en pie se quedaba atrás. Hay que ver lo que son las cosas de la vida.

Había un humo de mil diablos, y nos estrechábamos cada uno contra el hombro del compañero, apretando los

Seis o siete heridos que, en su mayor parte, se incorporaban cojeando…

dientes y las manos crispadas en torno al fusil con la bayoneta calada. Raas-zaca-bum-cling-clang una y otra vez, y nosotros procurando mantener el paso y la formación a pesar de lo que estaba cayendo. Varias filas por delante veíamos el sombrero del capitán García, buen tipo, un chusquero valiente, pequeñajo y duro como la madre que lo parió, de Soria, con aquellas patillas enormes, de boca de hacha, que casi le tapaban la cara. Raas-zaca-bum-cling-clang. Llevaba el sable en alto y de vez en cuando se volvía a gritarnos algo, pero con aquel jaleo no se oía un carajo, mi capitán, lo único que teníamos claro era adónde íbamos y para qué. A esas alturas suponíamos que los franchutes y los rusos y hasta el emperador de la China habrían visto ya nuestra maniobra y que algo tenía que pasar, pero con tanto humo y tanta leche no teníamos forma de saber lo que ocurría alrededor. Menos mal que a los artilleros ruskis debía de habérseles ido la mano con el vodka, porque tiraban fatal, y nosotros, los del segundo batallón del 326 de Línea, agradecíamos el humo que nos protegía un poco de vez en cuando.

Raaas-zaca-bum. Tanto va el cántaro a la fuente. Cling-clang. La primera granada que nos acertó de lleno hizo un agujero en el ala izquierda de la formación y convirtió en casquería surtida al sargento Peláez y a dos fulanos de su pelotón. Pobre sargento. Todo aquel largo camino, de Écija a Dinamarca por la antigua ruta de los Tercios, y la encerrona de Seelandia, y el campo de prisioneros, y Europa a pinrel para terminar palmando frente a Sbodonovo como un idiota, con el Enano y sus mariscales allá atrás en la colina, mirándote por el catalejo.

Llevaba el sable en alto y de vez en cuando se volvía a gritarnos…

En julio de 1808, cuando el primer motín de la División del Norte contra las tropas francesas —hasta ese momento aliadas—, fue Peláez quien le voló el cerebro de un pistoletazo al comandante Dufour, el gabacho adjunto, que era un perfecto cantamañanas. Habían llegado órdenes de Bernadotte y Pontecorvo para que los 15.000 españoles destacados en Dinamarca jurásemos lealtad a Pepe Botella, es decir, José Bonaparte, hermano del Petit Cabrón, y varios de los regimientos dijimos que ni hasta arriba de jumilla. Que éramos españoles y que los alonsanfán verdes las habían segado. Déjennos volver a España y que cada chucho se lama su propio órgano, mesié, dicho en fino, o sea. Entonces, con la tropa medio amotinada, a Dufour no se le ocurrió otra cosa que darnos el cante con su acento circunflejo:

—¡Peggos espagnoles! ¡Tgaidogues!... ¡Jugaguéis fidelidad al Empegadog y al gey de Espagna Gosé Bonapagte o seguéis fusilados!

En ese plan se puso el franchute. Y a todo esto el coronel Olasso, que era un poco para allá, o sea afrancesado, dudaba entre una cosa y otra. Que si Dufour tiene razón, que si esto y que si lo otro, que si nuestro honor es la disciplina. Total: venga a marear la perdiz. Entonces Peláez solucionó la papeleta yéndose derecho a Dufour y alumbrándole la sesera sin decir esta boca es mía, y al coronel se le quitaron las dudas de golpe. Y es que no hay nada como un buen pistoletazo a bocajarro en el momento oportuno. Es mano de santo.

Raas-zaca-bum-cling-clang. Allí seguían los cañones rusos dale que te pego, y nosotros cada vez más cerca. El pobre Peláez se iba quedando atrás, charcutería fresca entre los maizales quemados, y había llovido mucho desde el follón de Dinamarca. Ustedes no están en antecedentes, claro, pero en su momento aquello dio mucho de qué hablar. Podría resumirse la historia en pocas líneas: Godoy lamiéndole las botas al Enano, Trafalgar, alianza hispano-francesa, quince regimientos españoles destacados en Dinamarca bajo el mando del marqués de La Romana, dos de mayo en Madrid y resulta que los aliados se convierten en sospechosos. Y el Emperador con la mosca tras la oreja.

—Vigílemelos, Bernadotte.

—A la orden, Sire.

—Esos hijoputas ya son difíciles como aliados, así que cuando sepan que les estamos fusilando a los paisanos para que los pinte al óleo ese tipo, Goya, figúrese la que nos pueden organizar.

—Me lo figuro, Sire. Gente bárbara, inculta. Vuestra Majestad sabe lo que necesitan: un rey justo y noble, como vuestro augusto hermano José.

—Deje de darme coba y mueva el culo, Bernadotte. Lo hago a usted responsable.

Fue más o menos así. A todo esto, nosotros estábamos dispersos un poco por aquí y por allá guarneciendo Jutlandia y Fionia. Había pasado ya el tiempo feliz de las cogorzas de ginebra y las Gretchen rubias, de caderas confortables, que nos revolcábamos —a menudo ellas a nosotros— en los pajares locales. Ahora se olía próxima la chamusquina, las Gretchen se encerraban en sus casas con los legítimos, y los barcos ingleses patrullaban la costa sin que nosotros tuviésemos muy claro si había que darles candela cumpliendo órdenes o pedirles que nos recibieran a bordo para ir a España. El caso es que a partir de mayo los gabachos empezaron a desconfiar de nuestros contactos con los británicos. Que si usted le ha enviado un mensaje a aquel barco inglés. Que a usted qué coño le importa, Duchamp, lo que yo envíe o deje de enviar. Que si tal y que si cual, mondieu. Que yo me carteo con quien me da la gana. Que si su honog de soldado, Magtinez. Que si me voy a tener que cagar en tus muertos, franchute de mierda. Total. Empezaron a detener oficiales, a desarmar unidades y a exigirnos juramento de lealtad, que a esas alturas era como pedirle peras al olmo. En vista del panorama, La Romana nos hizo jurar que permaneceríamos fieles a Fernando VII y que íbamos a intentar llegar a España como fuera, para ajustarles allí las cuentas a los gabachos.

—Nos abrimos, López. Disponga la evacuación.

—A la orden, mi general.

—Hay que largarse con lo puesto y aprisa, así que avise a los jefes y oficiales. El plan es capturar Langeland y concentrar en la isla a nuestros quince mil hombres para embarcar en la flota inglesa y salir por pies.

—Espero que los británicos cumplan su palabra, mi general.

—Eso esperamos todos. Sería muy incómodo liar la que vamos a liar para quedarnos en tierra.

—Viva España, mi general.

—Que sí, que viva. Pero espabile.

Fue bonito para quienes lo lograron. Nos hicimos con Langeland en un golpe de mano y todas las unidades dispersas por la costa danesa recibieron orden de acudir allí como quien acaba de patear un avispero. Los primeros en llegar fueron los del Batallón Ligero de Barcelona, y siguieron otros, infiltrándose entre las líneas y guarniciones francesas, desarmando a sus adjuntos gabachos y a las tropas danesas que no se quitaban de en medio. En varias ocasiones hubo que aplicar sin contemplaciones el sistema Peláez, pero el caso fue que entre el 7 y el 13 de agosto, en una de las mayores evasiones de la historia militar —el tal Jenofonte sólo se largó de Persia con 810 hombres más—, 9.190 españoles lograron llegar a Langeland para embarcar en los buques ingleses. Lo malo es que otros 5.175 nos quedamos a medio camino: los Regimientos de Guadalajara y Asturias —apresados por los daneses en Seelandia tras el motín donde Peláez disparó su pistoletazo—, el Regimiento del Algarve —atrapado en la ratonera de Jutlandia—, el destacamento que el mariscal Bernadotte tenía incorporado a su guardia personal, los heridos y los rezagados, amén de algunas pequeñas unidades que, como la nuestra, la sección ligera del Regimiento Montado de Villaviciosa, tuvieron mala suerte.

Lo cierto es que los de la Ligera estuvimos a punto de conseguirlo. Llegamos a la costa con el resto del regimiento y los daneses y los mondieus pegados a los talones, bang-bang y todo el mundo corriendo, maricón el último, para averiguar que los barcos daneses en los que íbamos a atravesar el brazo de mar hasta la isla se habían rajado, dejándonos sin transporte. Nuestros antiguos aliados estaban a punto de echarnos el guante como a los compañeros del Algarve, abandonados por sus jefes y conducidos hasta el embarcadero por un oscuro capitán con muchas agallas, el capitán Costa, donde tuvieron que rendirse —después de que Costa se pegara un tiro— cercados por los franchutes y sus mamporreros daneses. A nosotros estaba a punto de ocurrirnos lo mismo, pero nuestro coronel Armendáriz, que a pesar de ser barón los tenía bien puestos y no estaba dispuesto a pudrirse en un pontón gabacho, ordenó echar los caballos al agua y cruzar el canal nadando, agarrados a las crines y a las sillas. Y allá fue el regimiento. Algunos se ahogaron, otros fueron alejados por la corriente, o les fallaron las fuerzas. Nosotros, los de la sección ligera, recibimos la orden de sacrificarnos para proteger a los que se iban.

—Te ha tocado, Jiménez. Cubrís la retirada.

—No jodas.

—Como te lo cuento.

Y allí nos quedamos a regañadientes, en la playa, cubriendo la retaguardia, aguantando como pudimos más por el qué dirán que por otra cosa, peleando a la desesperada hasta que la mayor parte del Villaviciosa estuvo a salvo en la isla. Entonces los pocos de nosotros que sabían nadar echaron a correr para tirarse al agua con los últimos caballos, a probar suerte, aunque de éstos ya no llegó ninguno. El resto hicimos de tripas corazón, levantamos los brazos y nos rendimos.

Fuimos a Hamburgo, a inaugurar un campo de prisioneros nuevecito y asqueroso, para comernos cuatro años a pulso, con otros infelices deportados de la guerra de España. Tiene gracia: después, cuando Napoleón se cayó con todo el equipo, los alemanes juraban y perjuraban que ellos siempre estuvieron contra el Petit Cabrón. Pero había cantidad de ellos en el ejército gabacho. En Hamburgo, sin ir más lejos, nos vigilaban centinelas alemanes y franceses, y cuando alguno de nosotros lograba evadirse, eran los vecinos de los pueblos cercanos los que muchas veces nos denunciaban, o nos devolvían al campo a patadas en el culo. Ahora tengo entendido que allí nadie recuerda que haya habido nunca un campo de prisioneros españoles en Hamburgo, y es que los Fritz son estupendos para el paso de la oca, pero andan siempre fatal de memoria. En fin. El caso es que estábamos bien jodidos en nuestro campo de prisioneros cuando, en 1812, al Enano va y se le ocurre invadir Rusia. Cuando se preparan invasiones a gran escala, la carne de cañón se cotiza bien. Así que los veteranos de la División del Norte que habíamos sobrevivido al frío, el tifus y la tuberculosis, tuvimos nuestra oportunidad: seguir pudriéndonos allí o combatir con uniforme gabacho.

—A ver. Voluntarios para Rusia.

—¿Para dónde?

—Para Rusia.

Dos mil y pico preguntamos dónde había que firmar. Después de todo, de perdidos al río.

En cuanto a ríos, con la *Grande Armée* habíamos terminado vadeando unos cuantos. La santa Rusia estaba llena de rusos que nos disparaban y de malditos ríos donde nos mojábamos las botas. Antes del Moskova y Moscú, el último era aquel Vorosik que circundaba en parte Sbodonovo, por cuyo vado seguían colándose los escuadrones de cosacos que tenían el flanco derecho francés hecho una piltrafa, mientras en su colina del puesto de mando el Petit nos miraba admirado por el catalejo, preguntándole a Alaix quiénes coño éramos esos tipos estupendos que, a pesar de la que nos estaba cayendo encima, avanzábamos imperturbables, en perfecto orden, hacia las líneas enemigas.

Y sin embargo, la respuesta era sencilla. En medio del desastre del flanco derecho del ejército napoleónico, cruzando los maizales batidos por la artillería rusa, en formación y a paso de ataque, los cuatrocientos cincuenta españoles del segundo batallón del 326 de Infantería de Línea, no efectuábamos, en rigor, un acto de heroísmo. Para qué vamos a ponernos flores a estas alturas del asunto. La cosa era mucho más simple: ningún herido que pudiera andar se quedaba atrás, y avanzábamos en línea recta hacia las posiciones rusas, porque estábamos intentando desertar en masa. Aprovechando el barullo de la batalla, el segundo del 326, en buen orden y con tambores y banderas al viento, se estaba pasando al enemigo. Con dos cojones.

III

La sugerencia del mariscal Murat

Total. Que estábamos allá abajo, a dos palmos de las líneas rusas y aguantando candela mientras intentábamos pasarnos al enemigo como el que no quiere la cosa, y desde su colina, sin percatarse de nuestras intenciones, el Estado Mayor imperial nos tomaba por héroes. Los generales se miraban unos a otros sin dar crédito a lo que estaban viendo. Regardez, Dupont. Oh-la-la les espagnols, quién lo iba a decir. Siempre protestando, que si esta no es su guerra, que si vaya mierda de rancho, y ahora mírelos, atacando en plena derrota, con un par. Nomdedieu. Quién lo hubiera dicho cuando los alistamos para Rusia casi a la fuerza, o esto o pudrirse en Hamburgo. Y se daban unos a otros palmaditas en la espalda porque así, desde su punto de vista, no era para menos, con aquel flanco derecho que estaba literalmente hecho trizas, maizales humeantes llenos de muertos como si alguien se hubiera estado paseando por allí con una máquina de picar carne, los cañones de los Iván dale que te pego y el segundo del 326 siempre adelante, recto hacia el enemigo con la que estaba cayendo. Oh, les espagnols. Que son braves, los tíos. Quién nos lo iba a decir, Dubois. Vivir para ver. Togueadogues, eso es lo que son. Unos togueadogues.

Por su parte, el Enano no nos quitaba ojo. Cada vez que el humo de las granadas rusas cubría el valle frente a Sbodonovo, arrugaba la frente imperial pegándose el catalejo a la cara, inquieto por la suerte del pequeño batallón solitario que aguantaba el tipo frente a las líneas enemigas donde todos sus anfansdelapatrí habían salido por piernas. Ese gesto lo repetía a cada instante, pues aquella mañana los artilleros ruskis quemaban pólvora con entusiasmo, y con tanta granada y tanto raas-zacabum y tanto *pobieda tovarich* en el flanco derecho, había ratos en que el Petit y su Estado Mayor tenían la misma visión del flanco en cuestión que podía tener una fuente de salmonetes fritos. La verdad es que, desde aquella colina, el panorama del campo de batalla era impresionante: maizales chamuscados que humeaban, filas azules en retirada por la derecha o sosteniendo la línea en el centro y a la izquierda, los campos salpicados de manchitas azules más pequeñas, individuales e inmóviles. Heridos y muertos a granel, casi tres mil a aquellas alturas del asunto, y todavía quedaba tajo para un buen rato. De pronto los cañones del zar soltaban una andanada en condiciones, las filas azules del 326 desaparecían bajo la humareda, y todo el mundo en la colina, bordados y entorchados en pleno del mariscalato imperial, contenía el aliento imitando al fulano de capote gris y enorme sombrero que oteaba el paisaje con el ceño fruncido. Después, un poco de brisa abría claros entre el humo para mostrarles al 326 que proseguía su avance en buen orden, el Petit sonreía un poco, así, a su manera, torciendo la boca como si acabara de confirmar una corazonada, y todos los pechos galoneados en oro, todos los comparsas que lo rodeaban a la espera de un ducado en Holstein, una pensión vitalicia o un enchufe para su yerno en Fontainebleau, suspiraban a coro compartiendo solícitos su alivio, mais oui, Sire, voila les braves y todo eso.

—Los va-van a de-descuartizar —tartamudeó el general Labraguette, resumiendo el pensamiento de los que estaban en la colina.

Labraguette era el optimista del Estado Mayor imperial, así que la cosa estaba clara. El 326 tenía por delante menos futuro que María Antonieta la mañana que le cortaron el pelo en la Conciergerie. Sin embargo, al oír a Labraguette decir aquello, el Enano se puso el catalejo bajo el brazo y apoyó el mentón en un puño, frunciendo el ceño. Era el gesto que siempre ponía para salir en los grabados y ganar batallas, y solía costarle a Francia entre cinco y seis mil muertos y heridos cada vez.

—Hay que hacer algo por esos héroes —dijo por fin—. ¡Alaix!

—A la orden, Sire.

—Envíeles un mensaje para que retrocedan honorablemente. No merece la pena que se hagan matar de ese modo... Y usted, Labraguette, busque a alguien de la División Borderie para que proteja su retirada.

Labraguette dudaba en abrir la boca.

—Me te-temo que es imposible, Sire —se aventuró por fin.

—¿Imposible? —el Enano lo miraba con la simpatía de doce mosquetones en un pelotón de fusilamiento—. Esa palabra no existe en el diccionario.

Labraguette, que a pesar de ser general era un tipo leído, miraba al Ilustre, perplejo.

«Hay que hacer algo por esos héroes», dijo por fin…

—Yo ju-juraría que sí, Sire. Imposible: algo que no es po-posible.

—Le digo que no existe —el Enano fulminaba a Labraguette con la mirada—. Y si esa palabra existe, cosa que dudo, va usted a la Academia y me la borra... ¿Se entera, Labraguette?

Labraguette ya no estaba perplejo. Ahora se retorcía una patilla con visible angustia.

—Na-naturalmente, Sire.

—Los listillos me repatean el hígado, Labraguette.

—Di-disculpad, Sire —el general había pasado ya del estado de angustia al estado viscoso—. Fue un ma-malalentendido. Ejem. Un la-lapsus lingüe.

—Por un lapsus parecido a ese trasladé al coronel Coquelon a Sierra Morena, en España. Por allí anda, echando carreras por el monte con los guerrilleros.

—Glu-glups, Sire.

—Bien. ¿Qué pasa con la división Borderie?

—Que el 202 de Línea se lo he-hemos enviado a Ney a reconquistar la gr-gr-granja del Vorosik, Sire.

El Ilustre echó un vistazo en esa dirección y soltó entre dientes una de sus maldiciones corsas, algo del tipo mascalzone dil fetuccine de la puttana. Entre las llamas de la granja y la humareda de los maizales, junto al vado del Vorosik se veía algo azul mezclado con el centelleo de los sables de la caballería cosaca. En ese momento, el 202 de Línea no estaba para reforzar a nadie.

—¿Y qué hay del 34 Ligero?

—Hecho po-polvo, Sire. Ba-bajas del sesenta por ci-ciento.

—¿Qué me dice del 42 Regimiento de Granaderos a Caballo?

—Eso era ayer por la ma-mañana, Sire. Ahora son gr-granaderos a pie y apenas su-suman una co-compañía.

—¿Y el tercero de Dragones de Florencia?

—Pues corriendo van todos, Sire —Labraguette tragó saliva, señalando la dirección opuesta al campo de batalla—. Camino de Florencia.

El Ilustre miró al cielo y maldijo en arameo durante diez minutos sin que nadie osara interrumpirlo. Algo así como cazzo dil saltimboca de la madre que los parió y qué he hecho yo para merecer esto. Domingueros. Eso es lo que son todos. Unos domingueros de mierda que me van a hacer perder la batalla.

—Hay que hacer algo —dijo por fin, cuando recobró el aliento—. No puedo dejar solos a esos bravos allá abajo. Españoles o no, si luchan bajo mis águilas son hijos míos. Y mis hijos —hizo una pausa, y pareció que su mirada aquilina perforaba la humareda de pólvora del flanco derecho— son hijos de Francia.

El mariscalato en pleno mostró su aprobación con los murmullos apropiados. Hijos de Francia, naturalmente. Ese era el término justo. Brillante juego de palabras, Sire. Esa agudeza corsa, etcétera. El Enano cortó en seco el rumor de la claque levantando enérgico una mano.

—¿Alguna sugerencia? —preguntó, dirigiendo una mirada circular a los miembros de su Estado Mayor. Todos carraspearon adoptando gestos graves, igual que si tuviesen las sugerencias a montones en la punta de la lengua, pero nadie dijo esta boca es mía. La última vez que el Ilustre había hecho esa pregunta, en Smolensko, el general Cailloux había aconsejado «una táctica de flanqueo astuta como una zorra». Ejecutada sobre el terreno y encomendada a Cailloux su ejecución, la táctica había terminado convirtiéndose en un movimiento de retirada rápido como una liebre. Ahora, si es que aún continuaba vivo, degradado a capitán, Cailloux seguía un cursillo acelerado de tácticas de flanqueo sobre el terreno y en primera línea. Concretamente, en algún lugar del jodido flanco derecho.

—¡Murat!

El mariscal Murat, emperifollado como para un desfile, se cuadró con un taconazo. Iba de punta en blanco, con uniforme de húsar y entorchados hasta en la bragueta. Se rizaba el pelo con tenacillas y lucía un aro de oro en una oreja. Parecía un gitano guaperas vestido por madame Lulú para hacer de príncipe encantado en una opereta italiana.

—¿Sire?

El Enano hizo un gesto con la mano que sostenía el catalejo, en dirección al humo que en ese momento ocultaba de nuevo las filas azules del 326.

—Piense algo, Murat. Inmediatamente.

—¿Sire?

—Es una orden.

Murat arrugó el entrecejo y se puso a pensar, con visible esfuerzo. Era valiente como un choto joven, y punto. Lo suyo eran las cargas, la masacre, la vorágine. Le había costado mucho hacerse perdonar por el Ilustre su brillante gestión de orden público el 2 de mayo de 1808 en Madrid. *«Esto lo arreglo yo con dos escopetazos, Sire»,* había escrito, eufórico, ese mismo día a las doce de la

Parecía un gitano guaperas vestido por madame Lulú...

mañana. Todavía se atragantaba al recordar cómo después, cuando fue a rendir cuentas a su despacho de Fontainebleau, el Enano le había hecho comerse la famosa carta, a pedacitos.

—Estoy esperando, Murat.

El Enano se golpeaba el faldón del capote gris con el catalejo, impaciente, y los generales y mariscales asistían a la escena con mal disimulado regocijo, esperando por dónde se arrancaba el de los rizos. A ver si el niño bonito sugería también una táctica de flanqueo astuta como el pobre Cailloux. Voluntarios ni al rancho, rezaba el viejo dicho de cuartel. A ellos se la iban a dar, viejos chusqueros, con la mili que llevaban a cuestas desde el 92, el que más y el que menos ya era sargento cuando el Petit cazaba talentos en el sitio de Tolon y ellos asaltaban trincheras inglesas a la bayoneta, le-jour-de-gluar y todo eso, los buenos tiempos republicanos antes del Consulado y el Imperio y tanto ascender y amariconarse y echar tripa. Tampoco había llovido desde entonces, ni nada. Quién nos ha visto y quién nos ve, Laclós, ahora con galones y entorchados, mirando el flanco derecho por catalejo, o sea.

—Murat.

—Sí, Sire.

—Sugiera algo de una puñetera vez.

Se daban con el codo los mariscales, como cuando el coronel Alaix estuvo a punto de ganarse un paquete a la vuelta del reconocimiento. Lo bueno de esas cosas era que cuando el Petit estaba de malas, el escalafón corría que daba gusto. El secreto estaba en cerrar la boca, la gueule, mon vieux, y pasar desapercibido. Mire a Murat,

Lafleur, el rato que está pasando. El Rizos a punto de cagar las plumas. Seguro que sugiere una carga de caballería. Murat siempre está sugiriendo cargas. Tienen la ventaja de que se hacen en línea recta. No hay que calentarse mucho la cabeza, y después uno sale estupendo en los óleos de Meissonier. No hay como una carga de caballería para quedar bien delante del Enano.

—Sugiero una carga, Sire.

Los mariscales se guiñaban el ojo. Ya se lo dije, Leschamps, etcétera. Más simple que el mecanismo de un sonajero. El ilustre miró un par de segundos a Murat y después señaló hacia la humareda del valle con el pulgar, por encima del hombro.

—Perfecto. Hágalo.

El Rizos tragó saliva, con ruido. Una cosa era sugerir que alguien echara una galopada por el flanco derecho, y otra muy distinta descubrir que era él quien llevaba todas las papeletas en la tómbola.

—¿Perdón?

El Enano lo miró de arriba abajo. Tardó un rato.

—Parece un poco sordo esta mañana, Murat. ¿No acaba de proponerme una carga?… Pues suba a su caballo, póngase al frente de unos cuantos escuadrones, saque el sable y échele una mano a aquellos valientes del 326. Ya sabe. Tatarí tatarí. Usted tiene práctica en eso.

Murat hizo de tripas corazón, dio otro taconazo, se puso el colbac y subió a caballo. A media legua, al otro lado de la colina, estaban Fuckermann con el Cuarto de Húsares y Baisepeu con dos regimientos de caballería pesada con las corazas y los cascos reluciendo entre la hierba, acero bruñido como un espejo —fróteme eso,

Legrand— listo para cubrirse de polvo y de sangre según las ordenanzas. Así que, de perdidos al Vorosik, se fue para ellos con un trotecillo corto y elegante, la mano en la cadera y la pelliza bailándole con garbo sobre el hombro izquierdo, con todo el Estado Mayor imperial viéndolo irse, las cosas como son, Laclós, cenutrio y hortera sí que es, el tío, pero los tiene bien puestos. Y además, una suerte de cojón de pato. Igual hasta le sale bien la maniobra.

—Conspicua gesta —apuntó el general Donzet—. Aunque resulte estéril, será hermosa.

Y suspiró hondo, dramático, para la posteridad. Donzet siempre lo hacía todo pensando en la posteridad, un auténtico pelmazo que, por otra parte, nunca acertaba un pronóstico. Se escurría el magín durante horas y horas hasta idear una frase lapidaria, y las soltaba, a veces sin venir a cuento, con la secreta esperanza de que alguna terminase figurando en los libros de Historia. Es de justicia consignar que lo consiguió, por fin, tres años más tarde, en Waterloo. Aquello de *«Wellington está acabado, Sire. Muy mal se nos tiene que dar»*, lo dijo él. Fino estratega.

IV

La gitana del comandante Gerard

Cuentan los libros, al referirse a la campaña de 1812 en Rusia, que acudiendo en socorro de un batallón aislado —el nuestro—, Murat dirigió en Sbodonovo una de las más heroicas cargas de caballería de la Historia, ya saben, mucho sus y a ellos, galope de caballos y un zaszas de sablazos entre humo y toques de corneta. Después llega Gericault, es un suponer, pinta con eso un cuadro que van y cuelgan en el Louvre, y entonces todo el mundo, oh, celui-la, mondieu que es hermosa la guerra, tan heroica y demás.

Heroica mis narices, Dupont. Estábamos nosotros, si ustedes recuerdan, los del segundo batallón del 326 de Línea, a unas quinientas varas de las líneas rusas, y los de las primeras filas nos preguntábamos ya cómo diablos podía hacerse, en mitad de aquel fregado, para demostrarle al enemigo que íbamos en son de paz, dispuestos a pasarnos a sus filas con armas y bagajes. A esas alturas ya no quedaba en el regimiento ningún jefe ni oficial francés que lo impidiera. El primer batallón, compuesto por italianos y suizos, había sido aniquilado junto al Vorosik. El resto del 326 lo componíamos los del segundo, y en cuanto a jefes y oficiales no españoles el asunto estaba

No quedaba en el regimiento ningún jefe ni oficial francés…

resuelto desde hacía rato, porque justo antes de largarnos hacia el Iván, aprovechando el barullo cuando el flanco derecho empezó a irse al carajo, tanto el coronel Oudin como el comandante Gerard habían recibido cada uno su correspondiente tiro por la espalda. Una cosa limpia, bang y angelitos al cielo, más que nada por evitar que entorpecieran la maniobra. Lo del coronel era lo de menos, porque el tal Oudin era una mala bestia, normando, creo recordar, que no se fiaba ni de su padre, uno de esos que estaba todo el día dale que dale con lo de «peggos espagnoles, necesitáis disciplina» y cosas por el estilo. Ya cuando el paso del Niemen, Oudin había hecho fusilar a media docena de compañeros que intentaron tomar las de Villadiego y volver a España por su cuenta. Así que nadie lamentó verlo pararse de pronto, echar una mirada perpleja a la formación que marchaba cerrada a su espalda, y caer redondo en los maizales como un saco de patatas, el hijo de la gran puta, siempre dando la barrila como aquel idiota de comandante, Dufour, a quien el sargento Peláez le alumbró la sesera de un pistoletazo cuando el primer motín de Dinamarca.

Total, que pasamos por el maizal junto al fiambre del coronel y también junto al del comandante Gerard. Aquello si era una lástima porque Gerard no era mala gente, sino uno de esos franchutes alegres y amables que había combatido en España, mayo de 1808 en el parque de Monteleón —una escabechina que nos contaba con detalle, admirado del valor de nuestros paisanos—, y escapado después de Bailén por los pelos, cuando Castaños hizo que el ejército gabacho, con todos sus entorchados y sus águilas invictas, se comiera una derrota como el sombrero de un picador.

—Que conste, guenegal Castanios, que me guindo pog evitag deggamamiento de sangge...

—Que sí, hombre, que sí. Venga, entrégueme la espada de una vez.

Gerard tuvo la suerte de salir como correo, a caballo, cruzando entre enjambres de guerrilleros que bajaban del monte como lobos a un festín, y el desastre lo cogió al otro lado de Despeñaperros, evitándole ir a pudrirse a Cabrera con el resto de sus compañeros franceses. Pobre Gerard. Mala suerte: salvar el pellejo en Bailén, cruzar Despeñaperros sin que los guerrilleros se hicieran unas borlas para el zurrón con sus pelotas, para terminar con un tiro nuestro en la espalda, justo en el momento en que se disponía a volverse para decirnos vamos, chicos, será duro pero nos queremos unos a otros, hagamos un esfuerzo más, qué coño. Estamos intentando construir Europa y todo eso. En fin. Adiós al valiente Gerard, franchute que hablaba español y le gustaba sentarse a vivaquear con nosotros escuchando la guitarra de Pedro el cordobés y que una vez, nos contaba, se tiró a una española guapísima en el Sacromonte, una gitana de ojos verdes con la que aún soñaba en las noches al raso de esta jodida Rusia. Y ahora pasábamos a su lado, tendido en el maizal tras haberle pegado un tiro, y nuestro único homenaje era apartar la vista para no encontrar sus ojos abiertos como un reproche.

Raas-zaca-bum. Cling-clang. Otra granada rusa reventó a la izquierda, tirándonos encima metralla y cascotes, y alguien gritó en las filas sacad de una maldita vez una jodida bandera blanca porque los ruskis nos van a freír como sigamos así. Pero el tambor mantenía el ritmo de paso de ataque porque el plan era aguantar hasta el límite como si de veras estuviésemos atacando, con el águila al viento y toda la parafernalia, sin descubrir el pastel por si las cosas se torcían en el último momento. Nadie deseaba terminar como aquellos ciento treinta desgraciados del regimiento José Napoleón, entre Vilna y Vitebsk y hasta arriba ya de tanta marcha y tanta contramarcha y tanta *Grande Armée*, y tanto cascarles a los Popof. A fin de cuentas, como nuestros paisanos allá abajo, los ruskis se limitaban a defender su tierra contra el Enano y los mariscales y toda la pandilla de mangantes de París, los Fouchés y los Tayllerand, con sus medallas y sus combinaciones de salón y toda su mierda bajo los encajes y las medias de seda y las puntillas. No era un trabajo simpático, aunque teóricamente íbamos ganando nosotros, o nuestros casuales aliados franchutes. Te cepillabas un regimiento ruso y después, al rematar a los heridos a la bayoneta, veías las caras de campesinos que te recordaban a tus paisanos de Aragón o de La Mancha. *Niet, niet*, te rogaban los desgraciados, *tovarich, tovarich*, y levantaban desde el suelo las manos ensangrentadas, llorando. Algunos no eran más que críos con los mocos y los ojos desorbitados por el miedo, y a veces tú hacías como que dabas el bayonetazo, pinchando un terrón, o su mochila, y procurabas pasar de largo, pero otras tenías encima del cogote la mirada de algún jefazo gabacho, ya sabéis mes enfants, nada de cuartel. *Pas de quartier.* Se han cargado al general Nosequiencogne, y hay que vengarlo facturando a unos cientos de estos eslavos. Eso de

Una gitana de ojos verdes con la que aún soñaba…

vengar a los generales tenía lo suyo: cuando palmaba uno con gorro de plumas todo era hay que vengarlo y demás, que si el honor de la *Grande Armée* y todo eso. Pero a los cientos de desgraciados de a pie que cascábamos a diario en la tropa podían perfectamente darnos *boudin*, que es como en el ejército franchute llaman a la morcilla. Total. Que tú andabas por allí, tomando, es un suponer, el reducto de Borodino a puro huevo, y habías dejado en el camino y en el asalto a trescientos compañeros y no pasaba nada. Pero si los Iván le habían dado candela a uno de nuestros generales, siempre había un gilipollas que gritaba lo de *pas de quartier* cuando algún oficial estaba cerca de ti para comprobar cómo ejecutabas la orden, y bueno, pues suspirabas hondo y le metías al *niet tovarich* que se rendía la bayoneta por las tripas, y santas pascuas.

El caso es que entre Vilna y Vitebsk algunos de los españoles de Dinamarca ya estábamos hasta las polainas de todo aquello, y además las noticias que llegaban desde España no eran como para levantarnos la moral de combate: iglesias saqueadas, mujeres a las que compañías enteras se pasaban por la piedra, los sitios de Gerona y Zaragoza, la resistencia de Cádiz, los ingleses en la Península y la guerra de guerrillas. O sea, todo cristo luchando allí para echar a los gabachos, y nosotros con su uniforme y su bandera, acuchillando rusos sin que nadie nos hubiese dado vela en aquel entierro, que a poco que nos descuidáramos iba a ser el nuestro. La mayor parte lamentábamos ya no habernos quedado de prisioneros en Hamburgo, porque a ver con qué cara llegábamos a España cuando ya estuviese liberada, contándoles que habíamos estado luchando en Rusia con el otro bando. Imagínense la papeleta. Nosotros no queríamos, nos obligaron, etcétera. Se lo juro a usted, señor juez. Eso sí llegábamos hasta un juez, aunque fuera el de un consejo de guerra. Porque vete a contarle eso a un ex contrabandista de Carmona que lleva cuatro o seis años echado al monte, degollando franceses con la cachicuerna después de que le ahorcaran al padre, le mataran a la mujer y le violaran a la hija. Seguro que si asomábamos por allí las orejas, con nuestro curriculum íbamos derechos de Hendaya o Canfranc al paredón. Eso, rápido y con mucha suerte si le caíamos en gracia al del Carmona. Menudos eran nuestros paisanos.

Total que, entre Vilna y Vitez, ciento y pico españoles, no del 326 sino de otro regimiento, el José Napoleón, intentaron abrirse por las bravas. Salió mal la cosa y terminaron por meter la pata del todo al disparar sobre los franceses encargados de cortarles el paso. Así que, tras rendirse, los hicieron formar y fusilaron a uno de cada dos, por sorteo. Tú sí, tú no. Tú sí, tú no. Carguen, apunten, bang. Después nos hicieron desfilar junto a los fiambres para que el paisaje sirviera de escarmiento. Aquella noche, en el vivac, ni siquiera Pedro el cordobés tuvo ganas de tocar la guitarra, y el comandante Gerard se pasó todo el rato callado, por una vez sin darnos la paliza con la historia de su gitana de ojos verdes.

Así nos fuimos acercando a Moscú, cada vez más convencidos de pasarnos a los rusos a la primera ocasión. Después de la carnicería de Borodino estuvo más claro que nunca: treinta mil bajas nosotros entre muertos y heridos y sesenta mil los rusos. Aquello fue excesivo, y algunos mariscales empezaron a murmurar que el Ilustre estaba perdiendo los papeles. Y si los de los galones y entorchados se mosqueaban, pues figúrense nosotros, que nos habíamos comido el baile de cabo a rabo. Así que los españoles del 326 fuimos corriendo la voz, hay que quitarse de en medio a la primera ocasión, pero con más tacto. El aniquilamiento de nuestro primer batallón en Sbodonovo puso las cosas más fáciles, de modo que convencimos al capitán García, les arreglamos el cuerpo al coronel Oudin y al pobre comandante Gerard, y nos fuimos hacia los Iván aprovechando la coyuntura. El problema residía en escoger el momento adecuado para dar el cante. Demasiado pronto, nos cascaban los franceses. Demasiado tarde, los rusos. Lo difícil era encontrar el término medio. Lo malo de estas cosas es que, hasta que el rabo pasa, todo es toro.

Y en esas estábamos en el flanco derecho, con el Petit Cabrón mirándonos por el catalejo desde su colina, cuando de pronto, en la retaguardia, los húsares del Cuarto y los coraceros de Baisepeau, que llevan toda la batalla contemplando el paisaje, ven que aparece Murat muy airoso a caballo y se dicen unos a otros la jodimos, Labruyere, vienen a invitarnos al baile. Estar aquí pintándola era demasiado bonito para que durase. Y el Rizos que llega con el sable desenvainado y los arenga:

—¡Hijos de Francia! ¡El Emperador os está mirando!

Y los húsares y los coraceros moviendo la cabeza, hay que fastidiarse, Leduc, podía mirar para otra parte, el Enano, con lo grande que es el campo de batalla y toda la maldita Rusia, fíjate, y se pone a mirarnos precisamente a nosotros. Y Murat que apunta con el sable hacia el sitio de la batalla donde el humo es más espeso, o sea, el flanco derecho donde dicen que hay unos cuatrocientos zumbados que, en lugar de salir por pies como todo el mundo, se empeñan, con lo que está cayendo, en ganarse la Legión de Honor a título póstumo. Para que los hagan mortadela no nos necesitan a nosotros. Pero el caso es que Murat hace caracolear el caballo y dice eso que todos estaban viendo venir:

—¡Cuarto de Húsares! ¡Monten!... ¡Quinto y Décimo de Coraceros! ¡Monten!

O sea, traducido, Leduc, que hay que ganarse el jornal. Y todo son ahora trompetazos y tambores y relinchos y cagüentodo en voz baja, y el Rizos con sus alamares y sus floripondios saludado por Fuckermann y Baisepeau, que se ponen al frente de sus respectivas formaciones y sacan los sables. Y alguien comunica que la carga es contra los cañones rusos del flanco derecho y ya te lo decía yo, Labruyere, que esos españoles bajitos y morenos del 326 nos iban a buscar un día la ruina, ya me contarás qué coño hacen en Rusia esos fulanos, y encima tirándose el pegote como héroes, hay que fastidiarse, en vez de estar en su tierra con el Empecinado o pudriéndose en el campo de prisioneros de Hamburgo, como es su obligación.

—¡Listos para cargar! —grita Murat, que va a lo suyo.

—¡Desenvaineeeen... sables! —corean Fuckermann y Baisepeau.

Y unos mil doscientos sables, más o menos, hacen *riiis-ras* al salir de la vaina y en ese momento entre el humo y todo lo demás se apartan un poco las nubes y aparece el sol como en Austerlitz, un sol grande y redondo, rojizo, muy a lo ruso, y lo hace con una oportunidad que parece preparada de antemano, justo para iluminar las hojas de acero desnudas. Y todo ese bosque de sables reluce con un centelleo que casi ciega a los que están en la colina del Estado Mayor alrededor del Ilustre, y todos son parbleus y sacrebleus y qué emocionante espectáculo, Sire. Y el Petit sin decir esta boca es mía, observando con ojo crítico la extensión, cosa de media legua, que la caballería debe cruzar en apoyo del 326, y confiando en que el suelo esté lo bastante compacto a pesar de la lluvia de ayer para que no fastidie las patas de los caballos.

—¿Cómo lo ve, Labraguette?

—Estupendamente, Si-sire, gracias —responde Labraguette con prudente entusiasmo, por si al Enano se le ocurre la mala idea de enviarlo a ver el paisaje más de cerca.

—Digo que cómo lo ve. Qué le parece.

—Me pa-parece bien, Sire.

—¿Cuántas bajas calcula usted que le costará a Murat llegar hasta los cañones rusos?

—No sé, Sire. Así, a o-ojo, unos se-setecientos muertos y he-heridos, Sire. Quizá más.

—Eso calculo yo —el Enano suspira para la Historia—. Pero la gloria de Francia lo exige... ¡C'est la guerre, Labraguette!

—Muy ci-cierto, Sire.

—Triste, pero necesario. Ya sabe, la patria y todo eso.

—Ahí le du-duele, Sire.

Mientras esto se comentaba en la colina, los del segundo del 326 llegábamos a unas cuatrocientas varas de los cañones rusos. Lo que se mire como se mire, aunque sea desertando, era mucho llegar.

V

Los adverbios del mariscal Lafleur

A lo lejos estalló un polvorín, una especie de hongo de fuego que iluminó las nubes grises que se cernían sobre Sbodonovo, y el estampido llegó un poco más tarde, amortiguado por la distancia. Algo así como un *tuumpumba* sordo que hizo temblar las plumas en los sombreros de mariscales, generales y edecanes alrededor del Enano. El mariscal Lafleur, que en ese momento miraba por el catalejo, aseguró que en lo alto del hongo se veían figuritas humanas, pero Lafleur tenía fama de exagerado, así que nadie le hizo mucho caso. De todas formas, el pelotazo había sido tremendo.

—¿Son rusos o de los nuestros? —indagó el Ilustre, interesado.

—Rusos, Sire —aclaró alguien.

—Pues que se jodan.

Y siguió a lo suyo, que en ese momento consistía en seguir los movimientos del mariscal Ney. Después de despachar a Murat para que organizase su carga de caballería, el Enano había decidido olvidarse un rato del 326 de Línea para dedicar su atención a otros aspectos de la batalla. La cosa era que Ney, poniéndose a la cabeza de un par de regimientos de la Guardia, estaba a punto de tomar por cuarta vez, a la bayoneta, los escombros humeantes de la granja que dominaba el vado del Vorosik, por donde se nos habían estado colando durante toda la mañana los escuadrones de caballería cosaca que tanto daño hicieron en el flanco derecho. En ese preciso instante, Ney, como siempre despechugado y sin sombrero, con la casaca hecha trizas y la cara tiznada de pólvora, peleaba al arma blanca como un soldado más después de que le hubieran matado cuatro caballos frente a la granja, uno por asalto, contra los rusos que todavía aguantaban a esta parte del vado. La granja del Vorosik se había convertido en una de esas carnicerías memorables, sablazo va y sablazo viene, bayonetas por todas partes, fulanos gritando de furia o de pavor y sangre chorreando a espuertas, como si entre los muros calcinados de aquel recinto de locura hubiesen degollado a una piara de cerdos. Y en esto que los rusos empiezan a chaquetear, *tovarich*, *tovarich*, y a largarse hacia el río, y Ney les dice a los suyos apretad que es pan comido, muchachos, dadles lo suyo y que no vuelvan a por más, y los granaderos de la Guardia con los bigotazos y los aros de oro en la oreja y los gorros de pelo de oso y las bayonetas de cuatro palmos que avanzan como segando hierba, zas, zas, no deis cuartel, grita Ney cabreado porque lleva toda la mañana atascado en la puñetera granja, y a los ruskis les meten el *niet niet* en el cuerpo a bayonetazos, salvo a los jefes y oficiales que se rinden. A esos la orden es cogerlos vivos porque los oficiales son unos caballeros, Marcel, que no te enteras, cómo se te ocurre volarle la sesera a ese capitán que se rendía, acabas de cargarte a un caballero, pedazo de imbécil, a ver si crees que todos son como tú, carne de cañón, o sea, chusma.

Arriba, en la colina del puesto de mando, el Petit le pidió el catalejo a Lafleur y echó un vistazo. Sonreía a medias, como cuando recibió la carta del emperador austríaco diciendo que sí, que María Luisa estaba en edad de merecer y él aceptaba, qué remedio, convertirse en suegro del Ilustre. No hay como ganar Marengos y Austerlices para emparentar con la realeza y marcarte un rigodón en Viena, o tal vez fuera un vals, con todas las frauleins mirándole el paquete al apuesto Murat, *donner und blitzen* con el feldmariscal, siempre tan ceñidito él y eructando a los postres, mientras el emperador de los osterreiches tragaba quina por un tubo, mordiéndose el cetro de humillación con los franchutes de amos del cotarro y el Enano con su uniforme de los domingos dándole palmaditas en la espalda, ese suegro simpático y rumboso, Papi, cómo lo ves. La única pega para el Enano era que la tal María Luisa respondía más bien al tipo cómo pretendes que yo te haga eso, esposo mío, ¿qué diría Metternich si me viera en esta postura? Mucho oig y mucho remilgo, eso era lo malo que tenían aquellas princesas tan educadas y tan Habsburgo. Poco imaginativa, a ver si me entienden, del tipo me duele la cabeza, querido, o bien ay, hola y adiós. En ese aspecto, el Enano seguía añorando a su ex, la Beauharnais, aquello sí era calor criollo a ritmo tropical. Llegaba, un suponer, de ganar la campaña de Italia, y allí estaba Josefina en la Malmaison, relinchando como una yegua, siempre lista para darle una carga de coraceros en condiciones. O dos.

—¡Lafleur!

—A la orden, Sire.

«El adverbio es superfluo, Sire», insinuó Lafleur…

—Escriba a París. Estimados, etcétera, dos puntos. Sbodonovo está a punto de caer, moral alta, victoria segura —echó un vistazo rápido al flanco derecho, donde el humo de las explosiones ocultaba en ese momento al 326—. Mejor escriba *prácticamente* segura, por si acaso.

—El adverbio es superfluo, Sire —insinuó Lafleur, que era un mariscal miserable y pelota.

—Bueno, pues elimine el adverbio. Y añada que Moscú es nuestro, o casi.

—Muy bien, Sire —Lafleur escribía a toda prisa, con la lengua en la comisura de la boca, muy aplicado—. ¿Qué frase histórica ponemos esta vez como fórmula de despedida?

—No sé —el Enano paseó la vista por el campo de batalla—. ¿Qué le parece *en el corazón de la vieja Rusia quince siglos nos contemplan?*

—Magnífica. Soberbia. Pero ya usasteis una parecida, Sire. En Egipto. ¿Recordáis?... Las pirámides y todo eso.

—¿De veras? Pues cualquier otra —el Enano echó un nuevo vistazo alrededor, deteniéndose otra vez en la humareda que ocultaba al 326—. Algo de las águilas imperiales. Siempre queda bien eso del águila. Tiene garra.

Y se rió de su propio chiste, coreado por el mariscalato en pleno. Muy bueno, Sire. Ja, ja. Siempre tan agudo, etcétera. Qué gracia tiene el jodío. Después, todo el Estado Mayor se apresuró a sugerir variantes, Sire, el águila vuela alto, las alas del águila, la nobleza del águila francesa, Sire.

—¿La so-sombra del águila? —apuntó el general Labraguette.

«Me gusta», asintió el Enano. «Eso está bien, Labraguette.
La sombra del águila…»

—Me gusta —asintió el Enano, aún con los ojos fijos en el flanco derecho—. Eso está bien, Labraguette. La sombra del águila, bajo la que se baten los valientes. Como esos españoles de allá abajo, en mi ejército de veinte naciones. Mírelos: bajitos, indisciplinados, con mala leche, siempre tirándose unos a otros los trastos a la cabeza… Y sin embargo, bajo la sombra del águila imperial van hacia la muerte como un solo hombre, en pos de la gloria.

Batió palmas el mariscalato.

—Sublime, Sire.

—Lo ha dicho un gran hombre.

—Es que el que vale, vale. Y el que no, con Wellington.

—Menos coba, Lafleur. No sea imbécil —el ilustre requirió el catalejo y echó una ojeada a retaguardia—. Por cierto. ¿Qué pasa con Murat?

Todos los mariscales empezaron a ir y venir aparentando estar muy ocupados en el asunto, a despachar batidores a caballo con mensajes para acá y para allá, Murat, a ver qué pasa con Murat, ya estáis oyendo que se impacienta el Emperador, esa carga es para hoy o para mañana, mondieu, así no hay cristo que gane esta guerra. Y los batidores galopando hacia cualquier parte sin saber adónde ir, agachándose bajo los cañonazos y jurando en francés, con los mensajes ilegibles e inútiles en la vuelta de la manga del dolmán agujereado por los tiros y la metralla, acordándose de la madre que parió a aquel primo suyo que los enchufó como enlaces en el Estado Mayor imperial.

El caso es que visto así, en panorámica, el Estado Mayor daba la impresión de tener una actividad del carajo,

con todo el mundo pendiente otra vez del flanco derecho, donde los fogonazos de artillería se intensificaban
de modo alarmante entre la humareda de pólvora. Allá
abajo, los cuatrocientos y pico españoles del segundo batallón del 326 de Línea habíamos gozado hasta ese momento de la relativa protección de una contrapendiente
suave entre los maizales, una especie de desnivel con
cuatro o cinco pajares ardiendo y tres o cuatrocientos
muertos repartidos un poco por aquí y por allá, el rastro
de los muchos ataques sin éxito que la división había lle-
vado a cabo sobre ese punto durante la mañana, y en la
que el mismo general Le Cimbel se había cambiado el
fusil de hombro, ya me entienden, nosotros los españoles decíamos *dejar de fumar*, o sea morirse. Cada uno eu-
femiza como puede, mi general. El caso es que Le Cimbel era uno de aquellos cuatrocientos despojos que
marcaban el punto más avanzado de la progresión francesa en el flanco derecho frente a Sbodonovo: tal vez
aquel fiambre sin cabeza junto al que pasábamos en ese
momento. El punto más avanzado de la progresión. Tó-
queme la flor, corneta. Lo del punto suena muy técnico:
eso es lenguaje oficial de parte de guerra, como lo de *re-
pliegue táctico*, o aquello otro, no se lo pierdan, de *movimiento retrógrado hacia posiciones preestablecidas*, dos formas como otra cualquiera de decir, Sire, nuestra gente
ha salido giñando leches. En el flanco derecho ante Sbodonovo, el punto más avanzado de la progresión era el
punto en que la carnicería se volvió tan insoportable que
los supervivientes habían dicho pies para qué os quiero. Y
nosotros, los del 326, apretados unos contra otros en las
filas de la formación, blancos los nudillos de las manos

crispadas alrededor de los fusiles con las bayonetas, estábamos a pique de rebasar el punto más avanzado de la maldita progresión de las narices, es decir el desnivel que con el humo nos protegía un poco del grueso de la artillería ruski. Ahora íbamos a quedar al descubierto ante todas las bocas de fuego de la madre Rusia, imagínense el diálogo de los artilleros: Popof, mira quiénes asoman por ahí con la que va cayendo, están locos estos franzuskis, acércame el botafuego que voy a arreglarles el cuerpo con la pieza de a doce. Carga metralla, Popof, que a esta distancia es lo que más cunde. Ahí va eso, que aproveche. Ésta por la liberté, ésta por la egalité y ésta por la fraternité.

Raaas-zaca-bum. De pronto no hubo cling-clang porque el sartenazo de los ruskis cayó en medio de la formación, toda la metralla entró en blando, y es imposible saber a cuántos se llevó por delante entre el humo, los gritos y la sordera que viene cuando una granada te revienta a la espalda. A los de las primeras filas nos salpicó sangre encima, pero no era nuestra, y sólo Vicente el valenciano soltó el fusil con una mano pegada todavía a la culata, el fusil girando en el aire con la mano incluida y Vicente mirándose el muñón esperando que alguien le explicara aquello. Quisimos agarrarlo para que se mantuviera en pie, pero el valenciano fue cayéndose al suelo hasta quedar de rodillas, siempre mirándose la mano, y se quedó atrás y ya no volvimos a verlo. Igual tuvo suerte y alguien le hizo un torniquete y se emboscó allí con una Marujska de tetas grandes y se convirtió en campesino y fue feliz con muchos hijos y nietos y ya no volvió a ver una guerra en su puñetera vida. Igual.

Y en esto el capitán García, todo pequeñajo y enne-grecido por la pólvora, nuestro único oficial superior a aquellas alturas del asunto, que seguía sable en alto gri-tándonos palabras que no entendíamos con el estruendo de los cañonazos, empezó a decirle algo a Muñoz, el al-férez abanderado, a quien una esquirla rusa le había sus-tituido el chacó por un rastro de sangre deslizándosele por la frente y la nariz, que de vez en cuando se enjuga-ba con el dorso de la mano libre para que no le tapara el ojo izquierdo. No lo oíamos con los bombazos pero era fácil imaginarlo: Muñoz, atento a mi orden, en cuanto yo te dé el cante abates el águila de los cojones y le pones la bandera blanca, la sábana que llevas doblada bajo la casaca, y la agitas bien en alto para que la vean los Iván, y entonces ya sabes, todos a correr levantando en alto los fusiles para que sepan de qué vamos y no nos ametrallen a bocajarro, los hijoputas. Y en las filas pasándonos la voz, atentos, en cuanto el capitán dé la orden y Muñoz ice bandera blanca, fusiles en alto y a correr hacia los ruskis como si nos quitáramos avispas del culo, a ver si terminamos de una vez este calvario. Y otra granada ru-sa que pasa rasgando sobre nuestras cabezas, ahora va al-ta, muy atrás, y otra que llega más corta, cuidado con esa que las trae negras, y acertamos, y la granada también acierta, y más compañeros que se largan a verle el blanco de los ojos al diablo. Y el *ras-ras* de nuestras polainas ro-zando los maizales tronchados, negros de carbón y san-gre, chamuscados por las bombas y las llamas escuchan-do el redoble del tambor que nos ayuda a mantener el paso en aquella locura. Y Popof que empieza a afinar la puntería mientras remontamos los últimos metros de contrapendiente. Y más raaaca-zas-bum y más cling-clang. Y ahora estamos casi al descubierto y nos están dando los rusos una que te cagas, y García grita algo que seguimos sin entender, mi capitán, no se moleste en abrir la boca hasta que no llegue el momento de salir arreando. Y el tambor que arrecia su redoble y las filas que se estrechan más, a ver si hay suerte y la siguiente granada le toca a otro, porque Dios dijo hermanos pero no primos. Y más raaca-zas y más bum-cling-clang y más compañeros que se quedan atrás en los maizales. Y la contrapendiente que se acaba, y humo por todos sitios, y ya tenemos las bocas de los cañones rusos a un palmo de la cara, y García que se vuelve y parece que nos mira uno por uno duro como el pedernal, aquí nos la jugamos, hijos míos, aquí nos sacan el último naipe, a correr que llueve. Y el alférez Muñoz se limpia por última vez la sangre de los ojos y mete la mano en la casaca para sacar la bandera blanca, y abate el águila para sustituir la bandera mientras sudamos a chorros bajo la ropa, mordiéndonos los labios de tensión y miedo. Y de pronto empieza a caernos metralla rusa a espuertas, por todos sitios, y todos gritan terminemos de una vez, y ya estamos a punto, no de levantar, sino de tirar los fusiles al suelo y correr hacia los rusos con las manos en alto, *españolski, españolski*, cuando suenan trompetas por todas partes, a nuestra espalda, y nos quedamos de piedra cuando vemos aparecer una nube de jinetes, banderas y sables en alto, cargando por nuestros dos flancos contra los cañones rusos.

VI

La carga de Sbodonovo

Desde su colina, el Enano había visto abatirse la bandera del 326 a pocas varas de los cañones rusos, justo en el momento en que el alférez Muñoz se disponía a sustituirla por la sábana blanca y todos nos preparábamos allá abajo para consumar la deserción echando a correr hacia los Iván sin disimulo alguno. Era tanto lo que en ese momento nos caía encima, raas-zaca-bum y cling-clang por todas partes, que la humareda de los sartenazos ruskis cubría el avance del batallón, ocultándolo de nuevo a los ojos del Estado Mayor imperial. Con el catalejo incrustado bajo la ceja derecha, el Petit Cabrón fruncía el ceño.

—Ha caído el águila —dijo, taciturno y grave.

A su alrededor, todos los mariscales y generales se apresuraron a poner cara de circunstancias. Triste pero inevitable, Sire. Heroicos muchachos, Sire. Se veía venir, etcétera.

—Ejemplar sa-sacrificio —resumió el general Labraguette, emocionado.

De abajo llegaban unos estampidos horrorosos. Ahora era una especie de *pumba-pumba* en cadena. Toda la artillería rusa parecía ametrallar a bocajarro al batallón, o lo que quedara de él a tales alturas del episodio.

—Escabeche —dijo el mariscal Lafleur, siempre frívolo—. Los van a hacer escabeche… ¿Recordáis, Sire? Aquel adobo que nos sirvieron en Somosierra. ¿Cómo era? Laurel, aceite…

—Cierre el pico, Lafleur.

—Ejem, naturalmente, Sire.

—Es usted un bocazas, Lafleur —el Petit lo miró con la misma simpatía que habría dedicado a la boñiga de un caballo de coraceros—. Están a punto de hacer trizas a un puñado de valientes y usted se pone a disertar sobre gastronomía.

—Disculpad, Sire. En realidad, yo…

—Merece que lo degrade a cabo primero y lo envíe allá abajo, al maldito flanco derecho, a ver si se le pega a usted algo del patriotismo de esos pobres chicos del 326.

—Yo… Ejem. Sire… —Lafleur se aflojaba el cuello de la casaca, con ojos extraviados de angustia—. Naturalmente. Si no fuera por mi hernia…

—Las hernias se curan como soldado de infantería, en primera línea. Es mano de santo.

—Acertada apreciación, Sire.

—Imbécil. Tolili. Cagamandurrias.

—Ese soy yo, Sire. Me retratáis. Clavadito.

Y el pobre Lafleur sonreía, conciliador, entre la chunga guasona del mariscalato, siempre solidario en este tipo de cosas.

—A ver, Labraguette —el Ilustre había vuelto a mirar por el catalejo—. Anote: Legión de Honor colectiva para esos muchachos del 326 en caso de que alguno quede vivo, cosa que me sorprendería mucho. En todo caso, mención especial en la orden del día de mañana, por heroísmo inaudito ante el enemigo.

—He-hecho, Sire.

—Otra cosa. Carta a mi hermano José Bonaparte, palacio real de Madrid, etcétera. Querido hermano. Dos puntos.

Y el Ilustre se puso a dictar con destino a su pariente, ese que los españoles llamábamos Pepe Botella por aquello del trinque o la maledicencia, vaya usted a saber, dicen que le daba al rioja pero que tampoco era para tanto. El caso es que el Petit se despachó a gusto aquella mañana en la modalidad epistolar desde la colina de Sbodonovo y con Labraguette dándole al lápiz a toda leche. Hermanito del alma, tanto llorarme sobre tus súbditos, que si no hay quien gobierne con esta gente y que si tal y que si cual, a ver quién se las arregla en un país donde no hay dos que tomen café de la misma forma, o sea, solo, cortado, corto de café, largo, doble, con leche, para mí un poleo. Donde los curas se remangan la sotana, pegan tiros y dicen que despachar franchutes no es pecado, y donde la afición nacional consiste en darle un navajazo al primero que dobla la esquina, o arrastrar por las calles a quien sólo cinco minutos antes se ha estado aplaudiendo, y a menudo con idéntico entusiasmo. Me cuentas eso en cada carta, querido hermanito, dale que te pego con lo de que vaya regalo envenenado te hice, y que antes que rey de España hubieras preferido que te nombrara arzobispo de Canterbury, nos ha jodido. Pero, entre otras cosas, Canterbury no lo hemos conquistado todavía, y España, aunque esté llena de españoles, es un país con mucho futuro. Así que ya está bien de tanta queja y de tanto chivarte a Mamá de lo mal que lo pasas en Madrid. Para que te enteres, un batallón de tus súbditos acaba de cubrirse de gloria a las puertas de Moscú, por la cara. Así que ve tomando nota, Pepe. Que no te enteras. Un capullo, eso es lo que eres. Desde pequeño siempre has sido un capullo.

—Pásemelo a la firma, Labraguette. Y despáchelo.

—A la orden, Si-sire.

—Y ahora, ¿alguien puede decirme dónde está Murat?

No hizo falta. Un marcial toque de corneta ascendía hacia la colina desde el flanco derecho, y mariscales, generales, edecanes, ayudantes y correveidiles al completo saludaron con alborozo la buena nueva. Hablando del rey de Roma, es decir el de Nápoles, Sire, ahí lo tiene en plena carga, lento pero seguro ese Murat, observe el espectáculo que tiene tela. Y abajo, en la llanura de maizales chamuscados del flanco derecho, desplegándose en escuadrones multicolores, los húsares y los coraceros, mil y pico sables desenvainados y sobre el hombro derecho, tararí-tararí, listos para la memorable carnicería que los haría entrar de perfil, a los vivos y a los muertos, en los libros de Historia. Y acercándonos a vista de pájaro al meollo del asunto, volando sobre las apretadas formaciones donde los caballos relinchaban impacientes, tenemos a Murat, todo bordados y floripondios, con una capacidad mental de menos quince pero valiente como un toro español cuando los toros españoles salen valientes, levantando el sable sobre la cabeza rizada con tenacillas y diciendo sus y a ellos, muchachos, ese batallón español necesita ayuda y los vamos a ayudar, voto al Chápiro

Verde. Y Murat, con su dólmán de seda y sus rizos de madame Lulú y su menos seso que un mosquito y todo lo que ustedes quieran, pero, eso sí, al frente de sus tropas en un tiempo en que los generales y los mariscales aún la diñan así y no de indigestión en la retaguardia, Murat, decíamos, se vuelve a su cornetín de órdenes y le dice venga, chaval, toca de una vez esa maldita carga y que el diablo nos lleve a todos. Y el chaval que escupe para mojarse los labios que tiene secos y toca carga y Fuckermann y Baisepeau que les gritan a sus húsares y coraceros aquello de al paso, al trote y al galope, y mil y pico caballos que se mueven hacia adelante, acompasando el ruido de los cascos y herraduras. Y Murat grita *Viva el Emperador* y los mil y pico jinetes corean que sí, que vale, que viva el Petit Cabrón pero que aquí podía estar, más cerca, para compartir en persona aunque fuese un trocito de la gloria que a ellos les van a endilgar los cañones ruskis a chorros dentro de nada, gloria para dar y tomar, un empacho de gloria, mi primero, lo que vamos a tener en cinco minutos. Vamos a cagar gloria de aquí a Lima.

Y entonces hay como un trueno largo y sordo que retumba en el flanco derecho, y los doce escuadrones de caballería se extienden por la llanura mientras ganan velocidad, y los artilleros rusos que empiezan a espabilarse, Popof, mira lo que viene por ahí, esa sí que no me la esperaba, *tovarich*, la virgen santa, nunca imaginé que tantos caballos y jinetes y sables pudieran moverse juntos al mismo tiempo, nosotros tan entretenidos tirando al blanco con ese batallón de mierda cuando lo que se nos venía encima era esto otro, a ver esa pieza, apunta que las cosas van a ponerse serias, mira cómo grita ahora el capitán Smirnoff, con lo tranquilo y contento que estaba hace sólo cinco minutos, el hijoputa. A ver esas piezas de a doce, apunten, fuego. Dales caña, Popof. Dales, que mira la que nos cae.

Total. Que los artilleros rusos cambian de objetivo y empiezan a arrimarle candela a Murat y sus muchachos, y el primer cañonazo va y arranca de su caballo al general Fuckermann y lo proyecta en cachitos rojos sobre sus húsares que van detrás, ahí nos las den todas, pero hay muchas más, raaas-zaca, raaas-zaca, y ya corren caballos sin jinete adelantándose a las filas cerradas de los escuadrones, bota con bota y el sable extendido al frente mientras suena el tararí tararí, y los húsares sujetan las riendas con los dientes y empuñan en la mano izquierda la pistola, y los coraceros con destellos metálicos en el pecho y la cabeza, con boquetes redondos que se abren de pronto en mitad de la coraza y todo se vuelve de pronto kilos de chatarra que rueda por el suelo, tiznándose de hollín y barro mientras sigue el tararí tararí y Murat, ciego como un toro, sigue al frente del asunto y está casi a la altura del 326, húsares por la derecha, coraceros por la izquierda y allá en su frente Estambul, o sea, Moscú, o sea, Sbodonovo, o sea los cañones rusos que escupen metralla como por un grifo. Y por fin llega, galopando a lomos de su caballo que va desencajado e imparable como una bala, cubierto de sudor y espuma, junto a las filas del heroico 326, y entre el humo y la velocidad ve fugazmente los rostros de esos valientes que lo miran boquiabiertos, socorridos en el último instante cuando libraban su último y heroico combate sin esperanza. Y a Murat, que en el fondo es tierno como el día de la Madre, se le pone la carne de gallina y grita, enardecido:

—¡Viva el 326! ¡Viva Francia!

Y todos sus húsares y coraceros, que ya rebasan al 326 por los flancos cargando contra los cañones rusos, todos esos jinetes rudos y veteranos que acuden a compartir el hartazgo de metralla que se están llevando los bravos camaradas del 326, corean con entusiasmo el grito de Murat y, a pesar de la que está lloviendo, saludan con sus sables a esos héroes bajitos y morenos, los fieles infantes del batallón español, al pasar junto a ellos galopando en línea recta hacia el enemigo. Y los del 326, mudos de agradecimiento, se ve que no encuentran palabras para expresar lo que sienten.

Y es que no hay palabras, Muñoz, quince minutos aguantando el cañoneo a quemarropa de los ruskis y, a punto de conseguirlo, justo en el momento en que bajas la bandera para sustituirla por la sábana blanca que llevas oculta en la casaca, con todos los compañeros acuciándote, date prisa, mi alférez, espabila que nos caemos con todo el equipo, suenan los trompetazos y Murat y mil doscientos franchutes aparecen cargando a uno y otro lado del batallón y encima pasan vitoreándote, los tíos, hégoes espagnoles, te dicen, camagadas y todo lo demás mientras acuden al encuentro de la metralla rusa, mira, lo positivo es que ahora tocaremos a menos cada uno, al repartir. Y todo el batallón que se queda de piedra viéndose en medio de una carga de caballería, y Murat saludando con el sable y su corneta dale al tararí tararí, de qué van estos fulanos, mi capitán, aquí hay un malentendido.

Ve fugazmente los rostros de esos valientes que lo miran
boquiabiertos…

Lo que está claro es que nos han fastidiado la maniobra, los gilipollas. Nos han jodido el invento. A ver quién es el guapo que deserta ahora, rodeado por mil doscientos húsares y coraceros que te dan palmaditas en la espalda.

Total. Que todos nos paramos un momento, aturdidos y sin saber qué hacer, pendientes de lo que dice el capitán García, y el capitán, pequeñajo y tiznado de pólvora, nos dirige una mirada de tranquila desesperación y después se encoge de hombros y le grita a Muñoz, eso sí lo oímos bien, alférez, levanta otra vez la bandera franchute, levanta el águila de los cojones y esa sábana blanca la haces cachitos y nos la podemos ir metiendo todos por el culo. Y el águila que se levanta de nuevo, y los coraceros y los húsares que siguen pasando a nuestro lado venga a dar vítores a los valegosos espagnoles, y García que nos dice hijos míos, suena la música así que a bailar tocan, echemos a correr hacia adelante y que sea lo que Dios quiera, allá cada cual, y vamos a meternos tanto en las filas de los Iván que al final no tengan más remedio que cogernos prisioneros. Conque levanta el sable, apunta a los artilleros rusos y dice eso de *¡Vivaspaña!* que es la única cosa nuestra que nos queda en mitad de toda esta mierda. Y Luisillo, nuestro tambor de quince años, redobla toque de carga, y los fulanos del 326 apretamos fuerte el fusil con la bayoneta y echamos a correr entre los jinetes hacia los cañones rusos, aunque antes de caer prisioneros alguien va a tener que pagar muy cara la mala leche que se nos ha puesto con el patinazo de esta mañana. Si no fuera por tanto cañonazo y tanta murga ya estaríamos trincando vodka en plan tovarich después de habéroslo explicado todo, cretinos. Así que ya puedes

«¡Viva el 326! ¡Viva Francia!...»

darte por jodido, Popof. Cagüentodo. Como llegue hasta ahí, por lo menos a los de las primeras filas os voy a dejar listos de papeles.

Y los artilleros ruskis, que ya tienen a los húsares y los coraceros encima y se defienden como pueden sobre sus cañones, echan un vistazo al frente y ven que por la cuesta suben cuatrocientos energúmenos erizados de bayonetas y gritando como posesos, cuatrocientos tipos con la cara tiznada por el humo y ojos enrojecidos de miedo y rabia, y se dicen: fíjate lo que sube por ahí, camarada, esos no necesitan decir que no hay cuartel, lo llevan pintado en la cara, así que date por jodido, Popof, pero bien. Y el primero que llega hasta ellos es un capitán pequeño y negro de pólvora que grita algo así como *¡Vaspaña!*, *¡Vaspaña!*, que nadie sabe muy bien lo que quiere decir, y ese capitán se tira encima de los primeros cañones como una mala bestia, y se lía a sablazos, y al capitán Smirnoff, que se ha puesto delante haciendo posturas de esgrima, le patea los huevos y después le abre la cabeza de un sablazo, y ahora llegan todos los demás gritando como salvajes, y a golpe de culata y bayonetazos, desesperados, como si nada tuvieran que perder, empitonan a Popof y a su santa madre, vuelcan los cañones, rematan a todo el que se mueve y, llevados por el impulso, mientras Murat y sus jinetes retroceden para reorganizar las filas desordenadas por la carga, siguen corriendo entre gritos y blasfemias hacia las filas de los regimientos rusos que, formados a la entrada de Sbodonovo, los miran acercarse inmóviles, incapaces de reaccionar, paralizados de estupor ante el espectáculo.

VII

La resaca del príncipe Rudolfkovski

Durante mucho tiempo, los historiadores militares han intentando explicarse lo que ocurrió en Sbodonovo, sin resultado. Sir Mortimer Flanagan, el famoso analista británico, afirma que se trató de una brillante improvisación táctica de Napoleón, la última chispa de su genio militar antes de extinguirse en Moscú y en la desastrosa retirada de Rusia. Por su parte, el francés Gerard de la Soufflebitez plantea las cosas desde otra óptica más limitada, o sea casera, atribuyendo a Murat el exclusivo mérito en la acción de Sbodonovo y evitando mencionar, incluso, la presencia del segundo batallón del 326 de Línea en la batalla. Sólo en la correspondencia privada del mariscal Lafleur —dirigida a su amante, la conocida soprano Mimí la Garce— se encuentra una irrefutable prueba del papel desempeñado por los españoles, cuando do el mariscal escribe: «*Les sanglots longs des baïonnettes des espagnols blessent les russes d'une langueur monotone...*», en clara alusión al asunto. Más explícito se muestra en sus memorias (*De Borodino a Pigalle*, San Petersburgo 1830) el mariscal Eristof, que reconoce sin rodeos el importante papel jugado por los españoles en los acontecimientos de la jornada, sobre todo cuando el viejo león escribe aquello de: «*En Sbodonovo, el 326 de Línea nos puteó bien*».

Y ahora pónganse ustedes en el lugar de los rusos. Tres o cuatro regimientos formados en perfecto orden a las puertas del pueblo, inactivos durante toda la mañana porque ya se habían encargado las baterías artilleras y la caballería cosaca de pulverizar el flanco derecho francés. Unos cuatro o cinco mil hombres tumbados en la hierba viendo los toros desde la barrera, fíjate, Vladimir, la que les está cayendo a los herejes, eso para que aprendan a invadir lo que no deben, Dios salve al zar y todo eso. Dame cartas. A ver, la sota de copas. Vaya día llevas, *tovarich*. Acabas de ganarme otro rublo. ¿A qué hora dices que sirven el rancho?... Y los oficiales tres cuartos de lo mismo: cómo lo lleva, conde Nicolai, bien, gracias. Estaba yo acordándome de aquella velada en San Petersburgo, en casa de Ana Pavlovna, junto a la princesa Bolkonskaia. Exquisito caviar, vive Dios. Lástima de inactividad, Boris, aquí toda la mañana con nuestros artilleros haciendo el trabajo y nosotros mano sobre mano, sin poder cubrirnos de gloria. A ver cómo diantre vuelvo yo a San Petersburgo sin un brazo en cabestrillo, o un heroico vendaje en torno a la cabeza para lucir en el palacio de la gran duquesa Catalina. Así no hay quien se coma una rosca por muy bien que uno baile el vals.

Y ese era el panorama a las puertas de Sbodonovo, con el pueblo ardiendo un poco al otro lado, hacia el vado del Vorosik, pero en esa parte estaba tranquilo, todo bajo control de los Iván. Hasta el príncipe Rudolfkovski, que mandaba la división, se había bajado del caballo y echaba una siestecita bajo un abedul. Ese era el panorama, repito, cuando de pronto empezó a oírse algo de barullo por la parte de los cañones. Entonces el príncipe Rudolfkovski, que por cierto era primo segundo del zar Alejandro, abrió un ojo y requirió a su ordenanza, el fiel Igor:

—Igor, ¿qué ocurre?

—No lo sé, padrecito —respondió el leal subalterno.

—Pues echa un vistazo, imbécil.

Quizá si el príncipe Rudolfkovski hubiese echado el vistazo personalmente habría cambiado el curso de los acontecimientos, pero vaya usted a saber. De hecho, Rudolfkovski dormía la siesta porque la noche anterior había estado despierto hasta altas horas beneficiándose a una robusta campesina a la que sus dragones habían descubierto oculta en un pajar de Sbodonovo. Además, al príncipe se le había ido un poco la mano con el vodka, cuyo consumo excesivo solía producirle una espantosa jaqueca. El caso es que el fiel Igor Igorovich pasó junto a los oficiales del estado mayor de Rudolfkovski, que charlaban en un grupito, y se acercó a echar un vistazo por la parte de los cañones. La familia del fiel Igor había servido a la familia Rudolfkovskaia desde tiempo inmemorial, y cada vez que un Rudolfkovski defendió a sus zares en un campo de batalla, hubo junto a él un Igorovich para limpiarle las botas y echarle agua caliente en la bañera. Lo cierto es que el príncipe no era demasiado duro con su leal siervo, y sólo lo azotaba por faltas muy graves como plancharle mal el cuello de una camisa, no bruñirle la hoja del sable de modo conveniente, o retrasarse en las marchas en vez de correr junto a su estribo derecho con una botella de champaña razonablemente frío a mano. Por lo demás, el príncipe Rudolfkovski era un amo justo y cabal. Quizá por eso, cuando el fiel Igor anduvo un cuarto de *versta* más y le echó un vistazo a lo que ocurría donde los cañones rusos, se detuvo un momento, miró hacia el lejano abedul donde el príncipe Rudolfkovski dormía la mona, y soltando una extraña risita entre dientes puso pies en polvorosa.

Así que las primeras señales de lo que iba a ocurrir llegaron un poco más tarde, cuando los cuatro o cinco mil rusos que holgazaneaban sobre la hierba vieron aparecer, de pronto, una compacta fila de uniformes azules que se dirigía hacia ellos a la carrera y pegando unos gritos que helaban la sangre. Mucho se ha discutido después la reacción de los ruskis, pero en esencia fue del tipo anda, Vladimir, qué cosa más rara, por ese lado debían estar nuestros artilleros y resulta que aparecen otros con uniforme azul, yo creía que iban de verde los nuestros, te vas a reír pero por un momento he creído que eran franceses, fíjate, si hasta la bandera parece francesa, estoy de lo más tonto esta mañana, cómo van a ser franceses si están hechos polvo en el flanco derecho. El caso es que, bien mirado, esa bandera no parece nuestra, ¿verdad? Oye, pues ahora que lo dices, tampoco eso que gritan me suena a ruso. *Vaspaña*, algo así como *Vaspaña*, pero francés tampoco es. A ver. Espera. Trae el catalejo. Hostia, Vladimir. Los franceses.

Unos dicen que gritábamos *Viva España* y otros que *Vámonos a España*, pero el caso es que los cuatrocientos, o lo que quedaba de nosotros, desembocamos en la llanura frente a Sbodonovo a la carrera, con las bayonetas por delante y la furiosa energía que te proporciona la desesperación. Mucho se discutió después el asunto, y la mayor parte coincidimos en afirmar que pretendíamos caer prisioneros para terminar de una vez, antes de que los húsares y los coraceros de Murat volviesen a cargar a nuestro lado creyendo ayudarnos contra los ruskis. Es cierto que los cañones de los Iván nos habían hecho sufrir mucho y todavía íbamos calientes a pesar de haber empitonado a los artilleros; pero la verdad es que al llegar a la llanura nuestra intención era seguir hasta las filas rusas y allí adentro, una vez a salvo de nuestra propia caballería, arrojar las armas. El problema fue que los Iván se lo tomaron por la tremenda y mantuvieron el equívoco, o sea, nadie ataca así, en línea recta y a la bayoneta, a puro huevo, si no lo tiene muy claro. Así que espérame un momento, Vladimir, que ahora vuelvo. Sí, a retaguardia voy. A por tabaco.

Cuatro mil hombres saliendo por pies ante cuatrocientos es un espectáculo que no se dio con frecuencia en la campaña de Rusia. El movimiento de pánico se propagó como una ola, y las primeras filas ruskis echaron a correr. Las segundas hicieron lo mismo al pasar junto a ellas las primeras, y los de las últimas, que vieron a toda la vanguardia dar la vuelta y venírseles encima, se volvieron atropellándose unos a otros, desbordados los oficiales, y salieron zumbando hacia Sbodonovo, maricón el último, metiéndose por las calles del pueblo en dirección al río y al puente de la carretera de Moscú. Y nosotros corriendo detrás, esperad, pringaos, aquí hay un malentendido. Pero claro, en eso que algunos rusos se vuelven y nos descerrajan unos cuantos tiros, y a Manolo el maño y a Paco el sevillano los dejan secos en plena carrera, y empezamos a cabrearnos mientras vemos caer a unos cuantos más, colegas de los tiempos de Dinamarca, tiene guasa escaparte de unos y de otros para que un tovarich te pegue un tiro a última hora. Y en esas que llegamos junto a un abedul para darnos de boca con un ruski lleno de cordones y entorchados, con cara de resaca y pinta de mandar mucho, que no para de preguntar por un tal Igor, vete tú a saber quién coño es el Igor de las narices. Total, que el sargento Ortega intenta explicarle que nos rendimos, pero el otro dice algo de que los Rudolfkovski mueren pero no se rinden. Ortega, que es un buenazo, intenta explicarle pacientemente que no, míster, quienes nos rendimos somos nosotros, aquí, *españolski tovarich*, a ver si te enteras. Napoleón *kaput*, nosotros querer ir a España, *¿capito?* O sea que *fini la guerre*. Pero el ruski mira alrededor, ve a toda su tropa corriendo como conejos y a nosotros tiznados de humo, con las bayonetas manchadas de sangre de los artilleros que acabamos de cepillarnos allá atrás, y se cree que le estamos vacilando, o sea, estos hijoputoskis quieren quedarse conmigo. Así que saca una pistola y le descerraja al sargento Ortega un tiro a bocajarro, pumba, que le chamusca las patillas, menos mal que el Iván tenía el pulso fatal aquella mañana. Y claro, Ortega se cabrea y ensarta al ruski en el abedul de un sablazo, para que aprendas, gilipollas, que no se puede ir de buena fe, hay que joderse, chavales, con aquí el capitán general. Y eso que se lo dije bien clarito. A todo esto, los Iván corren por ahí diciendo que nos hemos cargado al príncipe Rudolfnosequé, y todos venga a correr más todavía, y en estas llegamos ya a las primeras casas del pueblo, con los rusos cruzándolo a toda prisa hacia el puente y la carretera de

Moscú, entrando por un extremo y saliendo por el otro como si fueran a hacer un recado, a toda leche. Y en todo ese trajín no mantiene la calma más que la reserva de caballería cosaca, a la que alguien ordena que cubra la retirada. Así que, de pronto, cuando los del 326 vamos corriendo tras los rezagados rusos por la calle principal, todavía con intención de encontrar alguien a quien rendirnos, vemos aparecer dos escuadrones cosacos cargándonos de frente, sables en alto, atiza Gorostiza, esos no huyen sino que atacan. Y nos miramos unos a otros para decirnos hasta aquí hemos llegado, compadres, vete a explicarles nada a éstos. Se acabó lo que se daba.

O sea, que nos caen encima doscientos y pico jinetes cosacos haciendo molinetes con los sables y las lanzas, y el capitán García se da cuenta de que no hay espacio para formar el cuadro. Entonces nos ordena hacer fuego por secciones porque aquí no hay *tovarich* que valga, hijos míos, así que ya nos rendiremos otro día. Y tenemos el tiempo justo de escalonarnos la mitad del 326 en la calle, mientras la otra mitad se reagrupa detrás con la lengua fuera, y ya tenemos a los cosacos a treinta varas mientras García se planta a la derecha, sable en mano, y el teniente Arregui a la izquierda. Y cuando lo cosacos están a quince varas, García va y ordena primera descarga a los caballos, hijos míos, endiñársela por lo bajini para taponarles la calle a esos hijoputas. Y los de la primera fila, arrodillados, nos llevamos el fusil a la cara diciendo madre santísima, de esta no salimos ni hartos de sopa.

—Primera sección, ¡fuego!

García los tiene bien puestos, las cosas como son. Y es un profesional. La primera descarga abate una veintena

La primera descarga abate una veintena de caballos…

de caballos, formando un obstáculo para los jinetes que vienen detrás.

—Segunda sección, ¡fuego!

Ahí va eso. La segunda sección dispara sobre nuestros chacós mientras los de la primera seguimos las órdenes del teniente Arregui: primera sección, rodilla en tierra, carguen. Y tú vas, muerdes el cartucho igual que muerdes el miedo, lo metes en el cañón caliente, ahora la bala, golpe de baqueta y otra vez el fusil a la cara mientras los de la segunda, ya arrodillados también a tu espalda, cargan a su vez. Ahora son los de la tercera fila los que apuntan sobre nuestras cabezas.

—Tercera sección, ¡fuego!

Toma candela, Iván. Tres descargas en quince segundos, plomo barriendo la calle principal, patas y relinchos por el aire, cosacos por el suelo a un palmo de nosotros, angelitos al cielo. Pero siguen llegando más y más cuyos caballos tropiezan, se encabritan sobre los caídos. A nuestra espalda, Luisillo redobla sobre su parcheado tambor para darnos ánimos. Y la voz ronca del capitán García, no es para menos lo de ronca, con la mañana que lleva, se alterna con la del teniente Arregui mientras seguimos soltando descarga tras descarga:

—¡Tercera sección, carguen armas!

—¡Primera sección en pie! ¡Apunten! ¡Fuego!

El humo de pólvora negra empieza a cubrir la calle y las andanadas parten a ciegas, hacia el lugar de donde vienen los alaridos y los relinchos, fusilando a los cosacos a bocajarro.

—¡Primera sección, rodilla en tierra, carguen armas!

—¡Segunda sección, en pie! ¡Fuego!

Unos jinetes cosacos consiguen llegar hasta nuestra izquierda…

—¡Segunda sección, rodilla en tierra! ¡Carguen armas!

—¡Tercera sección, en pie! ¡Fuego!

Así cinco minutos. Ahora ya no se ve nada de nada, y todos estamos dentro de una humareda oscura y acre, disparando contra un muro de niebla del que brotan alaridos, lamentos, detonaciones. La pólvora negra quemada se mete por las narices y aturde los sentidos, y ya no sabes dónde diablos estás, y tu único contacto con la realidad son las voces que te llegan, el capitán García de la derecha, el teniente Arregui de la izquierda, diciéndote que cargues y dispares, que cargues y dispares, que cargues y dispares. Y el otro contacto real es la culata, el gatillo, la baqueta del fusil que te quema las manos al tocar el cañón donde hasta la bayoneta parece al rojo. Y entonces, de pronto, unos jinetes cosacos consiguen llegar hasta nuestra izquierda, hay fogonazos y alaridos y *chas-chas* de sablazos que dan en blando, la fila parece estremecerse por ese lado y el teniente Arregui ya no dice nada y no vuelves a oírlo más, el tambor de Luisillo deja de pronto de redoblar, y es García quien te dice ahora que cargues y dispares, en pie o rodilla en tierra, que cargues y dispares. Y después oyes su voz, un grito desgarrado y brutal ordenando al ataque a la bayoneta, vamos de una vez a terminar con esos ruskis de mierda. Y a tu lado notas que los compañeros, a los que tampoco ves, se mueven contigo, adelante, y aúllan vamos a por ellos a masticarles los hígados, cagüentodo, rediós y la Virgen santa, y aprietas fuerte el fusil con la bayoneta y corres entre la niebla oscura de la pólvora hasta tropezar con cuerpos de caballos y de hombres, unos inmóviles y otros agitándose cuando trepas por encima de ellos, cuando escalas el montón y distingues brillos de acero entre la humareda espesa, y percibes sombras que también gritan en otra lengua, y tú empiezas a clavar la bayoneta en todo cuanto se pone delante, *¡Vaspaña!*, *¡Vaspaña!*, y nuevos fogonazos de pólvora te chamuscan la cara mientras sigues adelante entre patas de caballos y cuerpos de hombres que se debaten ante ti, *¡Vaspaña!*, *¡Vaspaña!*, y entre golpe y golpe de bayoneta tienes la visión fugaz de la cara de un crío que te espera en alguna parte, de una silueta de mujer que llora mientras te vas del pueblo camino abajo, o el rostro de tu madre junto al fuego, cuando eras zagalico. *¡Vaspaña!* O a lo mejor esas imágenes no son tuyas, no te pertenecen a ti sino a la memoria de los hombres que tienes enfrente, y tú se las vas arrancando a tajos de bayoneta.

Por fin la niebla empieza a disiparse y sigues corriendo con la garganta en carne viva de gritar, y el cuerpo destrozado de fatiga, hasta llegar a la otra punta del pueblo. Entonces te apoyas en el pretil de un puente hacia el que convergen por ambos lados muchos jinetes con gran estruendo de cascos y trompetas. Y ya te dispones a levantar la bayoneta para acuchillarlos también y llevarte lo que puedas por delante antes de ir a Dios y descansar de una puñetera vez, cuando te das cuenta de que son coraceros y húsares franceses, de tu bando, si es que a estas alturas puedes todavía sentirte en bando alguno, y que te aclaman entusiasmados porque acabas de cruzar Sbodonovo de punta a punta, haciendo huir a cuatro regimientos rusos y aniquilando a dos escuadrones cosacos.

VIII

Confidencias en Santa Helena

Años más tarde, después de Rusia, Leipzig y Waterloo, en Santa Helena y a punto de palmarla, el Enano le confiaría a su fiel compañero de destierro, Les Cases, que en Sbodonovo se le apareció la Virgen. A ver si no cómo se lo explica uno, Les Cases: un batallón que ni siquiera es francés y cambia el signo de la batalla dándole a los rusos las suyas y las de un bombero, o sea, pasándose por la piedra de amolar toda una batería artillera de piezas de a doce y cuatro o cinco regimientos, príncipe Rudolfkovski incluido. Según sus últimos biógrafos, el Ilustre hacía estas confidencias mientras clavaba agujas en un muñequito de cera representando la efigie de su carcelero sir Hudson Lowe, el malvado inglés a quien el gobierno de Su Majestad Británica encomendó el confinamiento y liquidación, en aquel islote del Atlántico convertido en cárcel, del hombre que había pasado veinte años jugando a los bolos con las coronas de Europa. Allí, en las largas veladas invernales, rodeado por sus últimos fieles, el Petit Cabrón pasaba revista a los recuerdos gloriosos mientras Les Cases y Bertrand tomaban oporto y notas para la posteridad. Algunos de sus juicios arrojan luz sobre rincones oscuros de la Historia, o revelan facetas desconocidas de los personajes. Que si Wellington no era más que un sargento chusquero con mucha potra. Que si Fouché un trepa y un pelota, Talleyrand una rata de cloaca y Metternich un perfecto gilipollas. También rememoraba el Ilustre cuestiones más íntimas. Las piernas de Desirée, por ejemplo, Les Cases, aquello era gloria bendita, mujer de bandera, se lo dice uno que de banderas entiende un rato. Lástima que tuviese aquel marido, Bernadotte, al final se colocó bien, ¿verdad? Rey de Suecia, y eso que era un completo soplador de vidrio. Los hay con suerte. En cuanto al príncipe Fernando, el hijo de Carlos IV, menudo personaje, Bertrand. Mi mayor venganza tras la guerra de España fue devolvérselo a sus paisanos. ¿No queréis Fernando VII? Pues que os aproveche. ¿Sabe usted, Les Cases, que cuando lo tuve preso en Valençay tardé algún tiempo en averiguar su estatura *real* porque siempre entraba en mi despacho de rodillas?… Brillante muchacho, el tal Fernando. Creo que lleva fusilada a media España. ¿No gritaban *viva las caenas*? Pues toma caenas. *La joya de la corona*, lo llamaba aquel tipo grande y simpaticote, ¿recuerda, Bertrand? Godoy, creo recordar. El que chuleaba a la madre.

Al llegar a este punto, recordando los años de gloria, el Enano miraba el fuego de la chimenea y después sonreía a sus últimos fieles. Sobre España recordaba haber leído algo una vez, mientras esperaba que su caballería polaca despejara Somosierra. Una traducción sobre el *Poema de Mío Cid*, o algo por el estilo, Les Cases, resulta difícil acordarse bien ahora, con lo que ha llovido desde Somosierra y aquel puntazo que se marcó Poniatowski, ¿recuerda?, sus jinetes cargando ladera arriba con los españoles cogidos de través y Madrid a un paso, creíamos que eso lo dejaba todo resuelto, y ya ve. En ese momento, el Ilustre se quedaba pensativo y suspiraba mirando la chimenea. España. Maldito el día que decidí meterme en semejante berenjenal. Eso ni era guerra ni era nada; una pesadilla es lo que era, con el calor y las moscas y aquellos frailes con canana y pistoleras, y los guerrilleros cazándonos correos en cada vereda, y cuatro baturros con una bota de vino y una guitarra descalabrándome a las tropas imperiales a las puertas de Zaragoza mientras los ingleses sacaban tajada como de costumbre. Cada vez que miro uno de esos grabados del tal Goya me vienen a la memoria aquellos desgraciados con sus ojos de desesperación, engañados por reyes, generales y ministros durante siglos de hambre y miseria, analfabetos e ingobernables, con su orgullo y su furia homicida como único patrimonio. ¡Aquellas navajas, Les Cases, que daba miedo verlas! Mis generales todavía tienen pesadillas en que salen esas navajas donde ponía *Viva mi dueño* y hacían siete veces *clac* al abrirse. Esos bárbaros heridos de muerte, cegados por su propia sangre, que aún buscaban a tientas las junturas del peto del coracero para meterle la hoja de dos palmos hasta las cachas y llevárselo por delante, con ellos, al infierno. En España metimos bien la gamba, Bertrand. Cometí el error de darles a esos fulanos lo único que les devuelve su dignidad y su orgullo: un enemigo contra el que unirse, una guerra salvaje, un objeto para desahogar su indignación y su rabia. En Rusia me venció el invierno, pero quien me venció en España fueron aquellos campesinos bajitos y morenos que nos escupían a la cara mientras los

Su fiel compañero de destierro, Les Cases...

fusilábamos. Aquellos hijoputas me llevaron al huerto a base de bien, se lo aseguro. España es un país con muy mala leche.

En fin. Que allí, en Santa Helena, el Enano seguía haciendo memoria. A vueltas con los españoles y el Cid, la cita era algo del tipo *«qué buen vasallo que fuera si tuviese buen señor»*. Y es que hay que fastidiarse, Les Cases: a veces uno encuentra escritas verdades como puños. Una gente como aquella, que hasta las mujeres empujaban cañones y tiraban de navaja para degollar franceses, y fíjese qué gobernantes ha tenido durante toda su desgraciada historia. Mientras el futuro Fernando VII me lamía las botas en Valençay, sus compatriotas destripaban franceses en las guerrillas o tomaban Sbodonovo a puro huevo, como aquel batallón, ¿cuál era? El segundo del 326 de Línea. Hermosa jornada, Bertrand, vive Dios, a las puertas de Moscú. El último vuelo del águila. Aún me parece estar en la colina, respirando el humo de pólvora que subía del campo de batalla, etcétera —en este punto, el Enano torcía la boca en una mueca nostálgica, y las llamas de la chimenea agitaban en su rostro sombras parecidas a recuerdos—. Aquel olor a pólvora, Les Cases. No hay nada que huela igual. El olor de la gloria.

—¿Y sabe qué le digo, Les Cases? Que me quiten lo bailado.

En ese punto, con la imaginación, el Petit Cabrón se trasladaba de nuevo a la colina frente a Sbodonovo, con el campo de batalla extendido a sus pies, recién conquistada por Ney la granja en el vado del Vorosik y el pueblo en manos francesas por la tozudez de un pintoresco batallón de españoles, con todos los mariscales,

Clavaba agujas en un muñequito de cera...

generales y edecanes aplaudiendo la gesta en el Estado Mayor imperial, extraordinario, Sire, glorioso día y demás, felicitando al ilustre como si Sbodonovo lo hubiera tomado él personalmente y no cuatrocientos desgraciados actuando por su cuenta.

—Gran día, Sire.

—He-hermosa ge-gesta, Sire.

—Chupado, Sire. Ahora, tomar Moscú lo tenemos chupado.

Y batían palmas, plas-plas, mientras acudían los ordenanzas con champaña y todo el mariscalato y generalato del Imperio brindaba por la victoria de Sbodonovo haciéndole al Ilustre de claque. Alonsafán, Sire. El zar Alejandro está listo de papeles y cosas como ésa.

Entonces aparece Murat por la falda de la colina. Y las cosas como son: tarugo y fantasma sí que era un rato, el nota, con aquellos rizos y el aire de príncipe gitano vestido para una opereta, cargando a la izquierda en los ajustados pantalones de húsar y con los zarcillos de oro en las orejas, un chapero de lujo es lo que parecía aquella prenda del arte ecuestre. Pero entre él y Ney sumaban, a cada cual lo suyo, el mayor volumen de redaños por metro cuadrado de toda la *Grande Armée*. El caso es que estando los mariscales en plena celebración en torno al Petit, llega Murat negro de pólvora, con la pelliza hecha jirones, tres balazos agujeréandole el dolmán y esa mirada que se les pone a los que acaban de echarse una carrera con el cuarto jinete del Apocalipsis, ya saben, uno se levanta y echa a correr, o espolea el caballo para cruzar los mil metros más largos de su vida, sin saber si llegará al final o van a picarle el billete a mitad de camino. El caso es que Murat había bajado a la boca del infierno y ahora estaba de regreso, con un manojo de banderas rusas como trofeo.

—Llegué, vi y vencí, Sire.

Murat no era exactamente lo que entendemos por un tipo modesto. En cuanto a erudición, nunca había ido más allá de deletrear, no sin esfuerzo, el *Manual Táctico de Caballería* del ejército francés, que tampoco era precisamente la *Crítica de la razón pura* de don Emmanuel Kant. «*El arma básica de la Caballería* —empezaba el manual— *se divide en dos: caballo y jinete…*», y así durante doscientas cincuenta páginas. Respecto a lo del llegué y vi, Murat se lo había apropiado de un libro de estampas de sus hijos, algo que un general griego, o tal vez fuera romano, había dicho frente a las murallas de Troya cuando aquella zorra dejó a su marido para escaparse con un tal Virgilio, después de meterse dentro de un caballo de madera. O viceversa. Murat estaba muy orgulloso de haber retenido esa frase, que con la de «*Y sin embargo, se mueve*», de aquel famoso *condottiero* florentino, el general Leonardo Da Vinci, inventor del cañón, constituían la cumbre de sus conocimientos sobre literatura castrense y de la otra.

El caso es que Murat llegó a la cima de la colina, arrojó a los pies del Enano la media docena de banderas rusas que sus húsares y coraceros habían recolectado del campo de batalla tras la feroz carga del 326 de Línea, y dijo aquello de llegué, vi, etcétera, con los generales y mariscales mordiéndose de envidia las charreteras mientras lo criticaban por lo bajini, no te fastidia, Duroc, el niño bonito de las narices. Cualquiera diría que ha ganado la guerra él solo, total por darse una vuelta a caballo por el campo de batalla, cuando eso lo hace cualquier imbécil. Peste de tiempos, Morand, ya va siendo hora de que la Historia aprecie el esfuerzo intelectual que hacemos los de Estado Mayor, parece que en la guerra lo único importante sea ir de un lado a otro pegando tiros como un vulgar cabo furriel. Y encima va y hace frases, el tío, llegó y vio, dice, menudo enchufe tiene ese cabrón. Me pregunto qué le habrá visto el Ilustre para darle tanto cuartelillo. A lo mejor es que, guapo y con ese culo tan ceñido... Usted ya me entiende, Lafleur, aunque no creo yo que el Ilustre navegue a vela y vapor a estas alturas: me fijé en la dama rusa que le mamporreó usted anoche en el vivac, sí, aquella de las tetas grandes que disfrazó de oficial de coraceros para meterla de matute en su tienda. Muy bueno lo de la coraza, Lafleur, je, je. Muy logrado. Todos nos percatamos de que le venía un poco justa. En fin, que ahí tiene usted a Murat, triunfando con sus rizos y sus banderas y sus *veni, vidi, vici*. Lástima que los artilleros rusos no le hayan hecho la raya en medio con una granada del doce.

Mientras los mariscales intercambiaban *sotto voce* tales muestras de camaradería militar, Murat desmontaba e iba, contoneándose, a cuadrarse ante el Enano.

—Misión cumplida, Sire.

—Me alegro, Murat. Buen trabajo. Glorioso hecho de armas. Una carga heroica y todo eso.

—Gracias, Sire.

El Petit se colocó el catalejo bajo la ceja izquierda para echarle otro vistazo a Sbodonovo. Desde la granja del vado del Vorosik la división de Ney avanzaba, por fin, tras el hundimiento del flanco izquierdo ruso. Al otro lado del río, por la carretera de Moscú, las masas de infantería del zar se retiraban en desorden, hostigadas por la caballería ligera francesa, mientras en las afueras del pueblo, junto al puente, se concentraban las minúsculas manchitas azules del 326 de Línea tras su increíble carga a la bayoneta. Aquello era una victoria más imponente que la de Samotracia. Satisfecho, el Ilustre esbozó media sonrisa, le pasó al mariscal Lafleur el catalejo y, abriéndose el capote de cazadores de la Guardia, introdujo una mano entre los botones del chaleco.

—Cuéntemelo, Murat. Despacito y sin aturullarse, ya sabe. Sujeto, verbo y predicado.

Murat enarcó con dificultad una ceja y se puso a contar. Lo nunca visto, Sire. Toque de carga, mil doscientos jinetes tararí-tararí, o sea, indescriptible, o sea. Y en esto que llegamos junto a los cuatrocientos españoles del 326 justo cuando están a pocas varas de los cañones rusos, o sea, como quien dice, Sire, y resulta de que. Dispuestos a echárseles encima a puro huevo, Sire, supongo que capta el tono del asunto. Bueno, el caso es que cargamos vitoreándolos por su valor, y ellos nos miran con cara de sorpresa, o sea. Parecían incluso indignados, como si mismamente fuéramos a joderles la marrana. No sé si me explico.

—Se explica, Murat. Con cierta dificultad, como de costumbre. Pero se explica. Prosiga.

Y Murat prosigue narrando con su proverbial fluidez, o sea, Sire, los del 326 no esperaban ningún tipo de ayuda, o sea, dispuestos como estaban a hacer todo el trabajo con sus propias bayonetas. Así, tal cual. Por la cara. Mismamente como si fueran autómatas, Sire.

—Autónomos, Murat —corrigió el Enano.

—Bueno, Sire. Autónomos o como se diga. El caso es de que algunos incluso nos insultaban, Sire. «Hijoputas», decían, «qué hacéis aquí. A ver quién os ha dado vela en este entierro».

El Petit hizo un gesto augusto y comprensivo.

—Es lógico, Murat. Ya sabe lo quisquillosos que son los españoles. Honor y demás. Sin duda querían toda la gloria para ellos solos.

—Será eso, Sire —el Rizos fruncía el ceño, no muy convencido—. Porque nos llamaron de todo, o sea, de todo. Y nos hacían cortes de mangas, tal que así, con perdón, Sire. O sea. Algunos mismamente nos apuntaron con sus fusiles, como dudando si pegarnos un tiro.

Nueva sonrisa del Enano, a quien las victorias lo volvían de un indulgente que daba asco:

—Ahí los reconozco, Murat. Sangre fogosa. La furia española.

Murat asintió sin demasiado entusiasmo. Sus recuerdos sobre la furia española databan del 2 de mayo de 1808, jornada que vivió como gobernador militar de Madrid y que con gusto habría cambiado, a ciegas, por una jornada como gobernador militar en Papúa-Nueva Guinea. Por un momento recordó a las majas y chisperos metiéndose entre las patas de los caballos, las viejas tirándole macetas desde los balcones, los chuloputas y los jaques de los barrios bajos convergiendo hacia la Puerta del Sol con aquellas navajas enormes empalmadas, listos para acuchillar a sus mamelucos y coraceros. Fue muy comentado el caso de media docena de granaderos libres de servicio que no se habían enterado del alzamiento ni de nada, los infelices, y seguían tranquilamente sentados a la puerta de una tasca de Lavapiés, bebiendo limonada y diciéndole piropos a la cantinera, cosas del tipo guapa espagnola, si tú quegueg yo te hagué muy feliz y todo eso. Con la que se había liado por la ciudad y ellos allí, practicando idiomas. Hasta que de pronto vieron doblar la esquina a unos quinientos mil paisanos indignados llevando en brazos el cuerpo de una tal Manolita Malasaña. Cuando, un par de horas después, los compañeros de los granaderos fueron en su busca, los trozos más grandes que pudieron localizar consistían en doce criadillas ensartadas con un espetón en la puerta de la tasca. Sí. A Murat iban a contarle lo que era la furia española.

—El caso, Sire —continuó— es que cargamos con ellos contra los cañones, o sea, de aquella manera, y después, cuando yo reagrupaba a mis jinetes, siguieron corriendo a su aire hacia el pueblo, mismamente detrás de los rusos, y lo cruzaron de punta a punta, tal que así, enrollando a dos escuadrones de caballería cosaca.

—Arrollando, Murat.

—Bueno, Sire. Arrollando o enrollando, el caso es de que a los rusos se los pasaron por la piedra. Fue, o sea... —el Rizos frunció de nuevo el entrecejo, buscando una frase que resumiera gráficamente el espectáculo—. Fue osmérico.

—¿Osmérico?

—Sí. Ya sabéis, Sire: Osmero. Aquel general tuerto que conquistó Troya. El de los elefantes.

IX

Una noche en el Kremlin

El 15 de septiembre de 1812, en la vanguardia de las tropas francesas que entraron en Moscú, íbamos marcando el paso los supervivientes del segundo batallón del 326 de Infantería de Línea, a esas alturas menos de trescientos hombres en razonable estado de salud. El resto se había quedado por el camino, de Dinamarca al campo de prisioneros de Hamburgo, de allí a Vitebsk y Smolensko, y después Valutina y Borodino, con parada y fonda en las baterías rusas y la calle principal de Sbodonovo. La noche anterior la habíamos pasado a orillas del Vorosik, vendando nuestras heridas y enterrando a nuestros muertos, que eran unos cuantos; aproximadamente uno de cada cuatro, pues con tanto raaas-zaca y bang-bang, los cañones rusos y luego los cosacos en la calle principal nos habían dado también lo suyo antes de que los mandáramos a criar malvas. Todavía impresionado por el asunto, el Enano nos había hecho enviar un centenar de botellas de vodka de su tren de campaña personal para felicitarnos por la heroica gesta: cuídeme a esos valientes, Lafleur, antes de que los condecore personalmente en la plaza del Kremlin, ya sabe, dígales de mi parte que olé sus cojones y todo eso. Así que el mariscal

Lafleur vino personalmente a traernos el vodka —«bgavos espagnolés, el Empegadog y la Patgia están oggullosos de vosotgos»—, mientras nos cachondeábamos entre las filas, aún tiznados de pólvora, la Patria dice aquí, mi primo, a ver a qué patria se refiere. Y a todo esto sin enterarse todavía de que la intención de los bgavos espagnoles era darse el piro, o sea, abrirnos. Así que dígale a la Madre Patria que me agarre de aquí, mi mariscal, silvuplé. Y es que hay que ser gabacho, o sea, gilipollas.

En fin. El caso es que al menos el vodka era vodka y que, como nos dijo el capitán García en cuanto Lafleur se quitó de en medio, al mal tiempo buena cara, hijos míos, de momento parece que somos héroes, así que paciencia y a barajar. Ya desertaremos más adelante. Entonces nos quitamos el gusto a pólvora de la boca despachando las cien botellas del Ilustre a la luz de las fogatas. Al beber nos mirábamos unos a otros el careto en silencio, mientras Pedro el cordobés pulsaba las cuerdas de su guitarra, por bulerías.

—Por lo menos —resumió el capitán, que se atizaba unos lingotazos de vodka horrorosos— seguimos vivos.

Era evidente. Seguíamos vivos todos, menos los muertos. Lo peor era que en Sbodonovo habíamos estado a punto de largarnos, y hubiéramos logrado desertar de no ser por la carga de caballería del Petit Cabrón. Como decía el fusilero Mínguez, un gaditano de San Fernando con más pluma que el sombrero de Murat, el Rizos podía haber ido a socorrer a la madre que lo parió, la muy zorra, con todos sus apuestos húsares y coraceros y toda la parafernalia, a un palmo habíamos estado de librarnos de los franchutes y mira, allí seguíamos pintándola, con más mili por delante que el cabo Machichaco. Nos habían jodido Murat y mayo con las flores.

Mínguez hacía estas reflexiones mientras nos zurcía los desgarrones de metralla en las casacas. Tenía buena mano para la aguja y el hilo, y le encantaba echarle una mano al cocinero con el rancho. Era de los veteranos del regimiento de Villaviciosa, alistado voluntario para ir a Dinamarca.

—Con ese nombre, me dije, *Villaviciosa*, tiene que ser un regimiento de lo más guarro.

Mínguez era muy maricón, pero en combate se volvía bravo como una fiera. Amaba en secreto al capitán García, aunque el suyo era un secreto a voces, y en cuando empezaban los tiros procuraba situarse cerca, bayoneta en mano, dispuesto a defenderlo hasta la muerte como un tigre de Bengala, quítese de ahí, mi capitán, que van a darle un tiro, por Dios, al ruso que se acerque le saco los ojos. En Sbodonovo, Mínguez se había multiplicado alrededor del capitán, disparando, cargando el fusil, asestando bayonetazos a diestro y siniestro. Cuidado con ése, mi capitán, toma escopetazo, ruso malvado. Cúbrase, mi capitán, que me lo van a desgraciar. Nada, ni caso. Qué cruz de hombre. Así, a lo tonto, Mínguez se había cargado él solo a una docena de cosacos. Al terminar la batalla le chorreaba la sangre por la bayoneta y el cañón del fusil, hasta los codos.

—Lástima de cosacos —se lamentaba después, junto al fuego, mientras zurcía la casaca del capitán—. Ya me hubiera gustado verlos más de cerca, con esas barbazas y tan peludos, los salvajes.

Y le sonreía respetuosamente al capitán, que se dejaba querer, bonachón, porque el fusilero Mínguez era buena persona y nunca se pasaba de la raya. El caso es que aquella noche, a orillas del Vorosik, la guitarra de Pedro el cordobés y el vodka del Petit Cabrón fueron nuestra compañía bajo el cielo de Rusia, mientras los muertos se enfriaban alrededor, descansando por fin en paz, y los vivos rumiábamos en silencio nuestra nostalgia de España y nuestras desgracias. Y al día siguiente, con la casaca zurcida por el fusilero Mínguez, el pequeño y duro capitán García entró en Moscú a la cabeza del 326 de Línea, o sea, nosotros.

La verdad es que fue una entrada con mal pie, sin vítores ni gente mirándonos. El ejército enemigo, mandado por Kutusov, se había retirado con casi toda la población civil, y nuestras botas remendadas sonaban en las calles desiertas, donde sólo el graznar de cientos de cuervos y grajos negros que revoloteaban por los tejados saludó a las victoriosas águilas napoleónicas. Así fuimos adentrándonos en la ciudad, fusil al hombro, preguntándonos adónde iba a llevarnos todo aquello. De momento nos llevó hasta una explanada a orillas del Moskova y junto al Kremlin, entre torres antiguas y cúpulas de iglesias doradas, donde tras las formalidades de rigor el Enano tomó posesión del asunto, muy cabreado porque todos los moscovitas se habían abierto con el ejército ruso y allí dentro no quedaba nadie a quien impresionar con el despliegue, o sea que nos han jorobado el número, Labraguette, ese Kutusov me la ha jugado, esperaba conquistar una ciudad llena de gente y me entregan otra vacía, como si hubiera pasado por aquí la peste negra. Menudos hijoputas, los ruskis.

—Por lo menos la han dejado intacta —apuntó el general Donzet, siempre oportuno—. Imaginaos si le hubieran prendido fuego, Sire.

El caso es que, con moscovitas o sin ellos, el Ilustre no estaba dispuesto a que le chafasen su parada militar. Así que se nos ordenó formar en la explanada del Kremlin, banderas al viento y demás, con los generales franchutes pasándonos revista para comprobar si estábamos en condiciones de comparecer ante el Petit Cabrón, a ver, cepíllense un poco las botas, saquen pecho, esos chacós erguidos, capitán, qué coño de soldados tiene usted aquí. ¿Cómo dice? Ah, sí, los españoles del 326. Ya veo. Pero que sean ustedes los héroes de Sbodonovo no es excusa para que vayan con esa pinta, las casacas desabrochadas y sin afeitar. El Emperador estará muy impresionado con su bravura y todo lo que quieran, pero como no se aseen un poco les vamos a meter un paquete que se van a cagar por la pata abajo. Así que de frente, ar. Uno dos, up aro, uno dos, up aro. Alto. Fiiiir-mes. Así me gusta, capitán. Disciplina, eso es lo que ustedes necesitan. Mucha disciplina. A ver qué se han creído, aquí, los héroes.

—A mí me la van a dar estos salvajes, Leclerc. A mí, que perdí un primo segundo en Zaragoza y un cuñado en Bailén.

En eso, trompetas y clarines, vista a la derecha y todo lo demás, y el Enano que aparece pasando revista escoltado por los granaderos de la Vieja Guardia, magnífico día, Murat, a ver dónde tiene a esos valientes muchachos. Y todo el gallinero emplumado del Ilustre y compañía que se acerca al 326, oh, mais oui, son éstos, Sire, quién lo iba a decir, tan bajitos y con esas pintas infames, si no lo veo no lo creo, cuántos rusos dice usted que se cargaron en Sbodonovo. Y el capitán García que nos grita presenten

Se nos ordenó formar en la explanada del Kremlin...

armas y se cuadra saludando con el sable, pequeño y moreno con sus patillas de boca de hacha tapándole media cara, diciéndonos entre dientes poned cara de soldados, hijos míos, que no se os note mucho de qué vais. Más vale ser héroes a la fuerza que fusilados por sorteo, uno de cada dos, como aquellos compañeros a los que les echaron el guante en Vitebsk. Y a todo esto el Enano que se para ante García y lo mira de arriba abajo, con una mano entre los botones del chaleco y otra en la espalda, como en las estampas.

—Dígame su nombre, capitán.

—García, mi general. Ejem. Eminencia. Sire.

—A ver, Labraguette. Acérqueme una de esas legiones de honor que tengo reservadas para los valientes.

Sonaron redobles de tambores y un par de toques de corneta, a ver esas condecoraciones que son para hoy, pero las susodichas no aparecían por ninguna parte. El Enano despachó a Labraguette a hacer averiguaciones, y lo vimos regresar al cabo, más corrido que una mona, deshaciéndose en excusas. Las le-legiones de honor se habían pe-perdido en el campo de batalla de Sbodonovo, Sire. Una caja entera, nu-nuevecitas, en el fondo del río. Imperdonable descuido y de-demás.

El Petit fruncía el imperial ceño.

—No importa. Déme la suya.

—¿Perdón?

—Su legión de honor. Démela para este bravo capitán. A usted ya le buscaré otra cuando volvamos a París —el Petit miró la ciudad desierta a su alrededor y pareció estremecerse bajo el capote gris marengo—… Si volvemos.

Labraguette y los mariscales rieron aquello como si fuera una gracia, jé, jé, Sire, muy bueno el chiste. Siempre tan agudo. Pero el Enano miraba a los ojos del capitán García, y éste nunca estuvo muy seguro de si aquella vez, en la plaza del Kremlin, el Enano hablaba en broma o hablaba en serio. El caso es que después de colgarle al cuello la cruz, el Petit pasó entre nuestras filas estrechando algunas manos, bien hecho, muchachos, estoy orgulloso de vosotros. Os vi desde la colina. Algo magnífico. Francia os lo agradece y todo eso.

—¿De dónde eres, hijo?

—De Lepe, Zire.

Después hubo unos trompetazos más, redoble de tambores, y el Ilustre se retiró a ocuparse de sus cosas, no sin antes volverse a su Estado Mayor, tome nota, Labraguette, paga doble para el 326, déjenlos saquear un rato la ciudad con el resto de la tropa, y esta noche los quiero de guardia de honor en el Kremlin. Viva Francia y rompan filas. Ar.

Así que nos fuimos a dar una vuelta por Moscú y practicar un poco el pillaje, que a esas horas estaba siendo ejercido con entusiasmo por todo el ejército franchute. En la ciudad habían quedado pocos civiles, pero suficientes para que algunos soldados encontrasen rusas a las que violar, con lo que, bueno, se produjeron ciertas escenas poco agradables, de esas que nunca se mencionan en los heroicos partes de guerra militares. En cuanto al 326, después de pasar en Sbodonovo por la máquina de picar carne, no estábamos en condiciones de violar a nadie. Además, seguíamos dispuestos a largarnos a las primeras de cambio, y tampoco era conveniente dejar mal cartel entre los ruskis, que para eso de las violaciones tienen tan buena memoria como el que más. Así que, a renglón seguido de que el capitán García le rompiera la mandíbula de un puñetazo a Emilio el navarro, que intentó propasarse con una mujer en la calle Nikitskaia, todos nos conformamos con vodka, comida y echar mano a vajillas de plata y cosas de esas, incluido un cofre de monedas de oro que descubrimos en casa de un comerciante tras hacerle, durante un rato, cosquillas con las bayonetas. Nos encaminamos al Kremlin al atardecer, cargados de botín, con gorros y abrigos de piel, piezas de seda e iconos de plata. Todos sabíamos que tendríamos que abandonar aquello si lográbamos salir por pies y pasarnos por fin a los rusos, pero hicimos buena provisión, por si acaso. Y durante unas pocas horas, infelices de nosotros, fuimos los soldados más ricos de Europa.

Esa noche montamos guardia en las murallas exteriores del recinto sagrado, en el corazón del imperio ruso, lo que a tales alturas del asunto nos impresionaba un carajo de la vela, mi capitán, para impresión la de los cañones ruskis dándonos cera en Sbodonovo, o los dos escuadrones cosacos cargándonos por las bravas en la calle principal. Después de eso, tanto nos daba estar en el Kremlin o en el Vaticano. El caso es que, impresionados o no, cumplimos el honor que nos dispensaba el Ilustre asomados a las murallas, escuchando los cantos y la juerga de los franchutes que iban con antorchas de un lado para otro por la ciudad desierta. De vez en cuando llegaban hasta nosotros ruido de tiros aislados, carcajadas o el grito de una mujer.

A eso de la medianoche, el capitán García estaba apoyado en las almenas que daban a la ciudad vieja,

«Os vi desde la colina. Algo magnífico…»

encendiendo una tagarnina que había encontrado el día anterior en los bolsillos de un oficial de cosacos muerto. Sonaba en la oscuridad la guitarra de Pedro el cordobés, y alguien, uno de los centinelas inmóviles como sombras negras, tarareaba entre dientes una copla. Algo de una niña que espera y un hombre que está lejos, huido a la sierra. En esto García oyó unos pasos y, cuando se disponía a preguntar alto quién vive, santo y seña y toda esa jerga que suele barajarse antes de descerrajar un tiro, apareció el Enano en persona. Iba envuelto en su capote gris, inconfundible a pesar de la oscuridad. No había nadie tan bajito ni con un sombrero tan enorme en toda la *Grande Armée*.

—Buenas noches, capitán.

—A sus órdenes, Sire —García, cortadísimo, se cuadraba con un taconazo—. Sin novedad en la guardia.

—Ya veo —el Ilustre se apoyó en la muralla, a su lado—. Descanse. Y puede seguir fumando.

—Gracias, Sire.

Estuvieron un rato inmóviles los dos, el uno junto al otro, escuchando la guitarra del cordobés y la copla del centinela. García, que no las tenía todas consigo, observaba de reojo el perfil del Ilustre, iluminado apenas desde abajo por una hoguera que ardía al pie de la muralla. A quien le digan, pensaba, que estoy a dos palmos del fulano que tiene en el bolsillo a media Europa y acojonada a la otra media. Instintivamente rozó la culata de la pistola que llevaba al cinto, imaginando lo que ocurriría si le soltaba un tiro al Petit Cabrón así, por las buenas. ¿Qué dirían los libros de Historia?... *Napoleón Bonaparte, nacido en Córcega, muerto en las murallas del Kremlin por un capitán español. Véase Capitán García...* Y en la letra G: *García, Roque. Capitán de infantería. Mató a Napoleón de un pistoletazo en las murallas del Kremlin. Eso aceleró la liberación de España, pero García no estaba allí para disfrutar del asunto. Juzgado sumariamente por un tribunal militar francés, fue fusilado al amanecer...* Con un suspiro, el capitán apartó la mano de la culata. Figurar en los libros de Historia no era la pasión de su vida.

—¿Por qué lo hicieron, capitán?

Sobresaltado, García tragó saliva.

—¿Por qué hicimos qué, Sire?

—Aquello de Sbodonovo, ya sabe —el Enano hizo una pausa y al capitán le pareció que reía quedamente, en la penumbra—. Avanzar así hacia el enemigo.

García tragó más saliva mientras se rascaba el cogote, indeciso. Más tarde, al contarnos el episodio, confesaría que hubiera preferido hallarse otra vez frente a los cañones rusos que allí, intimando con la realeza imperial. Por qué lo hicimos, preguntaba el Petit Cabrón. Sin embargo, unos cuantos porqués sí tenía nuestro capitán en la punta de la lengua. Por ejemplo: porque pretendíamos largarnos y se nos fastidió el invento, Sire. Porque ya está bien de tanta gloria y tanta murga, tenemos gloria para dar y tomar, gloria por un tubo, Sire. Porque esto de la campaña de Rusia es una encerrona infame, Sire. Porque a estas horas tendríamos que estar en España, con nuestros paisanos y nuestras familias, en vez de estar metidos hasta las cejas en esta puñetera mierda, Sire. Porque la Frans nos la trae floja y Vuecencia nos la refanfinfla, Sire.

Eso es lo que tenía que haberle dicho el capitán García al Ilustre aquella noche en la muralla del Kremlin, con lo que nos hubieran fusilado a todos en el acto y santas pascuas, ahorrándonos la retirada de Rusia que nos esperaba días más tarde. Pero no se lo dijo, por las mismas razones que momentos antes le impidieron pegarle un tiro. Se limitó a dar una fuerte chupada a la tagarnina y dijo:

—No había otro sitio adonde ir, Sire.

Sobrevino un silencio. Entonces el Enano se volvió despacio a nuestro capitán, y en ese momento alguien avivó la hoguera de abajo y el resplandor iluminó un poco más el rostro de los dos hombres. Y el Ilustre sonreía a medias, entre irónico y comprensivo, como el viejo zorro que les da cuartelillo a las gallinas del corral. García sostuvo aquella sonrisa y la mirada del Ilustre sin apartar la vista ni pestañear, porque el capitán, a pesar de ser un pobre desgraciado como todos nosotros, era de Soria y tenía lo que hay que tener, y porque tanto él como el Petit, en el fondo, eran soldados profesionales y se estaban entendiendo sin palabras.

—Se dio cuenta —nos diría el capitán, más tarde—. Ese tío sabía que en Sbodonovo nos quisimos largar. Se dio cuenta pero le importa un carajo… Su instinto le dice que la *Grande Armée* tiene los días contados, y ni él mismo está seguro de salir bien de ésta.

Eso es lo que nos contó García. De una u otra forma, lo cierto es que al Enano debió de gustarle lo que había en los ojos de nuestro capitán, porque éste observó que le echaba un vistazo al cuello de la casaca, de donde García se había quitado por la tarde la legión de honor, y no hizo ningún comentario, sino que acentuó su extraña media sonrisa.

—Comprendo —se limitó a decir.

Y dando media vuelta, hizo ademán de alejarse. Pero a los dos pasos se detuvo, como si hubiese olvidado algo.

—¿Hay algo que pueda hacer por usted, capitán? —preguntó sin volverse.

García se encogió de hombros, consciente de que el Ilustre no podía ver su gesto:

—Mantenerme vivo, Sire.

Hubo un largo silencio. Después, la espalda del Petit Cabrón se movió imperceptiblemente.

—Eso no está en mi mano, capitán. Buenas noches.

Y el emperador de Francia se alejó lentamente por la muralla.

García lo estuvo mirando hasta que desapareció entre las sombras. Después se encogió de hombros por segunda vez. La tagarnina se había apagado, así que fue al resguardo de la almena para encender el chisquero. Entonces se dio cuenta de que la guitarra de Pedro el cordobés se había interrumpido y el centinela ya no cantaba su copla. Se asomó a la muralla, inquieto, y entonces vio el resplandor rojo que crecía en la zona este de la ciudad.

Moscú estaba en llamas.

X

El puente del Beresina

Fue un largo camino y una larga agonía. El 326 se
había ido diluyendo a retaguardia en el barro, la nieve y
la sangre desde aquella noche del incendio, cuando el capitán García cambió unas palabras con el Enano en las
murallas del Kremlin. Incapaz de sostenerse en la ciudad, con el invierno encima, el Ilustre convocó a sus mariscales y generales para tocar retirada, o sea, caballeros,
a casita que llueve. Y empezó el viacrucis: trescientos mil
hombres iban a quedarse en el camino, jalonando aquella tragedia con nombres de resonancia bárbara: Winko-
wo, Jaroslawetz, Wiasma, Krasnoe, Beresina... Columnas de rezagados, combates a quemarropa en la nieve,
hordas cosacas acuchillando a espectros en retirada demasiado embrutecidos por el frío, el hambre y el sufri-
miento para oponer resistencia, así que puede irse usted
directamente al carajo, mi coronel, no pienso dar un paso más, etcétera. Batallones exterminados sin piedad,
pueblos ardiendo, animales sacrificados para comer su
carne cruda, compañías enteras que se tendían exhaustas
en la nieve y ya no despertaban jamás. Y mientras caminábamos sobre los ríos helados, envueltos en harapos,
arrancando las ropas a los muertos, pasando junto a

Columnas de rezagados, combates a quemarropa en la nieve…

hombres sentados inmóviles y rígidos, con los copos de nieve cubriéndolos lentamente como estatuas blancas, el aullido de los lobos nos seguía a retaguardia, cebándose con los cuerpos que dejábamos atrás en la retirada. ¿Se imaginan el panorama...? No, no creo que puedan. Hay que haber estado allí para imaginar eso.

Un tercio de los soldados de la *Grande Armée* no éramos franceses, sino españoles, alemanes, italianos, holandeses, polacos, enrolados de grado o por fuerza en la empresa imperial. Algunos afortunados consiguieron largarse. Muchos compatriotas del regimiento José Napoleón lograron escabullirse en la retirada y terminaron alistados en el ejército ruso, donde con el tiempo tuvieron ocasión de devolverles ojo por ojo a los antiguos aliados gabachos. Emotivos diálogos del tipo hola, Dupont, qué sorpresa. ¿Te suena mi cara? Sí, hombre. Yo soy Jenaro el de Vitebsk, cómo no te vas a acordar, si cuando intentamos desertar y tú eras coronel ordenaste fusilar a uno de cada dos, haz memoria: uno, dos, bang, uno, dos, bang. Fue muy ingenioso, Dupont, de verdad. Todavía me estoy descojonando de risa. Y aquí me tienes ahora, al final lo hice, de sargento ruso a pesar de este acento malagueño mío que no se puede aguantar. Las vueltas que da la vida, Dupont, camarada, cómo lo ves. Mira, de momento te voy a rebanar los huevos despacito, en recuerdo de los viejos tiempos, sin prisas. Tenemos todo el invierno por delante.

Eso los que tuvieron suerte. Otros desaparecieron por las buenas, perdido su rastro para siempre entre los fugitivos, los rezagados y los muertos; cayeron prisioneros o fueron fusilados por los franchutes en los primeros momentos del desastre, cuando aún se intentaba mantener cierta apariencia de disciplina. En cuanto al 326 de Línea, los azares del destino y de la guerra nos impidieron repetir el intento de deserción en los primeros momentos de la retirada. Después, cuando todo empezó a desmoronarse y aquello se convirtió en una merienda de negros, los merodeadores rusos, la caballería cosaca y el odio de la población civil que dejábamos atrás desaconsejaban alejarnos del grueso del ejército. En nuestra misma división, los supervivientes de un batallón italiano que intentó entregarse a los ruskis fueron degollados, desde el comandante al corneta, sin darles tiempo a ofrecer explicaciones, o sea, ni *ochichornia tovarich* ni espaguettis en vinagre. Italiani degollati. Tutti. Vete a andarle con sutilezas a un cosaco.

Una vez, en el camino de Kaluga, creímos llegada la ocasión. Llovía a mantas como si se hubieran abierto de golpe todas las compuertas del cielo, ríos de agua repiqueteando en los charcos y el barro del camino donde nos hundíamos hasta los tobillos. El día anterior habíamos intercambiado disparos con infantería ligera rusa que se movía por nuestro flanco, e hicimos algunos prisioneros; así que, aprovechando la lluvia y la confusión de la jornada, al capitán García se le ocurrió utilizarlos para que aclarasen el asunto a sus compatriotas y éstos nos recibieran con los brazos abiertos en vez de a tiros. García convocó a dos de los prisioneros, un comandante y un teniente joven, y les explicó nuestro plan.

—Aquí todos *tovarich*, y los franzuskis a tomar por saco. ¿Me explico?

Los Iván dijeron que sí, que vale, que de acuerdo, y nos pusimos en marcha bajo la lluvia, por el camino que conducía a través de un bosque espeso y embarrado. Todo fue de maravilla hasta que se nos acabó la suerte, y en lugar de encontrarnos con tropas regulares rusas topamos de boca con una horda de caballería cosaca que no dio tiempo ni a gritar nos rendimos. Cargaron por todos lados aullando hurras como salvajes, con los caballos chapoteando en el barro. Al comandante ruso se lo cepillaron a las primeras de cambio, en el barullo, justo cuando abría la boca para decir hola. En cuanto al teniente, salió por piernas y no volvimos a verlo más. Aquello terminó en un sucio combate entre los árboles, ya saben, pistoletazos a bocajarro y sablazos, bang-bang y zas-zas dale que te pego, con los ruskis yendo y viniendo mientras nos ensartaban con aquellas jodidas lanzas suyas tan largas. El caso es que perdimos veinte hombres en la escaramuza, y salvamos la piel porque unos húsares que andaban cerca acudieron a echarnos una mano y pusieron en fuga a los Iván.

—Hay que joderse, François. En toda esta puta guerra nunca me he alegrado tanto de verle el careto a un gabacho como hoy a ti.

—¿Pardón? ¿Quesque-vou-dit?

—Nada, colega. Olvídalo.

En fin. Ya fuera por casualidad, o bien porque los húsares viesen algo extraño en la situación y transmitieran sus sospechas, a partir de entonces nos vimos mucho más vigilados. Dejaron de asignarnos misiones que nos alejaran del grueso de la tropa, y al 326 se le mantenía siempre entre otras unidades gabachas, imposibilitando cualquier nuevo intento de pasarnos al enemigo.

García, vencido, sorbiéndose lágrimas de impotencia y rabia…

Después vino la nieve, y el hielo, y el desastre. Los trescientos y pico españoles que habíamos salido de Moscú con el 326 quedamos reducidos a la mitad entre Smolensko y el Beresina. Cada amanecer, el capitán García, con un gorro cosaco de piel en la cabeza y estalactitas de escarcha en las patillas y el bigote, nos levantaba a patadas del suelo helado, arriba, joder, en pie, maldita sea vuestra estampa, idiotas, si os quedáis ahí estaréis muertos dentro de un par de horas, oíd cómo aúllan los lobos oliendo el desayuno. Arriba de una vez, pandilla de inútiles, aunque sea a patadas en el culo tengo que devolveros a España. Algunos, sin embargo, ya no se levantaban, y García, vencido, sorbiéndose lágrimas de impotencia y rabia que se le helaban en la cara, ordenaba coged los fusiles y vámonos de aquí, y la tropa se ponía en marcha sobre la llanura helada por la que soplaba un viento frío como la muerte, dejando atrás, cada vez, cuatro o cinco bultos inmóviles en la nieve. Caminábamos apiñados, inclinados hacia adelante, entornados los ojos para no quedar cegados por el resplandor blanco que nos quemaba los párpados. Y al rato escuchábamos a los lobos aullar de placer, disfrutando el festín que les abandonábamos a nuestra espalda. Se habían vuelto tan sibaritas y había tanto donde elegir que ya no jalaban sino de suboficial para arriba.

Una vez, la última que lo vimos, llegó el Enano cabalgando junto a nosotros. Ya nadie en lo que quedaba del ejército franchute levantaba el chacó para gritar viva el Emperador y todo eso, sino que se le acogía en todas partes con un hosco silencio. Los del 326 estábamos en un pueblo quemado hasta los cimientos, buscando inútilmente algo de comida entre los tizones que negreaban en la nieve, cuando apareció con varios oficiales de su Estado Mayor y una escolta de la Guardia. Ya no estaban allí el mariscal Lafleur ni el general Labraguette: el primero cayó prisionero de los rusos en Mojaisk, y el segundo había tartamudeado un último «po-podéis iros a la mi-mierda, Sire», antes de salir de la fila, sentarse bajo un abedul y saltarse la tapa de los sesos de un pistoletazo. El caso es que el Enano se dejó caer por allí, junto a aquel pueblo calcinado, y le preguntó al capitán García cómo se llamaba el lugar. Por supuesto que no reconoció al 326. Había pasado mucho tiempo desde Sbodonovo y la muralla del Kremlin, y además a García o a cualquiera de los que seguíamos vivos no nos hubiera reconocido en ese momento ni la santa madre que nos parió. El asunto es que García se quedó mirando al Petit Cabrón sin responder, allí de pie en el suelo helado, pequeño y cetrino con su gorro de cosaco y sus bigotes blancos de escarcha.

—¿No has oído la pregunta, soldado? —insistió el Enano.

García se encogió de hombros. Los que estaban cerca de él juran que reía entre dientes.

—No sé cómo se llama el pueblo —dijo—. Ni lo sé ni me importa.

No añadió Sire ni Vuecencias en vinagre. Lo que hizo fue sacar del bolsillo su legión de honor, aquella que el Ilustre le había colgado al cuello en el Kremlin, y arrojarla a sus pies, sobre la nieve. Un coronel de la Guardia hizo ademán de sacar el sable de la vaina, pero el Enano lo detuvo con un gesto. Miraba a nuestro capitán como si su rostro le fuera familiar, esforzándose inútilmente por reconocerlo, hasta que al fin se dio por vencido, volvió grupas y se alejó con su escolta.

—Hijo de la gran puta —dijo García entre dientes, mientras el Petit Cabrón salía para siempre de nuestras vidas. Y ese fue su último parte de guerra.

Proseguimos la marcha hacia el oeste. Ya apenas quedaban caballos. Algunos regimientos se reducían a unas docenas de hombres, y los mariscales y generales caminaban a pie, como la tropa, empuñando el fusil para defenderse del merodeo de los cosacos: es terrible, Duchamp, parbleu, dos mariscales de Francia como somos usted y yo, y aquí estamos, a pie y con nuestro curriculum, codeándonos con la soldadesca, imagine qué dirían en Fontainebleau si nos vieran con esta pinta. Se ha salido de madre el invento, Duchamp, se lo digo yo. Bien nos la endiñó doblada, el Ilustre. Y es que ya no hay guerras como las de antes, ¿verdad? Recuerde ese paso del San Bernardo. Ese sol de Austerlitz. Esos burdeles de El Cairo… Pero no presta usted atención a lo que le digo, estimado colega. ¿Cómo?… Anda, pues tiene razón. Los cosacos. A correr tocan. Más ritmo, Duchamp, más ritmo. Up, dos, up, dos. Más ritmo que nos trincan. Up, dos, cof, cof. Maldito tabaco, Duchamp. ¿Sabe lo que le digo…? Esta guerra es una puñetera mierda.

Oficiales y soldados desertaban por la vía rápida, o sea pegándose un tiro, mientras centenares de infelices nos seguían rezagados, sin armas, y a veces los Iván eran tan osados que llegaban hasta nosotros y se cargaban a alguno de un lanzazo o lo sacaban fuera de las filas para rematarlo a golpes de sable y apoderarse de lo que llevara encima, mientras el resto continuaba caminando, embrutecidos e indefensos como un rebaño de ovejas camino del matadero. A finales de noviembre, las unidades con capacidad de combatir en buen orden eran muy pocas en el ejército franchute. Y así llegamos a las orillas del Beresina.

La cuestión era simple. Los rusos intentaban cortar allí nuestra retirada, y durante tres días peleamos por salvar el pellejo contra un ejército enemigo que atacaba de frente para estorbar el paso, y contra otro que nos acometía por la espalda intentando empujarnos al río. Unos cuantos zapadores gabachos, metidos en el agua hasta la cintura y rompiendo el hielo a hachazos, mantuvieron en funcionamiento varios puentes de madera por los que, de modo casi milagroso, buena parte del ejército pudo ponerse a salvo. En cuanto a los supervivientes del 326, llegamos a la orilla izquierda del Beresina al atardecer del 28 de noviembre, combatiendo junto a los restos de un regimiento italiano que, sumado a nuestro centenar de hombres, apenas totalizaba los efectivos de una compañía. A los italianos los mandaba un coronel flaco que murió a media mañana, recayendo el mando en un comandante a quien le volaron la cabeza a media tarde. Eso convirtió a nuestro capitán García en jefe de la unidad. Algunos, italianos incluidos, abogábamos por tirar las armas y quedarnos en la margen izquierda del río hasta que los rusos se hicieran cargo del asunto, pero por todas partes encontrábamos grupos de rezagados que habían pensado lo mismo y que estaban siendo acuchillados por los cosacos borrachos de vodka y de victoria, cuyos *hurras* y *pobiedas* atronaban la cuenca del Beresina.

Así que, tras meditarlo un rato, nuestro capitán decidió ganar los puentes antes de que los franceses nos los volaran en las narices.

—La cosa está clara, hijos míos —dijo señalando hacia el oeste, al otro lado del río—. Tal y como están las cosas, a España sólo se va por ahí.

El sargento Ortega se puso a protestar, diciendo que lo mejor era quedarse atrás y entregarse a los rusos. Algunos de nosotros aún dudábamos, y García se dio cuenta. Se iba haciendo de noche y no quedaba mucho tiempo para dimes y diretes. Así que agarró un fusil, se fue hacia Ortega y le saltó los dientes de un culatazo.

—Insisto —dijo, volviendo a señalar hacia el otro lado del río—. A España se va por allí.

Después se cargó a hombros a Ortega, que estaba sin conocimiento, y nos pusimos de nuevo en marcha.

La noche fue espantosa. Peleamos sin tregua retrocediendo hacia el río con los rusos pegados a los talones, pasando entre cadáveres, heridos y agonizantes, carros volcados y cosacos entregados al saqueo y al degüello. Masas ingentes de rezagados, centenares de hombres harapientos, vagaban a merced de los ruskis, se calentaban en fogatas de fortuna, palmaban de frío sobre la nieve. Y al amanecer, cuando empezaron a volar los puentes, todos aquellos desgraciados parecieron despertar de su letargo y entre gritos se abalanzaron sobre los que quedaban en pie, cruzando mientras estallaban las cargas, pisoteándose unos a otros para precipitarse entre las llamas y el humo de las explosiones a las aguas heladas del río.

Fue la leche. Llegamos al último puente cuando los zapadores ya prendían fuego a las mechas de los explosivos.

Lo hicimos alejando con las bayonetas a los cosacos que pretendían cogernos prisioneros, retrocediendo a tropezones sobre los heridos y los muertos que nos obstruían el paso. Cruzamos el puente pegando tiros casi a ciegas, roncos de desesperación y pavor, con el capitán García que paraba y devolvía sablazos con la espalda apoyada en los maderos del lado izquierdo y azuzaba a los rezagados, vamos, cagüentodo, vamos, cruzad ya hijos de la gran puta, cruzad o no volveréis a casa jamás, cruzad antes de que el diablo nos lleve a todos. Y un pequeño grupo congregado a su alrededor, gritando *¡Vaspaña!, ¡Vaspaña!* para reconocernos unos a otros en mitad de aquella locura, bayonetazo va y bayonetazo viene, y la artillería ruski raaas-zaca-bum, y la metralla zumbando por todas partes, y los cosacos *¡Hurra, pobieda!*, clavándonos las lanzas y degollando a mansalva, en una orgía de vodka y sangre. Y el fusilero Mínguez disparando pistoletazos mientras le tira a García de la manga, vamos para atrás que están ardiendo las mechas, mi capitán. *¡Vaspaña!* Eso es, mi capitán, vámonos a España de una puta vez. Y en esto, de pronto, más cosacos que llegan y se amontonan en el lado izquierdo del puente, y el capitán con un sablazo en la cara, la hemorragia chorreándole por las patillas y el mostacho, esto se acaba, hijos míos, corred, salid de aquí, corred, maldita sea mi sangre. Y los últimos echamos a correr y él nos sigue cojeando, apoyándose en Mínguez que lo sostiene con una mano mientras en la otra lleva una bayoneta. *¡Vaspaña! ¡Vaspaña!* Y Mínguez nos grita esperad, hijos de puta, no podéis dejar aquí al capitán, esperad. Y de pronto ya no puede más y deja caer sentado al capitán y se vuelve hacia los cosacos empuñando la bayoneta. Y los últimos del 326, que ya ganamos la otra orilla, nos volvemos a mirar por última vez a Mínguez de pie entre la humareda de pólvora, erguido en mitad del puente, las piernas abiertas con desafío y el capitán García agonizando abrazado a una de ellas. A Mínguez que está vuelto hacia los cosacos a los que corta el paso y grita *¡Vaspaña!* mientras le hunde la bayoneta a uno de ellos en la garganta y los demás le caen todos encima, y en esto que el puente salta por los aires bajo sus pies y Mínguez se larga, con su capitán, derecho a ese cielo donde van, con dos cojones, los maricones de San Fernando que también son pobres soldaditos valientes.

Epílogo

Un año y medio después del incendio de Moscú, la tarde del último día de abril de 1814, once hombres con una vieja guitarra cruzaron la frontera entre Francia y España. Algunos cargaban hatillos al hombro y aún podían reconocerse, en sus ropas hechas jirones, los restos azules del uniforme francés. Llevaban los pies envueltos en botas destrozadas y harapos. Enflaquecidos y exhaustos, barbudos, sucios, parecían una manada de lobos vagabundos y acosados, en busca de un lugar donde refugiarse, o donde morir.

Caminaban en grupos de dos o tres, con algún rezagado. Caía un sol de justicia, y los aduaneros franceses, protegidos bajo la garita donde ondeaba la flor de lis de los recién restaurados Borbones, los dejaron pasar con indiferencia al cabo de un breve diálogo del tipo mira, Dupont, ahí viene otro grupo, creo que no merece la pena pedirles papeles, ya se las entenderán con los de la aduana española. Y les permitieron seguir adelante, moviendo despectivos la cabeza hasta que se perdieron de vista. Ni eran los primeros, ni serían los últimos. Tras la caída del Monstruo, confinado ahora en la isla de Elba, los caminos de Europa estaban llenos de emigrados, antiguos prisioneros y soldados que regresaban a casa. Aquellos once escuálidos fantasmas, con las encías roídas por el escorbuto y ojos enrojecidos por la fiebre, eran cuanto quedaba en pie del Segundo batallón del 326 regimiento de Infantería de Línea, después de vagar por los campos de batalla de media Europa. Los héroes de Sbodonovo.

El sol caía vertical en el camino de Hendaya a Irún. Pedro el cordobés levantó la cabeza, palpándose la venda mugrienta que le cubría la cuenca del ojo perdido en el cruce del Beresina, y preguntó si ya estaban en España. Alguien dijo que sí, señalando una garita en la revuelta del camino, desde la que dos hoscos carabineros los miraban acercarse, observando con creciente desconfianza el aire francés de sus destrozados uniformes. Entonces Pedro el cordobés desató la guitarra de su espalda y, con cierta dificultad porque le faltaba una cuerda, pulsó las primeras notas de una melodía lenta, nostálgica. Algo sobre una mujer que espera, y un hombre huido a la sierra. Aquellas notas se habían dejado oír una vez en las murallas del Kremlin. Y ahora sonaban, apagadas y tristes, en el aire caliente de la tarde.

La Navata, julio de 1993

Índice

Praise for *The Essential Questions*

"*The Essential Questions* does an amazing thing. It takes something that most of us may regret someday—not knowing the narratives that shaped our closest relatives—and develops a beautifully written and elegant solution to it. Elizabeth Keating brings an anthropologist's eye and a humanist's heart to helping people collect and understand their own family stories. Don't just read this book; follow its instructions."

—Art Markman, professor of psychology at the University of Texas at Austin and author of *Smart Thinking*

"If you've ever heard anyone say, 'I wish I'd asked my mom about that,' then this is the book for you. In *The Essential Questions*, Elizabeth Keating reveals how, with empathy and curiosity, you can interview your family members to uncover previously hidden stories about the times and places that made them who they are, and strengthen your bond with them in the process. A gift to families everywhere!"

—Sarah Bird, author of *Daughter of a Daughter of a Queen*

"Some books feel profoundly necessary, though you can't pinpoint why. . . . This book is one of those. It goes beyond just family trees and helps you capture your elders' experiences before they slip away. This book is a love letter to anthropology itself, full of details about ways of life in other times and places. Down-to-earth and easy to use, it's a wonderful guide."

—Michael Erard, author of *Babel No More*

"With an innovative angle and compelling storytelling, *The Essential Questions* is an accessible and super-useful guide offering a multifaceted, poignant inquiry into our life stories, memory, identity, family, and intergenerational connections. It has been a long time since I read a book that felt as urgent, timely, necessary, and utterly relatable throughout. A page-turner!"

—Alexandra Georgakopoulou-Nunes, professor of discourse analysis and sociolinguistics at King's College London

The Essential
Questions

.

The Essential
Questions

....

Interview Your Family
to Uncover Stories and
Bridge Generations

ELIZABETH KEATING, PHD

A TarcherPerigee Book

tarcherperigee

An imprint of Penguin Random House LLC
penguinrandomhouse.com

Copyright © 2022 by Elizabeth Keating

Most TarcherPerigee books are available at special quantity discounts for bulk purchase for sales promotions, premiums, fund-raising, and educational needs. Special books or book excerpts also can be created to fit specific needs. For details, write: SpecialMarkets@penguinrandomhouse.com.

ISBN 9780593420928
eBook ISBN 9780593420935

Printed in the United States of America
3rd Printing

Book design by Lorie Pagnozzi

Some names and identifying details have been changed to protect the privacy of individuals.

To my students at the University of Texas at Austin
and
To the people who generously spent time answering
my questions about their lives
and
To families everywhere who want to find
deeper connections

CONTENTS

CHAPTER 1

Introduction:
The Anthropology of Family

Y ou might think you already know your family's stories pretty well—between childhood memories and reunions and holiday gatherings, you may have spent countless hours with your parents, grandparents, aunts, and uncles, soaking up family anecdotes and lore. As a professor of anthropology, I have always been fascinated by the stories that families tell, and a few years ago, I started researching family stories that are passed down from generation to generation. I have been astonished to find that many people actually know little of the lives of their parents and grandparents, even though they lived through some pretty interesting decades. Even when I asked my students, some of whom majored in history and excelled at it, about the history of their own families, they were in the dark. Our elders may share some familiar anecdotes over and over again, but still, many of us have no broader sense of the world they lived in, especially what it was like before we came along. What kind of world did our grandparents and parents inhabit as children and young adults? And how can we get them to open up about it?

It wasn't until my mother died in 2014 that I realized how much I didn't know about her life. This was all the more poignant because I had recorded several interviews with her when she was seventy-nine. Back then, I was curious about aunts, uncles, and cousins, people she knew and I didn't, and about the knowledge of our family she had gathered over a lifetime that I worried would be lost. And I wanted a record of her voice (I knew I would miss her husky, glamorous voice). At the time, I thought that if she just started talking for the tape recorder, everything I was curious about would spill out in one coherent narrative. Yet that idea turned out to be a fantasy. Rather than bringing us closer together, the experience underscored how differently our respective generations looked at the world. So, in spite of my efforts to dutifully record what my mother knew about various family members, I never asked the questions that haunt me now. Questions about her. Only after she died and her aura of "mother" receded did I wonder, did I really know her? Before she died, I—like many children, I suspect—avoided any potential clashes, wanting to preserve harmony rather than ask sensitive questions. Now I wish I had asked what formed her different generational beliefs. I'm curious about what it was like to live in her time, in the places she did, what interactions she had. I wish I had a fuller sense of her as a person, especially how she was when she was young with a lust for life. How would I have structured such a conversation? What questions should I have asked?

I've since heard other people express, with an emotion I recognize, that there are things they wished they'd asked their late parents and grandparents. Like me, they wanted to know more about their elders as people. Why did their grandmother leave home to work as a housemaid so far away at a time when this was extraordinary? Why did their parents buy that house with the big garden they never seemed that interested in?

I started to research how knowledge *isn't* passed down in families and why family members don't know more about one another. I realized there were three flaws in my failed interviews with my mother (never mind that I hadn't even thought to interview my grandparents). First, I formulated my questions based on information I already knew, meaning that my questions were based on fragments my mother had previously shared with me. As a result, she didn't tell me things I had no clue about. Second, I asked her about people in the family, when now I wish I'd asked about my mother herself, and her relationship to the world. And third, I was trapped in our mother-daughter dynamic, with all my impatience and discomfort with oppositional generational attitudes, for example, concerning how women should dress and what my behavior signified to others. I didn't ask my mother the kinds of questions that would have enabled me to step out of my own frame of reference and to take her perspective in order to better understand how she came to see things the way she did, and something of the experiences that made her who she was. In other words, I couldn't leverage the difference between us into something that gave me a new understanding of the times, places, and people that shaped her and my family history. I didn't have a way to see her in any role other than mother. I missed out on learning what my mother saw through her eyes as a young person, before five children dominated her time and aspirations.

I thought about this problem of how to learn more about the history of a person, how to enter a parent's or grandparent's world from their perspective, how to honor the language they choose to describe their experiences. And I started to think about my work as an anthropologist. I'm trained to gather information about people who are different from myself. I've done research on a remote Pacific island, on the Deaf community's skillful use of technologies, and on design projects conducted by engineers collaborating from four countries. But when interviewing my mother, I didn't apply what I knew. Despite being trained in anthropology, I lost an opportunity to do what an anthropologist does—to enter a different world of experience and interpretation.

In developing this book over five years after my mother's death and thirty years after my last grandparent's death, I have used what I know about anthropology and about studying diverse people with diverse beliefs to develop a set of topics and questions that would have treated my mother not just as the person who raised me but as an individual of a certain society and time: as a girl, a teenager, a young adult, a member of a generation.

Even though my mother didn't grow up in a different country, the world she knew when she was young was so different from mine as to seem that way, due to cultural change. Culture is hard to define because it is so big in scope, encompassing large-scale societal practices as well as small material things. And its influence is subtle. Though people are irrevocably shaped by culture, they are typically unaware of its influence. Anthropologist Pierre Bourdieu famously described culture as a set of practices that train our bodies and provide us with "dispositions" that structure everything we perceive.[1] By dispositions, he meant a sense of "how the game is played," how we make sense of and respond to what other people do. In researching this book, I've been surprised at the extent to which everyday aspects of culture have changed in just one or two generations. This rapid cultural change is what has given rise to the well-known phrase "generation gap." In fact, the phrase has only been a bellwether of people's experiences in America and Europe since the 1960s, when teenagers and their parents began to struggle with cultural differences. This struggle was recognized as something new or at least more common than ever before.

I started my research among families to find out more about this by interviewing people in the United States and other countries to find out how much they knew about their grandparents' or parents' early lives, such as how they were raised and what they experienced as young people. I soon realized that many of my interviewees, coming from a range of countries, knew hardly anything. Few could remember any personal stories about when their grandparents or parents were children, especially stories told from their point of view. Based on what people were telling me, it was clear that whole ways of life, and what made them unique within certain cultural and historical frameworks, were passing away unknown.

A kind of genealogical amnesia eats holes in family histories as permanently as moths eat holes in the sweaters lovingly knit by our ancestors and grandmothers.

As I interviewed more people, many of them parents or grandparents themselves, I became interested in hearing their *own* stories and learning about *their* childhoods. I developed a set of questions designed to get a person talking about the past in a way they never had before. The answers I got to the questions I asked opened whole new worlds to me and reflected each person's unique place in history and the extraordinary things that had happened to them. I heard some things I expected, but I was also surprised and delighted by what I learned. I gained a new appreciation for those I interviewed—and for humanity as a whole.

As I interviewed people about their families and about their own lives, and as the power of their eyewitness accounts became clear, I was convinced that the reason many people didn't know very much about their grandparents and even their parents was because they'd never thought to ask and didn't have the right questions. When I saw how much I was learning as I interviewed families, I started to share this approach with my students at the University of Texas at Austin. I gave them the assignment of interviewing one of their grandparents using the questions and topics that I've included in this book. My students loved interviewing their grandparents, and this exercise brought the generations closer together. The students' moving descriptions of what they had learned convinced me to write this book so that more people could have this experience and wouldn't miss out on hearing family histories that otherwise wouldn't have seen the light of day.

I wrote this book for you to better understand the cultural changes in your family, in a way that's intimate and personal. The book provides a step-by-step approach to guide your research on your own family so you don't experience the same regret I did. I use examples and descriptions of everyday life from the interviews I conducted with parents and grandparents from several countries, as well as cross-generational interviews I facilitated between parents and their adult children. They gave permission to have their words included, but none of the interviewees' real names are used (as is required by university research protocols on human subjects); rather, I've used pseudonyms. I also use quotes from papers written by some of my former students, whom I contacted as I was writing the book and who generously gave me permission to share their words, too. I've noted the titles of their papers in the endnotes, but I've used only their first names (in cases where they wanted to be identified) as we agreed. Both the students and the grandparents I interviewed were enthusiastic about being part of this book, and about sharing something of the experiences they had.

There are thirteen topics—and questions to support each of those topics—that I developed as I interviewed families and considered how to ask about their lives from an anthropological perspective, based on my years of research and teaching in the field. An anthropologist goes to a new place armed with curiosity and time. They try to shed the assumptions of their own culture and make the familiar strange, enabling them to see different perspectives of the same physical world. The goal with these questions is for you, too, to have the chance to see new sides of a world you've supposedly known all your life.

Getting to know your parents and grandparents on anthropological terms will enrich your understanding of your own beliefs and cultural habits, as well as the forces that have shaped your family history and, in turn, your own identity. The topics and questions are designed to lead to a new understanding of how the world looked to your elders when you weren't the center of their story. (If you're among the lucky ones, your grandparents have a tendency to focus totally on you when you're together.)

As counterintuitive as it sounds, the anthropological approach to getting to know someone near and dear to you can lead to their sharing details and anecdotes that many in your family have never heard. It's not only the questions in this book that help unearth stories about people, but the work you put into interviewing them, and the magic that happens when people get to talk about themselves to a curious listener who wants all the details. Cole, one of my students, explains this better than I could:

> While I would consider myself very close with my grandparents (as they live a mere 10 minutes from my house), I do not think I have ever had such a candid, in-depth conversation with them as I did from this interview. I learned things about them, their lives, and their relationship that I had never heard before. . . .

I was lucky to be able to do this and succeed at it as my grandfather has somewhat early-stage dementia. It has definitely started to affect his memory and cognition, though he still clearly remembers his childhood and adult life. I do not know how much longer he would be able to conduct an interview such as this one, so for that I want to thank you as I will always have this interview to hold on to as he progresses in his old age.[2]

Interviewing your elders by using the topics in this book will give you a personal glimpse into lived history. You'll get eyewitness reports that create a picture of your ancestors' past in a way that a family tree diagram never could. Your parent or grandparent might share stories of hunting and fishing with their father, wearing clothes their mother made out of feed sacks, cringing at the sound of cruise missiles overhead during World War II, helping during washday, or going barefoot from June to September.

In one interview, a grandmother shared that when she was a girl in Germany during the Nazi era, none of the adults would tell her why her nine-year-old friend and her family, who lived across the street, disappeared one day without saying goodbye. And this now ninety-year-old Oma told us about a sign she remembered seeing in a streetcar at the time depicting a man with a finger to his lips. One student's grandma talked about having to wait at the back of a restaurant to have her food handed through a window because she was Cajun and couldn't go inside.[3] These moments can create a sense of your grandparent's world. You'll recognize a child's uncanny feeling of living in a society punctuated with grim injuries to the spirit, and you'll learn how your grandparent still found the courage to go on. Or you may find your grandparent lived in a safer world, one where they roamed fearlessly, at least until the streetlights came on and they had to go home. You may suddenly see someone who isn't the frail person before you, but a lively teenager who was told that if she didn't hurry up and find a husband, the market for husbands would be gone; or a person who remembers his father's quiet desperation to put food on the table; or the young girl whose dream job to be a musician sustained her when she had to help her father run the farm during the war years, when the young men were away.

You will be surprised at how much your parents and grandparents haven't told you, perhaps because they thought you wouldn't be interested, or they weren't sure how you'd judge them. Just as the precious oral literatures and histories of whole communities are being lost the world over through rapid change, migration, language death, and a failure to ask, there is a risk that your family's personal stories, too, will be lost forever. Your parents and grandparents have unique snapshots and memories of the world they knew, and in this book, you'll learn to preserve them and create lasting meaning and connection in the process. Even if your first thought is "Grandma doesn't like to talk about herself," you'll be surprised by what these questions reveal even in the first half hour. In this book I've chosen to focus primarily on how to interview elder family members—parents, grandparents, uncles, and aunts. Typically, those with the most at stake in losing family stories are the younger generation, although certainly these techniques can be applied to interviews with younger relatives (or anyone, really). Your interview doesn't have to be formal—it can be designed to be more of a conversation. In chapter 2, I provide a detailed overview of what the interview process looks like. Chapters 3 through 15 cover interview topics and offer several questions related to each topic, including space at the end of each chapter for taking notes on what you've learned about your family through the questions in that chapter.

Because the thirteen interview topics in this book are rooted in cultural and linguistic anthropology, some of the questions might strike you and your interviewees (your parents or grandparents) as odd if you've never studied anthropology before. I teach hundreds of students about anthropology every year. These students have backgrounds in a variety of fields—including engineering, history, medicine, and business—but they often find that studying anthropology makes them more aware of themselves in new ways. You may have had this experience while learning a new language—suddenly the grammar of your own language becomes noticeable, though you hardly thought about it before.

Anthropology is not an old science. It wasn't until the early twentieth century that the first generation of professionally trained anthropologists began doing intensive fieldwork. Before that, missionaries, colonial administrators, and travelers supplied information about different ways of life around the world. The early anthropologists realized that in order to get beyond a brief account of lives different from their own, they had to spend time with people, observing and asking questions. One of these early anthropologists was Bronislaw Malinowski, who traveled to Papua New Guinea and then to the Trobriand Islands. He pitched his tent in the middle of a small village, learned the language, and observed what his neighbors did throughout an ordinary hot tropical day.[4] He spent time talking with them and asking questions about their practices and beliefs. His views about trying to inhabit the unique perspective of another, especially a person very different from himself, had enormous influence.

You won't be able to literally pitch your tent in the same place where your parent or grandparent grew up, but the questions in this book will help re-create that life for you. I've included background information on the anthropological framework behind the topics and questions in every chapter. You already know more about anthropology than you might realize.

I'm sure your parent or grandparent hasn't been asked some of these questions before and might not be used to describing their lives in an interview setting. For example, they might never have described in much detail the spaces they grew up in, and it may have been years since they last thought about how they interacted with people when they were growing up. This is all for the good, though, since the questions are intended to reveal things they've forgotten about or never thought you might be interested in knowing. It's this unfamiliarity with an anthropological approach that can lead your grandparent or parent to remember things that will surprise you (and even them).

Although the topics may seem abstract at first, you'll find they elicit very interesting descriptions of daily life "back then." When you ask for descriptions of your elder's childhood home and the neighborhoods they roamed around in, you'll hear stories that place you in a rich sensory world you knew little about.

You might find that how you usually perceive your grandparent doesn't actually align with how they perceive themselves. You may see your grandmother as religiously minded and cautious, while she sees herself as still having a young girl's spirit and is rather unaware of her aging. Taking an anthropological approach depends on resisting any characterizations or labels for people or their behavior that you might have formed before your interview. For example, you may have the preconception that "Grandpa is the black sheep of the family," or "Grandma has always been the strong one." My grandfather worked in a bank, and I always saw him as a person who was most at home at a desk. When my mother told me that he'd been a semiprofessional baseball player when he was younger, I realized there was a side of him I never knew. If I'd interviewed him, which I now wish I had, I hope I'd have set aside the bank label I'd given him and been able to hear something of his passion for a different game.

When interviewing your elders, you're the anthropologist who wants to understand the world from someone else's point of view, and the key is getting details about ordinary life. Sometimes parents, grandparents, and other family members are puzzled by your interest in the ordinary. They may feel that their everyday doings won't be interesting enough for you. One grandparent I interviewed said, "I had a very commonplace sort of upbringing." People we interview know much more than they realize, and they overestimate how much we have in common with them. Studies have shown that people consistently *over*estimate how many other people can recognize the same things they can and consistently *under*estimate how many can identify things they can't. Each of us has a more particular view of normal than we realize. It may be "normal" for one person to experience the deaths of five out of seven children. Someone else might consider it "normal" to be recruited by an Ivy League women's college on the East Coast, only to be told by her father that ladies don't leave the South. Ordinary life doesn't get much attention. But it's where people spend their time and make sense of things. And it's what we miss the most when it's gone.

Your parents and grandparents have experienced modernization, new technologies, changes in parenting attitudes, and even political revolutions. You may hear fascinating snapshots of what it was like to be a child when World War II gasoline shortages suddenly brought back ponies and carts in Ireland, what it was like arriving on Ellis Island with only a few articles of clothing, or what it was like to be born on the day the stock market crashed in 1929 to a family suddenly struggling to survive in a world falling apart. You may hear about deep connections to the land, "growing up on horseback," worrying about the size of a dowry, picking crops in the summer, living meal to meal, and walking to school without heavy backpacks.

People are often surprised at just how much they enjoy

hearing memories about the customs and experiences of a previous generation. More than one student has told me that after interviewing a grandparent, they wished they could have experienced that old way of life. Grandparents were young and fit once, wielding their power to carve out a unique set of ideals and preferences. That spirit can still conjure up for you the exuberance of their youth, or the scarcities that built a strength in them that they rarely talk about.

I didn't grow up in a generation where being twelve years old meant you were expected to function as an adult, and I never had to take a job to help with family bills. I wasn't like one grandparent, now seventy-two, who at fifteen was already a full-time apprentice electrician, or my student's grandmother, eighty-three, who remembered that a classmate of hers was asked to drive the school bus. According to one of my students, Henry:

> The school bus route started in the countryside, and one of the children would actually drive the bus from the beginning of the route to my grandmother's house, at which point her mother would take the wheel and drive the rest of the way. This was astounding to me, but since the country roads were all gravel, the child was able to drive the bus with relative ease.[5]

It was wartime and there was a shortage of adults.

Many grandparents I interviewed mentioned how they cherished the freedom they had to roam widely without supervision before dark, even at the age of five or six, which is quite different from the highly supervised way that six-year-olds play today. This was even true in cities like San Francisco. While early childhood was the time of greatest freedom for them, their grandchildren are probably experiencing their greatest freedom in their twenties or thirties, with increased opportunities for women and minorities, as well as more choices in lifestyle. The world is now more available for exploration due to many factors, including social media and technology.

As an anthropologist, you'll be interested in how your grandparent or parent makes sense of what happened to them within the world around them as they knew it. Maybe they had no electricity on the farm and that sounds like a hardship, but in the world they re-create for you through their memories, life without electricity can have a magical side as they tell you about being transported by the quality of moonlight on wheat fields, water, and leaves. When your grandparent talks about playing under the moon, the joys of a childhood self are re-created with the language of memory. There is richness in the details of human experience. The anthropologically oriented questions in this book will help you to know previous generations as members of unique worlds.

Different generations have a lot to say about one another. "Kids these days" don't act like grandparents think they should. This complaint isn't new. Apparently even Aristotle had the opinion that young people were annoyingly sure that they knew everything. And young people sometimes consider their elders to be grumpy and irritable. But stereotypes get in the way of knowing. In families and communities, there are secrets to be discovered.

INSIDER/OUTSIDER PERSPECTIVES

When anthropologists try to learn about a new culture, they seek to understand as an insider, or a native, does. Being an outsider is like being a tourist in another country. Tourists focus on how they see things—what's new to them, what they like and don't like—so they are the center of the story. A tourist might choose to stay at a hotel with amenities they're accustomed to (like heating in the winter), even though the locals live differently. In order to get an insider's view, an anthropologist would have to live without central heating and do as the locals do, bundling up and warming themselves by the fire. When one grandparent said to me, "I remember the weight of the blankets in the bed. You were almost flattened," those details gave me an insider view.

This anthropological approach was illustrated by my first experience "in the field" in Pohnpei, a tiny island in the Pacific, north of New Guinea and east of the Philippines. When I first went to Pohnpei, my usual ways of observing people and making judgments about what was going on were of no help to me—I didn't know what might happen next week or even after saying hello, nor could I interpret when an event, such as a feast or a celebration, was actually going to start. Decisions were made rapidly, without much advance announcement, based on many factors I don't even understand today. I know that clock time was the least important factor.

The way I dressed as a student in the US (in jeans) had to be abandoned when I got to Pohnpei, because a woman couldn't show the outline of her thighs. So, it had to be a skirt (my hosts made beautiful skirts for me, in the island's unique designs). It quickly became clear to me that my usual ways of dressing and eating were on hold. Habitual ways of thinking, in fact, got in the way of my communicating and connecting with and understanding a person from a different place. I had to cast aside my own cultural habits and see the world through a new lens.

In taking an anthropological approach to interviewing your parent or grandparent, your goal, too, is to leave aside your familiar thinking habits as you ask questions and listen. You'll want to become attuned to your parent's or grandparent's ways of seeing the world, including how they interact with people, what they find beautiful, or alarming, or infuriating. If your grandparent says about their childhood, "I didn't know we were poor until someone told me we were, and even after that I didn't feel I was disadvantaged or missing anything," you'll want to ask some questions to understand more about their way of framing the past.

You'll know that you're not taking the perspective of an insider if you find yourself forming judgments about your grandparent's behavior. If you were raised by parents who encouraged you to question authority, but your grandfather tells you that as a child, "you just did what you were told and there wasn't a lot of choice in the matter," it requires some mental flexibility to adopt your grandfather's perspective. But it's worth it.

The most successful interviewers in my classes were able to set aside their assumptions and be careful listeners. Excelling at the anthropological approach requires curiosity and patience with how the interviewee gathers their thoughts, letting them create a world in a way that suits them as a product of that world, although their story might wander or they might forget names or fail to explain contexts until you ask for more details. Getting details about a life, using questions that are rarely asked, will help you create a picture, and even a legacy.

THE IMPORTANCE OF ASKING

As the French novelist and playwright Simone Schwarz-Bart wrote, "When an old person dies, a whole library disappears."[6] My grandparents' lives are now available to me only through history books that offer insight into their generation, photos, and the fragments of paper they left behind, including a ship's manifest with my grandfather's name on it, which, let's face it, leaves too much to my imagination, influenced by my own ways of thinking.

I now wish I'd asked more questions about my grandparents when they were alive, to create a chain of knowledge between generations and a deeper understanding of the cultural changes we've experienced. Older generations are often dismissed, their perspectives considered outdated, but you'll be surprised by how much precious and undervalued knowledge resides in your family. By having the conversations suggested in the following chapters, you'll be able to learn things that aren't found in books. Often, we let official written histories, the grand narratives of famous people and conflicts, take center stage, but firsthand accounts from "ordinary" people can transmit emotional and intellectual contexts that are missing from official history. History books often paint whole decades in a way that makes it seem as though everyone experienced the same events the same way, but you'll find vivid new ways of understanding history through your parents' and grandparents' stories.

Author Diane Wilson described the importance of personal histories to families: "The loss of that oral tradition and the breakdown of communication between generations had set my family adrift, floating aimlessly without history and all its accumulated experience to guide us."[7] As she put it, our elders provide context so we can see "the invisible legacy that follows us, that tells us who we are." Oral historian Thomas Charlton describes an interview between generations as "an experience of unique, transactional (two-way) communication—a never-to-be-duplicated encounter between persons exchanging questions and answers."[8] Grandparents and parents need to be asked and given an opportunity to speak, even those who feel that the past sometimes isn't pretty, as one grandparent put it. We don't want only happy memories, although even among the difficult stories, there are often many more of awe and exploration.

The questions in this book are designed to elicit stories that offer context for events and the perspective of the teller, a sense of their hopes, doubts, confusion, struggles, and joys.[9] A story connects us with the storyteller on an emotional level, and inhabiting the role of an anthropologist means being open to what the interviewee considers important and letting them talk about that.

Now that we've established the goals for interviewing your family members, the next chapter covers important details on how best to prepare for and conduct your interview.

CHAPTER 2

Tips on Interviewing
Your Family

Most people welcome the chance to talk about their lives and their opinions. Every interview is an exciting, dynamic process, as you and your interviewee create what becomes a unique shared journey.

You can do the interview in several parts over time, getting to know your relative in relaxed conversations, or you can do the interview in one sitting. The advantage of breaking up the interview into several parts is that you will have more time, and you can pose more follow-up questions that may occur to you over the course of the conversations. Interviewees often remember new things between interviews and can share these details with you, too. Asking the questions over a longer time period can foster an even closer connection between you and your family.

AN OVERVIEW OF THE INTERVIEW

In this chapter, I offer a few simple guidelines to being a good interviewer. They are also the hallmarks of a curious and respectful listener, including paying attention, being open-minded and flexible, respecting silence, being thorough in obtaining details, and showing appreciation for your interviewee.

Anthropologists most often rely on semi-structured interviews to understand their subjects. The interview is organized around a set of questions prepared in advance, but new questions can emerge in the interview, the sequence in which the questions are asked is flexible, and the interviewer can reword the questions. The type of questions asked tend to be open-ended. There are opportunities for discussion between the interviewer and interviewee, and improvisations and digressions are welcome.

As you interview your family member, allow them to talk about what's important to them. As mentioned in the introduction, I've organized the questions around thirteen topics. Each topic begins with an Opening Question that is broad enough to give your interviewee space to answer however they'd like. I've also provided suggestions for follow-up questions to elaborate on the topic. Use them if you are interested in them, and if your interviewee hasn't already covered them in response to the Opening Question. At the end of the interview, give your relative time to ask any questions and to elaborate on anything they'd like. Be sure to express your appreciation for all that they've shared with you.

YOU, THE INTERVIEWER

In the role of interviewer, there are three positions you have to inhabit at the same time.[1] First, you must be a conversationalist facilitating a comfortable dialogue with your family member.

Second, you must be the regulator of conversation, managing which topics are covered by asking certain questions. It's important not to regulate too much, because you want your family member to talk freely about what they consider significant. While an ordinary conversation would require both people to do some regulating as they exchange questions, in an interview, you would want your family member to do all the talking (some people unfortunately do think that's a normal conversation).

Third, you must take the position of an anthropologist, suspending your opinions. As you hear what your grandparent or parent says in answer to your question, avoid showing bias in your thoughts and your responses. Usually, "being yourself" in a comfortable conversation doesn't mean holding back your opinions and reactions, but in this case, it's your relative's opinions and reactions that are central. People who've taken the anthropologist's approach to interviewing their parents and grandparents have described their satisfaction at creating an atmosphere in which their interviewee revealed opinions that surprised them. One student, William, said he hadn't expected his grandfather to speak with as much candor as he did; "I was surprised at how vulnerable and honest my grandfather was with me," he said.[2]

THE ASK

What might be the best way to ask your family member for an interview, to increase the likelihood that they'll agree to it? The good news is that most people welcome the opportunity to talk about their pasts.

In the unusual case that you encounter a person who is reluctant to be interviewed, you may find that they are unsure of what you are "looking for," or they may think they are just "too ordinary." Anthropologists since the time of Malinowski have encountered people who may not understand what an anthropologist wants to know or may fear that their own personal knowledge is not very deep or significant (you will find otherwise). Consider that by worrying about whether they can provide what you're looking for, they're trying to be helpful. Draw on this helpfulness to reassure them that they're the perfect candidate for your research. No doubt their consideration will make it an even smoother ride.

Some older relatives might be concerned about taking too much time (what a rich history they have!), so it's important to allay these concerns, if they have them, and assure them that there's nothing you would rather do than spend time learning more about them. Doing this interview with a family member strengthens your relationship with them and alleviates the loneliness that is especially common among older people—and increasing among younger ones, too.[3] Loneliness in the elderly is caused by a sense of invisibility, which in turn leads to sleeplessness, illness, and unhappiness. Asking your parent or grandparent about their life is a way to address feelings of invisibility, which is especially important in the US, where the contributions of older generations are regularly diminished. For people in the sixteen-to-twenty-four age group, who are the loneliest group in Western societies according to research psychologists, making a deeper connection with an older family member may be especially treasured.[4] As my student Taylor put it, "I was very excited, to say the least . . . when I was given the opportunity to do something I didn't even know I wanted to do until I read the instructions."[5] She went on to interview more than one grandparent.

Once your relative agrees, explain that you would prefer to record the interview, so as not to miss any important details. Usually people readily understand this.

WHOM TO INTERVIEW

Once you invite a person to have an interview, you may find that other family members want to participate or even just listen in. If so, consider that the presence of a third person in the room can be constraining to the interviewee, or bring in complex interpersonal dynamics that turn a private exchange into something more like a public performance. I suggest doing the interview on your own and sharing the recording later (with their permission).

Consider interviewing more than one relative, but it's best not to interview them at the same time.

PREPARATION

Once you have your interview scheduled, some preparation will ensure everything goes well. Select an interview environment free from distractions and where you and your interviewee will feel at ease.

Bring paper to take notes when something occurs to you as

you are listening, for example, if your parent or grandparent mentions something that you want to explore more later, without interrupting the flow of what they're saying in the moment. You can also make some notes about the setting, such as details about where and when the interview took place, as well as aspects of the person's mood or mannerisms.

I usually provide some water and snacks.

You'll want to test your recording equipment before you start, whether this is your phone or a separate recording device (more on recording later in this chapter). If you conduct the interview online, pay attention to lighting and the technical aspects. Once you have a good setting, a willing interviewee, a curious listener, and a recording device, there are a few things to keep in mind to ensure a successful interview.

BUILDING COMMON GROUND

Any good conversation depends on finding common ground. To build common ground between generations, I recommend doing a little research on the historical periods during which your interviewee was a child and young adult. For example, if your grandparent was a child during the Great Depression of the 1930s, you'll find photographs from that time showing people waiting in long breadlines for a small amount of free food. My parents were children during the Depression, called "the worst economic downturn in the history of the industrialized world."[6] They never lost their anxiety about money and always had a hard time spending any. If your parents or grandparents grew up in the US after Dr. Spock's *Common*

Sense Book of Baby and Child Care came out in 1946, they were likely influenced by this bestseller that shaped how children were raised for decades. And if your parents or grandparents were teenaged during the 1950s and '60s, they helped create what we now call "youth culture," which changes and is studied closely in each generation.

Glancing through magazines or newspapers from the period of your relative's upbringing (which can be found on the internet) will provide a glimpse of what was on people's minds back then. Don't forget to consider your interviewee's geographical location, too. When I was growing up in the Northeast US, I looked forward to snow days, when roads were impassible and school was closed, leaving a whole day to explore new snowdrifts or go skating on the pond at the bottom of the hill. Years later, my younger brothers spent their youth in Kingston, Jamaica, where there were no cold winters, and school closed for hurricanes.

STARTING THE INTERVIEW

Before you start, offer a brief explanation of your goals for the interview. For example, you could say, "I'd like to know about your childhood and to understand better what it was like to grow up when you did." Again, ask permission to record. Assure them that if there's anything they want to take out of the recording later, you will do so. After you start the recording, state the time and place of the interview and the name of the person you are interviewing. Ask your interviewee to state that they give you their permission to record them.

SILENCES AND INTERRUPTIONS

A successful interview depends on your ability to handle silence. Many interviewers may feel awkward if there are silences during an interview. The ability to tolerate silence varies from culture to culture. In Western Apache culture, for example, a period of silence is expected before someone answers a question or starts speaking.[7] And Japanese conversationalists recognize that a conversation isn't just about talking, but there is also a lot going on when words aren't being spoken.

When I first started interviewing, I had to unlearn my interpretation of silence as an expression of discomfort or an indication that something was wrong. I realized that silence, especially in the case of interviews like these, meant people were bringing memories to mind. If I flew in to fill the silence, I would redirect my interviewees' attention away from the memories they were trying to recall. When I gave people a chance to reflect in silence, they came up with details that were stunning in their power and immediacy.

I made a rule for myself that I wouldn't ever be the first one to end a silence during an interview. I came up with this rule after I listened to the audiotape of my first interview and was dismayed to hear the number of times I had filled a silence and redirected the flow of the conversation. I wished I had waited to see where the interviewee would go. It's good practice to develop the ability to hold a seven-second silence.

If you happen to ask a question that your relative answers with a simple yes or no, let some moments of silence elapse. Silence is an invitation for them to say more. If they say nothing after a while (these will seem like very long seconds to you, but they show that you are honoring the person's pace for answering), then try reframing the question or asking a follow-up question. There are some questions, though, that may be answered with a simple yes or no.

It's not just your interviewee's silences that you want to be patient with, but their stream of talk, too. It's easy to get excited and interrupt, but this disrupts what you're trying to facilitate, a journey into the past. As the interviewer, you are the tool for stimulating reminiscences.

CREATING A TRUSTING ATMOSPHERE

Besides taking care with silences and interruptions, another tool for creating a trusting atmosphere is showing compassion for your family member's experiences and attitudes. The world they'll describe isn't just the same world you know with different labels attached, but an entirely different world.[8] They may have different ideas than you about the moral uses of power, or how a person should balance the need for independence with responsibilities to other people.

One of my students told the class that as his interview proceeded, he began to realize that his grandmother was answering all his questions as though she were trying to prevent judgment, so he took steps to reassure her that he knew that there were different beliefs and expectations of behavior when she was growing up and that he was interested in learning more about them from her. If your parent or grandparent thinks you are judging them negatively or are critical of them, they will likely withhold or edit their views and stories of their past, out of deference to you. This unfortunately undermines your project to better understand your ancestors, and particularly how their beliefs might have shaped you.

You may hear your parent or grandparent express views that you feel yourself reacting to because they seem like a criticism of your generation. Since the goal of the interview is to better understand another generation's views and experiences, you have to hear more of their views and not less! That means not changing the subject to a more innocuous one, as I unfortunately did with my mother. If you find yourself feeling triggered by your parent's or grandparent's way of seeing things, try building common ground by asking questions that help you better understand their perspective. For example, I wish I had asked my mother to elaborate on her beliefs about women. Did her mother teach her the maxim that she repeated to me that a woman's status depended on being married? Did that affect her own decision to get married and leave a life she enjoyed when she was single and working? You want to create an environment where a person will feel comfortable revealing to you their experiences. Mirroring the interviewee's vocabulary or body comportment is one way that we often unconsciously show compassion and empathy for others.

APPRECIATION

Be sure to show your appreciation as you hear your relatives' stories. You can show appreciation through what social interaction scholars call expressions of alignment and expressions of affiliation. These are the sounds people make when they're showing they're attentive to a speaker, sounds like *uh-huh*, *hm*, and murmurs called continuers because they encourage the speaker to continue. You can use words like *yes, no, yeah*, and *really* for this purpose, too.

You can go further in showing not only acknowledgment but also affiliation through nonverbal signals like nodding your head, raising your eyebrows, or directing your gaze (at or away from them, depending on the culture) to show that you "get" their point of view and sympathize.[9] Using continuers, like *mm-hm*, and alignment gestures, such as smiling, nodding, and managing eye contact, are all great ways to show appreciation for how your parent's or grandparent's words have a unique relevance to you. The more interest you show in a particular topic, the more likely they will share about it, too.

PACING

Keep the pace slow and watch for signs of fatigue. Remember that the person you're interviewing is doing almost all the talking. If they begin to seem tired, take a break or set up another time to finish the interview. Usually, people can talk for quite some time about their childhoods and teenage years. Most people I interviewed talked easily and eagerly about all sorts of aspects of their past. And I found the interviews so fascinating I didn't want them to end. They often went on for several very enjoyable hours for both of us.

It might be necessary to break the interview into separate conversations at different times because of people's schedules or energy levels. I found that when I broke up interviews, people were just as enthusiastic to talk the next time. An advantage to doing several interviews over days or weeks or months is that you and your interviewee will have time to recharge after each conversation.

FLEXIBILITY

Sometimes a question needs to be rephrased because it reflects the perspective of the interviewer (or this author!). You might have to alter a question slightly so it makes sense to your interviewee.

Sometimes parents or grandparents will address several questions with the same anecdote. No problem, it's part of telling about their past experiences in their own way. My students told me that they learned a lot about their grandparents when they answered the questions with stories.

Some people I interviewed tended to talk very philosophically at first, without referring to specific incidents in their lives. With them, I asked for examples to illustrate what they'd been describing abstractly, so that I could see scenes of their childhood and the interactions that contributed to their beliefs. The details in their stories told me more about their childhood than their philosophical-life-lesson approach.

THE OPENING QUESTION

As I mentioned earlier, each topic chapter includes a main Opening Question, in addition to optional follow-up questions. The Opening Question is designed to be an entryway that invites your interviewee to remember. When some of my interviewees were in the middle of answering the Opening Question, they would pause and suddenly say, "Oh, I'm way off topic," but I loved how one memory led to another as they looked back, and I told them to please go on.

In my experience, interviewees typically had so much to say in response to the Opening Question that they actually answered many of the follow-up questions at the same time. But if interviewees gave short answers, I used the follow-up questions as prompts to say more.

When answering the Opening Question, people sometimes included stories related to other topics, which is understandable because any part of everyday life touches on many aspects of culture. For example, the chapter topic on space begins with an Opening Question asking the interviewee to describe their childhood home. When one person I interviewed mentioned the basement, it reminded her of washday. She explained that every Monday when she came home from school, she went directly to the basement to help her mother with the washing. It was her job to feed the washed clothes through a wringer that sat on top of the washtub. She remembered how hard her mother worked every day, taking care of four children with few of the modern appliances available today. The description of washday actually made it possible to imagine what it was like to live in that home.

I didn't see it as a problem when people combined multiple topics in one response because it was wonderful to hear how they related different aspects of their childhood. Later in the interview, when I came to a topic they had already mentioned in an earlier answer, I would acknowledge that they'd already told me something about the topic but asked if they could tell me a bit more.

As you ask your grandparent or parent about topics such as identity, rites of passage, belief, and kinship, you'll find, as Sean, a student in my anthropology class, described: "I was surprised by the number of things about my grandmother's life that I had no prior knowledge of. I knew very little about her childhood, and having her share narratives from that period of her life allowed me to have a real idea of what it was like, instead of just knowing the fact that she had lots of siblings and lived on a farm."[10]

I've had a couple of interviewees ask me to rephrase an Opening Question as a smaller-scope question. While I did rephrase the question, I still kept it fairly broad and assured them that they could answer however they wanted. Broad Opening Questions are important to elicit details and balance the power dynamics between the one asking the questions and the one answering them. With a broad question, your parent or grandparent has more autonomy to talk about what they want and shape their own approach to a topic. Narrowly focused questions might induce them to see the world from your point of view, and you might be pouring too many of your own ideas into the interview. I believe it's important for each interviewee to play the central role in telling their story. As one thought leads to another, a life takes shape in a way that much better captures what is significant and memorable to them. They are in control of the narrative.

FOLLOW-UP QUESTIONS

Follow-up questions are important to any interview. Asking someone to elaborate on what they've said saves you from the unfortunate realization later that you're not exactly sure what they meant or that there are some broken links in the story.

The follow-up questions I've asked vary according to what I've already learned from the person's answer to the Opening Question, what I'm curious to know more about, and what is appropriate for their special circumstances. Quite often, new follow-up questions occurred to me as the interviewee was speaking.

Follow-up questions can be as simple as asking for clarification, like "Could you explain what you mean by . . ." or "Let me see if I understand. . . ." You can also ask your interviewee to elaborate on something they've mentioned, like "Can you tell me more about your exploits with that childhood friend you mentioned?" or "Can you tell me more about where you used to go on your bicycle?" or "Can you tell me about some of the marriage prospects who came to your home?" These follow-up questions invite a story, and stories are a wonderful way to connect to someone's experience.

Follow-up questions can be specific or general. You can ask general questions to link the life of your family member with the others of their era. Before and during the interview, glance at the list of follow-up questions I've provided to see which interest you. They can be asked in any order.

You can also use follow-up questions to respond to a parent or grandparent who consciously or unconsciously adopts the formal, knowing tone of a patriarch or matriarch citing proverbs rather than taking you through the details of their life. Your job as an anthropological interviewer is to ask follow-up questions to get them back to a specific time and place in their youth.

Not only are proverbial ways of speaking full of contradictions (Clothes make the man vs. You can't judge a book by its cover), but they also close conversation rather than providing an opening. If your relative answers your question with a proverbial expression, ask for personal experiences that led them to believe the proverb was truthful.

I've found that the best follow-up questions are those that focus on how or who, and not why. People often answer a "why" question with something like "It's always been that way," or "I don't know." "How" questions, though, give people a chance to pass along skills and information that there might not otherwise be a context for revealing. And "who" questions often elicit stories with interesting details. When I am curious about why something is the case, I make sure the "why" question is about the interviewee's own motives or actions, rather than asking them to guess at other people's motives.

One of the best follow-up questions I've heard came from a daughter named Anne, who could have asked her ninety-year-old mother a why question, but instead transformed it into a who question. Rather than asking her mother, Georgina, why she'd decided to become a doctor in Britain at a time when this was unusual for women, Anne asked, "You became a doctor without an obvious science background, so who encouraged you?" Georgina replied with a surprising answer: "It was just me thinking to myself that maybe the thing I'd like most in life is to get married and have children. But I might not get to have that, so in case that doesn't happen, I want to have something to do that will be really interesting for the whole of my life, you know, something that will be really interesting and that will be obvious to others and not just to myself."

Georgina's answer revealed how important family was to her, since, in her view, a career had to be a particularly interesting calling in order to be as fulfilling as the role of wife and mother. Georgina also brought another generation into the picture when she added that she'd needed the support of her family to study medicine, but she'd never really known what her father thought about her choice until she'd been practicing medicine for some years. As she told it: "On one occasion Grandpa said to me—because I think I called on them after a working day, and they knew I'd been working all day—he said, 'Well, all my friends told me when I said my daughter's off to become a doctor, "Well, that's a waste of time; she'll just get married and that'll be the end of it. It's a waste for her, it's a waste." You've proved to me and to them that it wasn't in any way a waste.'"

Georgina told us, "It was quite nice to have him say to me that it hasn't been a waste. I guess he didn't discourage me." This story offers a picture of customary advice and thinking about marriage in Anne's grandfather's generation. The story also shows that the tendency for people in Western cultures to view each individual as a separate, autonomous force in determining their future is simplistic. Anne's follow-up question revealed a system of relationships that gives insight into the challenges Georgina faced.

If you get a short answer or an "I don't know" to a follow-up question, try a different way of asking. For example, if you ask when something happened but your grandparent doesn't know the exact date or year, ask the when question in relation to another event. For example, did the event take place before or after Granddad got married, or before or after his parents died? Or you could ask, "About how old were you when . . ."

If you find that your relative is giving only a "20/20 hindsight" view (that is, judging their past behavior by what they could only know now) or critiquing their past life by saying, "I should have . . ." it won't be as interesting an account to you. This kind of response overlooks the confusion a young person can feel. Try asking them a follow-up question that focuses on the moments leading up to a decision that they are now reevaluating.

If your parent or grandparent only speaks in very positive terms about the past, and you suspect that they may be trying to protect you from hearing about painful losses, you could try telling them about some challenges in your own life and asking if they have any experience you can draw from or advice for you based on their own life. Most people going to the trouble to interview their elders don't only want to hear the exemplary narratives demonstrating ideals about how to succeed. You want to avoid these mini lectures and proverbs that represent ideals rather than reality. Instead, you want to hear about vulnerabilities and how a person you love so much could continue to survive emotionally for sixty or seventy or even eighty-plus years! You want to hear about the full breadth of their experiences, including confusion, failures, joys, and sorrows, how they have wrestled with the mores of their times and the challenges of making their way. If you're bursting with curiosity, you may feel the impulse to ask more than one follow-up question at a time. Academics are famous for three-part questions. Unfortunately, a speaker trying to answer a three-part question typically leaves out one part or doesn't go into much depth. Slow down and ask only one question at a time.

ELICITING GREATER DETAIL FROM A STORY

The questions in this book are not designed to elicit a general historical description of a decade, but a very personal view. Getting vivid details from your interviewee is an essential part of experiencing the world through their eyes. Details make it possible to sidestep clichés.

One grandmother who grew up in Iceland told me that she and her youngest brother slept in their parents' room. When I asked more about it, she said, "I got the top bunk and my brother the bottom." Then she added that her mother had a knitting machine in the room, and more often than not, her mother would be knitting at night. "We'd go to sleep to the knitting machine, *prrrrr kssssssh prrrrr.*" These details brought that room to life for me.

Simply repeating a little of what your interviewee has said in question form can elicit more details, for instance, "So you slept in your parents' room?" If your interviewee describes the town girls and boys as a little uppity, acting as if they were better than the children raised in the country (something I heard from several grandparents), ask how this superior behavior showed itself.

EMOTIONAL BONDING

You may ask a question that causes an emotional reaction because your family member is sharing a moment so powerful that the emotions experienced decades ago can still touch them. As more than one student told me, asking their grandparents about the past brought back feelings they thought they had forgotten. It is very human to be surprised at the evocative power of our own memories. Emotions are best honored by not rushing past them or ignoring them. Emotional expressions between generations are very precious.

Emotional intimacy may be uncomfortable terrain for our parents and grandparents (and even for us). Showing emotion was thought to be childish or a sign of weakness in earlier generations, and still is in some societies. Grandfathers have told me that they were taught men weren't supposed to be emotional. But this doesn't mean that these same grandparents aren't eloquent observers of their life and times. You'll see how passionate a person can be about their life stories.

THE LANGUAGE OF YOUR ELDERS

Some of your grandparents may speak a different language than the one you know best. It's sadly common for many of us to lose our heritage language. Some of my students only realized while doing this assignment how much they were losing by not keeping up their language skills.

Even if you and your family all speak the same language fluently, your grandparents are probably going to use language that's no longer common, since speech is always changing. Your grandparents are wonderful repositories of language particular to a period and place.

THE IMPORTANCE OF RECORDING

I can't stress enough the importance of recording your grandparent's or parent's words rather than relying on notes. Recording frees you from the impossible task of writing down what someone just said while simultaneously focusing on what they are saying in the moment. By recording, you give the machine the responsibility to capture your interviewee's words, so you can focus on the interview. This will enable you to be a good listener and observer of body language and to formulate and ask appropriate follow-up questions. Not having to write constantly makes the conversation more natural. Notes are a poor representation of the many interesting ways people express their thoughts anyway.

The presence of a recorder is actually a way to demonstrate to someone that they and their words are important and that you take their time seriously. People often forget about the recording device once they get going. Of course, you can't hide the recorder from anyone, for ethical reasons.

Be sure to try out the recording device with a friend or family member before the interview to avoid any microphone problems. Find the best placement for the recorder. How far away do you and your interviewee need to be from the recorder to pick up good-quality sound? What effect might background noise have? Comfort with operating the controls is important. Make sure the recording device is fully charged or has fresh batteries or a power supply, and check that there is enough storage space on it. There have been times when I've realized at the last minute that I didn't have enough storage space on my recorder and was forced to delete something.

I have a number of digital recorders, some that are powered by separate batteries and others that have a built-in rechargeable battery. I always record with two devices, often my phone and another digital recorder. It's easy to transfer files from your recorder to your computer or storage device. When you conduct the interview, be sure to check several times to make sure the recording device shows that it is on "record."

You might even ask if your parent or grandparent is comfortable with being video recorded. This can be done from a phone or another type of video recording device. Either way, be sure to use a tripod, which is essential for getting a good-quality video. If using video, it's ideal to have an audio recorder, too, since the camera might need to be placed at a bit of a distance in order to get the person in the frame, and this can interfere with the audio quality. Afterward, be sure to make copies of your recordings and store them safely. As with any form of technology, familiarity is key for a smooth experience.

TRANSCRIBING

Transcribing your interviews is a fascinating exercise because you will find additional riches that you missed when you were focused on conducting the interview. There are easy-to-use software programs that can transcribe your tapes. If you use a software program, you'll need to go through the transcript to correct errors. And you'll gain immeasurably from going over the transcript yourself while listening to the recording; it'll give you the opportunity to rehear again not only the interviewee's words but also the sound of their voice, hesitations, and laughter. Their language and stories are influenced by the setting and interaction with you. While transcribing, listen for these beautiful influences. Author James Joyce called these moments the "epiphany of the ordinary." How a culture transmits itself through your family is the stuff of anthropology.

FORMING STRONGER BONDS WITH YOUR FAMILY

One of the greatest gifts of doing this interview is forming a stronger connection with your family. As one of the students, Henry, wrote, "Because of this interview I feel closer with my grandmother and more willing to share with her what is going on in my life."[11] Another student, William, said about interviewing his elder, "The interview allowed us to make a real, personal connection despite a language barrier that has existed for years. . . . I was the most surprised at the depth of the connection we were able to establish in such a short time."[12] You'll know you formed a strong bond if your parent or grandparent keeps calling or emailing you after the interview to tell you other things they remember.

The interview will help you see the multifaceted and

sometimes contradictory nature of your family. For example, your grandparent might wish they'd grown up with access to the internet but make little to no effort to gain proficiency when you give them an iPad. As my student Madeline said of her grandmother, "I find it very interesting that she described herself at a young age as wild, carefree, disobedient, and independent, yet at the same time those are the exact criticisms she offers to today's parents."[13]

As your elders speak from the heart, you'll be able to connect despite cultural and spatial differences in how you grew up. Carl Sagan eloquently describes human connectedness in this picture of the earth:

> Look again at that dot. That's here. That's home. That's us. On it everyone you love, everyone you know, everyone you ever heard of, every human being who ever was, lived out their lives. The aggregate of our joy and suffering, thousands of confident religions, ideologies, and economic doctrines, every hunter and forager, every hero and coward, every creator and destroyer of civilization, every king and peasant, every young couple in love, every mother and father, hopeful child, inventor and explorer, every teacher of morals, every corrupt politician, every "superstar," every "supreme leader," every saint and sinner in the history of our species lived there—on a mote of dust suspended in a sunbeam.[14]

Although a lot can change in just one generation, certain aspects of human experience remain constant. As another student, Alex, said, "What surprised me most over the course of the interview was the ways in which my own experiences have paralleled hers . . . this conversation gave me an intensified empathy for her experience."[15] But it's only through knowing the details of other generations' lives that these similarities will be revealed to you. So, let's get started!

CHAPTER 3

Questions to Get Some Basic Background

At the beginning of the interview, you'll ask some warm-up questions to ease your interviewee into the process and to get them in the rhythm of talking about themselves.

Opening Question

- *When were you born, and is there a story behind your name?*

Follow-up Questions

- *Where were you born?*
- *Have you heard any stories about your birth?*
- *How many brothers and sisters do/did you have, and where are you in the birth order?*
- *What's your favorite pastime?*
- *What's your favorite TV show or movie (past or present)?*
- *What book have you read recently that you enjoyed?*

You may already be able to sketch your grandparent's or parent's basic biography, but asking about their birth date and how they were named (followed by a few other basic biographical questions) is a way to set the tone for a relaxed start. Even simple biographical questions have the potential of generating unexpected stories. Asking about the day of the interviewee's birth can elicit tales of a winter blizzard, a spring flood, or a traffic jam that prevented their parents from getting to the doctor on time.

I've heard interesting stories about names, too. Melissa's parents were in a quandary about a name when one of their favorite singers, Melissa Manchester, came on the car radio. Her parents looked at each other and said, "That's it!"

In my own family, my parents clearly had run out of energy for naming kids by their fifth child because my sister, brothers, and I chose the name of my youngest brother while we were in the backseat of the station wagon on the way to the hospital to visit my mother and the new baby. (We named him William Edward. Upon hearing the name, my mother responded, "Okay, as long as he's not called Billy, but Bill.")

You may be surprised to dig up new information and fun stories with these basic Opening Questions.

NOTES FROM YOUR INTERVIEW

....

....

CHAPTER 4

Questions on Space: Learning About Where Your Elders Grew Up

The topic of space at first sounds very abstract, but becomes tangible and full of sensory details when you hear about the home your grandparent or parent grew up in. Houses and apartments are delightfully varied across time and region, and it's always fascinating to see how someone views "home." The memories of a person's life are entwined with space, and we better understand the lives of our parents and grandparents by knowing more about the spaces they moved about in.

Opening Question
- *Can you tell me about the home you grew up in?*

Follow-up Questions
- *How many bedrooms were there, and where did you sleep?*
- *Where did you eat your meals? Did the family eat together?*
- *What was your favorite part of your home?*
- *What did the windows look onto?*

- *What did you hear when you woke up in the morning?*
- *What was the home heated by?*
- *Was the home used differently in different seasons? (For example, in Texas, sometimes people sleep on the porch in the summertime.)*
- *Can you tell me any stories about the home, or surprising things that happened there?*
- *How was your home different from neighbors' homes?*
- *How did you get from home to school, and what did you see on the way?*
- *How does the neighborhood look today, compared to then?*
- *How would you compare your childhood home to the home you live in today?*

Through my anthropological fieldwork in Pohnpei, I saw firsthand how space is deeply interconnected with culture and life experience. When I first got to the island to live with the chief's family, I saw that my new home was a structure with walls on only three sides, one side completely open. Part of my new home had a bare earth floor, while another part had a raised platform, where we actually spent all our indoor time. I soon realized that the openness of the walls meant we would feel the sea breezes that made the sweltering equatorial heat bearable. Unlike where I'd grown up, there was no need for four walls to contain heat here! On the raised platform, we spent our days doing chores, chatting, eating, and playing with the toddler. At night, neighbors showed up to drink kava, catch up on news, and do the informal work of running the community. On formal occasions, like feasts and funeral ceremonies, the space in the house became an organizational chart of the community because people sat according to their rank; the floor was a picture of the island's family trees and all their branches, complex hierarchies of clans on an isolated fertile island in the Pacific. Afterward, we rolled out mats and slept on the platform.

Why is space so revealing? For one thing, homes and neighborhoods are repositories of family and cultural history. Someone interviewing their grandmother who grew up in India might see for the first time a childhood neighborhood where buildings from the British colonial period sit next to ancient temples, both still in use. Someone else interviewing their grandmother who grew up in Texas might see a deserted Main Street on Wednesday afternoon because the whole town is at Bible study. And still another person might see, through their grandparent's eyes, the American South during racial segregation, with separate water fountains for Black and White. One of the people I interviewed remembered how their front porch in Philadelphia was a place for hanging out and chatting with neighbors about baseball scores or where to buy ripe peaches.

Describing a childhood home can bring a person into focus in a new way and lead to talking about other aspects of daily life. In a single day, each person moves through many types of spaces, starting at home in the morning. In one grandmother's case, the day started with drawing back the curtain on the ice-crusted window in her bedroom, then grabbing her clothes and running downstairs on impossibly cold floors to get dressed in front of the thin flame of a fire just being lit.

Another mentioned heading off to school and then to "the horrid piano teacher's house," the one who banged their knuckles with a ruler and pinched their elbows when they made a mistake. Questions about space prompt descriptions that enable you to see a street with few cars, fields of wheat, a one-room schoolhouse, a sledding hill, the river, all linked with memories of people and things that happened.

I'm usually curious about how an interviewee's childhood home was heated not only because of what it reveals about technology but also because it creates a sense of the boundaries between inside and outside and the sensory experience of seasons and how someone adapted to them. One interviewee remembered the coal man coming and her mother counting the bags of coal using penny coins: "Every time a bag went in the coalhole, she would move a penny across. She said she had to keep track just in case they were diddling you." The coal fire died out while the family slept, so in the morning, the inside of the house was the same temperature as the outside, except under the warm bedcovers: "You really just wanted to climb back in bed to be warm, but you didn't."

The surroundings that each of us knows as a child form a sensory backdrop for the rest of our lives. Yet, the stories we tell about ourselves rarely include details of what we saw in the morning, the sounds we heard, the constancy of the wind, the smell of rain on the pavement. Instead, we usually give a chronicle of events. But if you think about when the lights go down in a movie theater, you'll realize that a thrill comes from the sudden sensory infusion as a scene fills the screen, and we're somewhere else. Similarly, the questions in this chapter are designed to prompt your family member to create scenes for you. One of my students, Jigyasa, told me, "My grandma started laughing when I asked this question. . . . At some points her eyes would light up when she started talking about herself as a child and the house that she grew up in. This really showed that she still remembers her childhood and the good moments she had during those years."[1]

As your parent or grandparent thinks back to earlier decades and describes their old surroundings, you'll realize that you're finding out details of their life that you never would have thought to ask about. What they used to see from the window when they woke up gives you an immediate sense of being there. Even if you grew up close to where your parent or grandparent lived as a child, you'll find that they experienced the same space very differently. A home can change radically even over the course of a few years. As one grandmother I interviewed, tells it,

> The first house I can remember is during the war. We shared a house with another family because my father and their father had gone, had been called up, gone to fight. We shared the house with them until the end of the war. I think it was necessity on both sides, because things were very difficult. . . . I don't think it was very great for Mum, but for me and the two girls, the daughters, it was fine, and there were loads of children around, and we all got on very, very well. . . . We were there seven years. Mr. Dunaid, he was away for the whole entire time of the war.

Your parent or grandparent might have grown up in what now would be considered a very small town, but to them, seemed huge because they remember roaming in what felt like vast woods populated with hidden societies of wildlife. This is the sort of childhood experience that caused one grandparent to describe his recently built grand Houston home as cramped, while his tiny childhood home in Corsicana, Texas, seemed limitless in size. The walls of his childhood home dissolved into the wide and beckoning open fields, where he spent his time once he had done his chores.

Many of our grandparents roamed through space at an early age without supervision, before the phrase "stranger danger" existed. Now children's mobility is more heavily supervised, although they may travel to far more places than their grandparents did. Many grandparents' stories allude to a sense of freedom and confidence they are now deeply nostalgic for. However, you might find on closer inspection that only the boys had this freedom. One grandmother described her jealous pangs watching her brothers roam wherever they chose, while for her, space meant confinement rather than freedom. There were counties in the US known for warning Black people against passing through after sunset lest they be killed, so their movements through space were severely curtailed.[2] Alex's grandmother remembered shopping with her two small kids in Tennessee and being told by a shopkeeper that he wouldn't sell her anything because she was a "Yankee Catholic." Another told me that she and her girlfriend were told to leave a pub in England because they didn't have a man with them, and "ladies didn't go into pubs" (without a man).[3] Power dynamics deeply affect a person's freedom and confidence in space. Not having the power to go where you'd like leads to feelings of isolation and dependency because others have to help you navigate space.

You might realize while talking to your grandparent how much your sense of identity and how you interact with others depend on mobility, and that being able to choose where to live, work, or play is a defining feature of who you are. People who have lived through the changing boundaries of wartime occupation, or had their home taken away, or experienced a pandemic have thought a lot about what space and mobility mean to them.

If your grandparents or parents grew up in a different country from where they live now, they've been confronted with differences in how space is organized. You might hear them describe feeling alienated within a space because they didn't know the language well. They may have limited where they went and avoided getting too close to people because they wanted to avoid the embarrassing situation of being clueless about what was said or not knowing how to respond.

Space has both natural and cultural boundaries, and we interpret our physical environment through the often invisible lenses of cultural beliefs and practices. Even if you imagine yourself standing alone in a forest, you are seeing the space through a cultural lens as you notice the types of trees around you and read the lines of the map that got you there. Back in town, you might notice while waiting in the checkout line of a grocery store that a child in the shopping cart behind you reaches out to touch your arm out of curiosity. Their parent might instruct the child on how each person has a kind of "sacred space" that others shouldn't intrude upon. Space is a powerful way to reflect belief.

People use spatial metaphors to describe human experience, such as being "trapped" in a relationship, or "running away from truth," as if truth were a physical place. People grow up in different moral spaces (for example, the community where everyone goes to Bible study). In northern Canada, the Athabaskan and Tlingit people, who are surrounded by glaciers, believe that the glaciers "listen, pay attention, and respond to human behavior—especially to indiscretion."[4] The spaces in which we live contribute to our sense of the world. Conversely, people also shape space, as evidenced in the wide variety of houses that people build around the world. Asking your parent or grandparent to describe their childhood home and neighborhood can open up many conversations about what growing up was like for them.

NOTES FROM YOUR INTERVIEW

CHAPTER 5

Questions on Time: Connecting with the History of Your Family

Asking about how your parents and grandparents experience time opens a door to connect with family history. Anyone who's achieved the age of a grandparent is keenly aware of time and how life can change at a breathtaking pace. They may feel time has passed faster than they expected and wish they could slow it down.

Opening Question

- *How did you perceive time when you were a child?*

Follow-up Questions

- *Was there a period in your life when time seemed to drag or when it seemed to speed up?*
- *What was a typical day like for you as a child?*
- *What was lunchtime at school like?*
- *What did you do in the evening?*
- *How did you entertain yourself as a child?*

- *What was a typical day like in your teenage years?*

- *Did you have a part-time job before you left home?*

- *What was your first day at your first job like?*

- *What was it like to plan your time when you first left home?*

- *How did marriage change your experience of time?*

- *How did being a parent change your experience of time?*

- *Is there a specific time that stands out in your life, and if so, what would that be and why?*

- *How do you plan your time differently now than when you were younger? Can you give examples?*

With questions on time, you'll learn about a person's sense of themselves in the order of things. Renowned cultural theorist Émile Durkheim considered time, like space, a fundamental category of our thought. The words *time*, *day*, and *year* are among the most frequently used nouns in the English language.[1]

Anthropologists are interested in what time means in different cultures and how time is measured, described, and influenced by contact with other cultures. The Barasana of the Amazon described to anthropologist Stephen Hugh-Jones how the passage of time and generations was like leaves piling up on the forest floor. As time passed, the layers of leaves took them further and further from their ancestors, so they conducted rituals to "squash" the leaves and bring relatives closer. Your interview with your living ancestor is a way of reducing distance, too, bringing them closer to you.

The Australian Aboriginals have managed to preserve

their unique view of time, where past, present, and future are indistinct from one another, a kind of "everywhen."[2] To them, time is integrated with space; it has an inside, underneath dimension.[3] But they aren't the only ones to make the idea of time less abstract by thinking of it in spatial terms; we may describe being late as being "behind," or apologize that we are short on time, or worry that we don't know "what's ahead" (although the future is behind in the Aymara language of Bolivia).[4] Economists make time less abstract by thinking of it as a finite resource—people in industrialized societies may experience a "time famine," while people in hunter-gatherer societies, now and in the past, have a "time surplus" or are time affluent, because they have fewer demands on their time.[5]

My students have been surprised to realize that time is not talked about or viewed the same way in every culture. People who live by the sea have tidal views of time; Geoffrey Chaucer famously wrote, "time and tide wait for no man." The tide follows the rhythms of the moon, while farmers follow the rhythms of the seasons. As one grandparent I interviewed told me, "Farmers worked from sunup to sundown except for maybe two months of the year in the middle of summer, when the crops were laid by and just growing. Then farmers went fishing. And when it was harvesttime, it was time to go back to work. Then it was time to cut wood. I'm telling you, I have split stovewood."

Anthropologist Nancy Munn pointed out that the clock has been endowed with a great deal of power in some societies. It's become a "moral timepiece," and being late has a moral value.[6] People react to their powerful clocks with equally powerful feelings, such as horror, resignation, excitement, and frustration.

When the anthropologist E. E. Evans-Pritchard studied the Nuer people in Africa, he was surprised to realize that they had no expression equivalent to time. They couldn't describe time as long or short or passing, or as something that could be saved or wasted. Activities always followed a sequence that everyone was expected to know.[7] Some outsiders might consider the Nuer lucky because they could escape the oppressive feeling of watching the clock.

Different senses of time echo through concepts like *mañana* in Spanish, literally "tomorrow" but known informally (and even by the Oxford English Dictionary) as an "unlimited future." People on the Isle of Man have a phrase that also describes limitless time, *Traa dy Liooar* (time enough), more affectionately referred to by people who are expected to do something than by people waiting for them.

People experience time in different ways at different ages. You may know how your grandparent or parent spends their time now, but their childhood and adolescence are mysteries to investigate. While you might have spent your childhood much the way you chose, your grandfather may have had little choice but to spend his time doing what the family needed him to do: feeding the chickens, cleaning out the barn, and watching his younger sister. A couple of grandparents I interviewed told me, "Time was not your own," and "I didn't have a life outside of school and music."

Other grandparents had little or no sense of time at all.

One told me, "I could follow my whims and my imagination, which took me places, following the magical world I lived in." Some of their lives were less structured because they weren't assigned as much homework as kids today and they didn't participate in organized sports, "so you were on your own or with your friends, and you would organize your own life."

Some interviewees compartmentalized time into life stages, like elementary school, high school, marriage, and children, with each new episode profoundly influencing their feelings about time. Yet the boundaries separating different seasons of life vary from person to person. For example, if a grandmother's first child "arrived" when she was barely out of girlhood herself, the child she'd known herself to be was suddenly gone.

Some of the people I interviewed remembered a lot of waiting—for the school day to end, for the weekend, for the summer. They would describe the rhythm of their time such that "The week would go by very slowly and the weekend would be very quick." They also described waiting "forever" to become one year older: "It was like ages and ages waiting from one birthday to another. It seemed like you were going to have to wait forever."

As people grow into adulthood, however, they often feel as though time is accelerating, like those childhood weekends that ended too soon. One grandparent described the change this way: "There was no urgency when I was a child, but there is always an element of urgency in my life these days."

When first questioned about the passage of time, your parent or grandparent may answer philosophically, describing time as a nonrefundable currency to be spent, or sentimentally, aware of how easily time is "lost." But as you ask for more details, you'll learn more about their unique relationship to this peculiar cultural phenomenon.

NOTES FROM YOUR INTERVIEW

CHAPTER 6

Questions on Social Interactions: The Importance of Everyday Encounters

With questions on social interactions, you'll invite your family member to thoughtfully reflect on everyday encounters. People are most conscious of how interactions work when something goes wrong, so the Opening Question focuses on what your interviewee finds annoying or surprising about interacting with people today.

Opening Question

- *In conversations and interactions with people now, do you find certain things surprising or annoying because they aren't how they used to be?*

Follow-up Questions

- *How do you think everyday interactions have changed since you were young?*

- *Can you describe the ways you interacted with older people or strangers when you were a child? (For example, were there special ways to greet them or act around them?)*

- *How did you and your parents greet one another first thing in the morning when you were a child?*
- *Were there people you were taught to avoid, or weren't allowed to interact with as a child?*
- *Can you remember any particular encounter with an older person from your childhood that is really memorable?*
- *Are there any brief encounters with other people in your childhood you particularly remember?*
- *Who did you spend the most time playing with when you were a child?*
- *Can you tell me about a time when you were angry because someone treated you as insignificant?*
- *What barriers existed between boys and girls or men and women when they were interacting during your childhood?*
- *Who did you spend the most time interacting with as a teenager?*
- *When you were a teenager, what was a party or similar gathering of young people like?*
- *Can you compare your interactions on social media today with how you interacted with people before social media?*

If you're like most people, you don't think much about how you interact with others because it's so routine. Yet people effortlessly manage many different types of interactions in a single day, using language crafted for each situation. We know how to say about forty different types of hellos in English,[1] which we deploy depending on whether we're greeting a close friend, or someone we met the other day whose name we forgot, or a talent scout from MGM. You'll no doubt have noticed, though, how new technology can change the way you interact with others. When mobile phones first became widely available, newspaper headlines were full of warnings about how cell phones were disrupting human interaction.[2] Your grandparents, though, grew up in communities without internet, social media, and access to images and stories from around the world in the palm of their hand. Grandparents I interviewed remembered fondly the days before cell phones, when you "talked to people more." One grandparent remembered thinking life was as good as it could get until his family got a TV. The images he saw on the screen made him envy other ways of life that he'd never imagined, including work opportunities that were far less backbreaking.

One grandparent, raised in a small town, said that until she moved to the city, she'd thought that everyone interacted the same way. There, she was shocked to receive strange looks in response to her greetings; not only did people in the city ignore her greetings, but they rarely made eye contact, which would have been unthinkable back in her small town. She experienced a typical urban style of interaction that sociologist Erving Goffman described as "civil inattention," where people come into close contact on crowded sidewalks and elevators without showing much recognition of one another, apart from acknowledging someone else's right to be there, and everyone's careful not to encourage any dialogue.

Social class also affects how people interact with those around them. One grandparent in the UK told me about winning a scholarship to grammar school, the school for kids headed to university:

> I was the first person in my road to pass the scholarship. It was a working-class neighborhood. Actually, some others might have passed it, but they were not allowed to go to grammar school by their parents, because working class didn't go to grammar school, but rather to the local secondary modern school. My parents being of Scottish descent were more educationally minded. And they wanted their children to succeed academically. But once I went to grammar school, nobody in the road played with me ever again. They were quite polite and didn't pull my hair or anything, but they didn't hang out with me ever again. I was nine.

When grandparents talk about changes in interaction styles, they often focus on respect. One grandparent told me that she feels both parents and children showed more respect for one another when she was a child, and parents gave children more responsibility, too: "We'd go in the barn and we made all kinds of things. Nobody worried back then; it was so free, you know. We had hammers and saws and nails and stuff. We would take old apple boxes, put old roller skates on the bottom, kind of like an early-day skateboard, and we'd take those over to the hills nearby and go down and you know, crash and burn a few times." Other grandparents feel that children are treated with greater respect now, that parents accept children "for who they are" in a way the grandparents never experienced. Some grandparents have remarked to me that American parents show more open affection to their kids these days.

How you're taught to interact with others can tell you a lot about a society's "theory of the person," meaning what kind of social behavior is considered moral and honorable. While researching this book, I was surprised at the differences that can exist between different generations' theories of the person, affecting their ideas of how people should interact with one another. In my interviews, I found that grandparents' theory of how a moral person should behave was sometimes so different from their grandchildren's as to be almost opposite. For example, you may believe that people should make choices independently of their family, while someone on the opposite end of the spectrum may believe that they should remain subject to their parents' wishes as long as their parents are alive.

Differences in views of moral personhood are especially evident in immigrant families in the US. Children raised in America grow up in a very different environment than their immigrant parents did. For example, the parents may have been raised in a culture where teenage girls and boys didn't go out on dates or interact with one another much at all, but now their children are growing up in a culture where this is expected. The children of immigrants are caught in two different systems. Doing what is "normal" in American culture may clash with their parents' customary ways of showing moral personhood. Notions of how a moral person should interact with others aren't easy to change because people learn these actions and protocols at an early age.

Immigrant adults have to adjust their own interactions, too. One person from Japan told me that after moving to the US, she discovered that even asking a question was quite a different experience in Japan from the US, dictated by different ideas of how a moral person was supposed to behave in each country. In Japan, observing others' needs first is paramount, while in the US, it is important to "help yourself." She said,

> It's much easier for me to ask a question here [in the US].
> In Japan, I have to take one or maybe two steps before I
> ask a question. I cannot change this. I must always
> observe first before I express myself—that's a very
> typical Japanese way. You have to see what's around first
> before putting yourself on the table. I don't need to
> change that and I don't think I can change that; it's part
> of me. When I want to ask a question, I still always
> observe quickly around me and my situation first and
> then ask a question. But when I visit Japan these days,
> they see me not looking around enough before asking a
> question! But if I keep that Japanese speed here in the US,
> I don't get to say anything! Here you have to speed up to
> get to the point. The time that I spend as an observer
> before asking a question is different within these two
> cultures. In Japan I cannot help but look at other people,
> what the people in front of me are doing, or what a
> person senior to me expects.

You might find that when you listen to your older family members tell you about interactions in their childhood, that their theory of the person *has* changed over time. While they may have once considered it unthinkable for women to be involved in politics because public interactions degraded a woman (and by extension, her family), your grandmother may be proud of women in politics today. As one grandmother said, "I think things have evolved so much in how we now interact with the world, things which we didn't do before."

Although I've emphasized contrasts in how different generations and cultures interact, you might be surprised to learn that when sociologists and anthropologists started closely analyzing everyday interactions in the 1960s, they found that people are actually very agreeable across generations. Human interactions are full of murmurs of assent and acknowledgments of what others have said. Sociologist Erving Goffman remarked that even when things get off track, people quickly apologize and take the blame, working together to get the interaction righted again.[3]

The amount of time we spend in everyday interactions far outweighs the time we spend at formal events. Yet it's the formal events that are recorded in family histories. The everyday interactions that make up the bulk of our lives get lost. That's why this topic is so important. Asking your older family members about social interactions when they were children shows something of the time and culture, as well as how your family members have evolved with the changing times.

NOTES FROM YOUR INTERVIEW

CHAPTER 7

Questions on Becoming: Rites of Passage and How Your Elders Were Raised

....

When one of my students, Jacob, asked his grandfather about how children were raised in his generation, his grandfather responded with, "Wow, thank you, that is a beautiful question and I am happy to answer this."[1] Anthropologists also consider how children are raised to be a beautiful subject because it's the key to how cultures survive and how ways of doing things get passed down.

Opening Question

- *How would you describe your parents' parenting style?*

Follow-up Questions

- *How is child-rearing different today than when you were a child?*
- *Can you tell me about a time as a child when you were scolded for doing the wrong thing?*
- *Were your parents' rules of behavior the same for sons and daughters?*

- *What were you taught about expressing emotion?*
- *What were family dinners like?*
- *When you were growing up, who were the key authority figures in your life?*
- *Who were the important teachers in your life?*
- *When did you feel most independent as a child?*
- *What experiences did your parents consider crucial for you to have?*
- *What coming-of-age events (and other rites of passage) were important to you, and can you describe one of them (for example, getting a driver's license, wearing makeup, going hunting, getting your first car, leaving home, etc.)?*
- *What was schooling like?*
- *How did the world look to you as you entered it as an adult?*
- *What was leaving home like?*
- *What current social norms/accepted behaviors would you have thought unimaginable before today?*
- *Did you raise your children the same way you were raised?*
- *What do you wish you'd known when you were younger?*
- *How would you advise your younger self?*

You've probably heard the metaphorical term "raising children" more often than the more formal term "socialization," the process of learning the values, habits, and moral codes of your community as you grow up. The idea of "raising" captures the years of care and nurturing children need, as well as the perhaps uncertain outcome, influenced by environment and chance. Learning culture is a dynamic process. As the anthropologist Margaret Mead said, a baby born into the world has few behaviors, no language, and "neither beliefs nor enthusiasms." Yet each one succeeds in becoming their culture's adult "in every particular."[2]

From the moment of conception, our existence is already part of a web of relationships in an existing world. To study these relationships and how people are socialized, linguistic anthropologists some years ago began to study how family members talk to one another during family dinners. So, when one person I interviewed, Kay, told me a story of a family dinner she remembered from when she was a child in London during wartime, I was especially interested. Kay told me that food was scarce, "you couldn't get anything." On one particular day, all that was in the cupboard was a bit of cheese and the eggs the chickens had laid that day. Her mother decided to make a cheese soufflé. When it was finished cooking and she put it on the table, Kay's father looked at it and said angrily, "That's not a meal for a man." The children were sent to bed, and Kay said, "I imagine they had a row." Her story is a good example of the socialization that takes place at family dinners. As the children learned that day, it was the symbolism of the food that counted more than the sustenance for Kay's father.

Although humans share many biological similarities with the animal world, including birth, death, reproduction, and the need for food, humans are remarkable in how we create social and symbolic meaning around those biological processes. You can see from Kay's example that the rhythms of culture can distort the rhythms of biology, so that even though everyone was hungry (because food was rationed), Kay's father rejected the food because of its social meaning. As Margaret Mead put it, culturally induced "needs" are so important that when a person fails to acquire these social needs, like success, wealth, authority, approval, or the right food, this can "produce more unhappiness and frustration in the human breast" than the physiological demands of hunger.[3] The learned values of the human world, how we've been socialized, take precedence over the hunger we share with the animal world.

The big job of socialization primarily falls to parents, but others—including friends, siblings, teachers, work colleagues, religious leaders, journalists, and even web content creators— also play a role. One parent who grew up in the 1950s in the Midwest said, "Teachers were second only to parents," when it came to telling you what to do. For some kids who attended boarding school in England, teachers were in fact more important than parents, since children only saw their parents on holidays, and life was mostly lived at school. I was told that the local bobby (police officer) also took on a parenting role: "He'd just give you a clip 'round the ears, you see." If you thought you could complain about it later to your parents, "you'd get another clip for it, you see." One grandparent told me that her mother in Hong Kong had complained to her, "You listen to the nuns more than you listen to me." Who were the important teachers in your parents' and grandparents' lives?

It's clear that we all have an extraordinary ability to learn, a process that fascinates anthropologists and psychologists, but according to Margaret Mead, it's the human ability to *teach* that is our most impressive skill: "As we are coming to understand better the circular processes through which culture is developed and transmitted, we recognize that man's most human characteristic is not his ability to learn, which he shares with many other species, but his ability to teach and store what others have developed and taught him. Learning, which is based on human dependency, is relatively simple. But human capacities for creating elaborate teachable systems, for understanding and utilizing the resources of the natural world, and for governing society and creating imaginary worlds, all these are very complex."[4]

The special teaching ability Mead is referring to starts very early. Even young children teach other children. One grandparent raised in Iceland, Maria, gave me a great example of this. When Maria was four, her best friend was two years older and already in school. Every afternoon after school, Maria and her friend got together to "play school" at the friend's insistence. When it was time for Maria to enroll in the real school, she tested two grade levels above the rest of the children in her age group.

What's taught to children varies across generations and cultures. Parents used to instruct children, "Never touch the gas mantle on the lamp" (the mantle was a thin, fragile cloth that was ignited and hung like a cloak in the lamp), but this knowledge is no longer relevant. Parents also teach values, as described by one interviewee who had been chided for spending a penny to get on the bus, instead of using "the perfectly good bicycle in the shed." Another grandparent told me about a favorite teacher who'd been in the Marines and used to talk about war:

> He told us what it was about, and how it was—how the men starved to death on Guadalcanal. He would tell us; he wouldn't tell it to the girls. I just thought it was so interesting. You know little boys; we want to talk about war. But when he talked about war, it didn't seem like as much fun as we thought. He talked about the time he touched his buddy and his buddy was dead. So, war was not nearly so glamorous anymore.

In the decades during which your parents and grandparents grew up, gender was an important part of the socialization process, and a lens through which children's behavior was judged. Socialization to male or female started from the moment of birth. A study published in 2002 showed that children then had very clear knowledge of being a boy or girl by the time they were three.[5] One grandmother told me, "My father was almost Victorian in his views of the world. He really didn't believe that women needed to do very much. He expected me to come top of the class, but he didn't expect me to do very much with it." Grandfathers remember that while growing up, they continually asked themselves, "Am I man enough?" Nowadays categories of gender are being re-evaluated in some places as a means of inducting people into cultural ways of doing things and making sense of a world.

The level of independence we are socialized to exhibit varies quite a bit across cultures and generations, too. Take

Japanese children, who are encouraged to ride the subway by themselves from as young as age seven.[6] In Australia, state-funded sleep schools help parents who haven't managed to teach their children to sleep independently.[7] In Pohnpei, independence training doesn't start as early (the idea of separating mother and baby at night, or letting a baby cry itself to sleep is quite alarming to them); but around age three, independence training starts in earnest, and children aren't indulged anymore or allowed to be as dependent on their mothers, a process the children don't like at all.

Quite a few grandparents I interviewed reported being parented in a way encapsulated by the phrase "Spare the rod and spoil the child." A few interviewees vividly recalled the image of their parent approaching them with a certain belt after some misbehavior, a form of punishment that would get the parent referred to child protection services today. Physical punishment wasn't unusual at school, either. According to one interviewee, "In one class in junior school, I used to get the slap every day for talking in class. It couldn't have done me much good because I carried on the next day." Some grandparents used metaphors like an "iron fist" to convey the rigidity and harshness of the socialization process back then. One grandparent told me he'd realized recently that the traditional lullabies he grew up with are really quite violent, like "Hush-a-by baby on the tree top, when the wind blows, the cradle will rock; when the bough breaks, the cradle will fall, down will come baby, cradle and all." He also mentioned a prayer that I was taught, too, which, when I think about it, meant that every night as children, he and I imagined that we might die in our sleep: "Now I lay me down to sleep, I pray the Lord my soul to keep, if I should die before I wake, I pray the Lord my soul to take. Amen." Sweet dreams! Today, by contrast, in the same cultures, parents believe in taking the opposite approach: that it's not *sparing* the rod that causes damage, but *using* it.

Socialization also affects universal emotional responses. Perhaps your grandparent will observe, as one did to me, that in childhood, it was rare for anyone to show physical affection or to say, "I love you." Anthropologist Charles Briggs wrote that during his fieldwork in a Mexicano community in New Mexico, people continually lectured him on the dangers of causing his little daughter to laugh too much. They explained that if infants or young children laughed loudly for too long, they would be a target for supernatural illness.[8] Children weren't comforted if they were "roughed up" by other children, either, because parents there believed children would fail in life if they didn't learn to stand up for their own rights and reputation.

Through socialization, each particular world becomes so familiar and even natural that questioning the ways we've been taught seems nearly impossible. As the anthropologist Pierre Bourdieu put it, it's almost as if we become enchanted by our own culture. He felt "enchantment" was the best way to describe how, in their socialization process, people become so accustomed to a certain way of doing things that it's difficult to accept alternative ways of doing them or of being in the world. This is evidenced in how some grandparents are concerned, for example, about a new culture of "disposability," in which one can change jobs, houses, friends, devices, and interests with ease.

Rites of passage are another aspect of socialization and include Confirmation, Bar and Bat Mitzvah, Quinceañera, Okuyi, retirement, weddings, Walkabout, graduation, and more. Anthropologist Arnold van Gennep originated the phrase "rite of passage" to describe a process of socialization in which people move between life stages. He visualized the different stages as rooms with passages or corridors that separated them (a nice spatial metaphor). It was the passages that interested him—how people are forced into the next stage, accompanied by a ritual. One grandparent I interviewed described how joining a trades union in Great Britain in the 1960s was a rite of passage:

> There's one rite of passage that's an important one, but it's so disappeared out of the world today that I lost sight of it. I grew up in a family of what you'd call political activists today. They were members of the trades union and I admired them because they accomplished extraordinary things. And when you became a member of the trades union you passed into a more mature world, a world where your opinion became important in a way that it never is as a child. You had to wait until you were sixteen years of age to be accepted into the trades union; I didn't join the same trades union my dad was in but nevertheless I joined a trades union.

Some grandparents remember the move from home to boarding school at age nine as a rite of passage. The comfort of home was replaced by a sudden institutionalization of life, "rows of iron beds with thin blankets." But many rites of passage have disappeared, especially the mandatory ones. Getting a driver's license is voluntary, but still has intense meaning as a passage from childhood to adulthood.

Your grandparent will have interesting stories to tell about growing up, how a child was positioned in society and shaped into a person. They'll likely remember key phrases that were used to impart wisdom to children. Asking questions related to socialization, or how culture is learned, offers an opportunity to hear about the intentional nature of your grandparent's or parent's choices in raising children, and the beliefs that motivated those choices, which affected who you are. Multiple grandparents told me that they've learned that values are less universal than they seemed to be when they were young.

NOTES FROM YOUR INTERVIEW

CHAPTER 8

Questions on Identity: The Factors That Made You Who You Are

Based on how you may have heard identity discussed in the media, it may seem like identity is limited to attributes like race, religion, politics, and socioeconomic status, but the questions in this chapter encourage your family members to tell a fuller, more interesting story of how their sense of self has changed over time.

Opening Question

- *Can you remember a moment when you first became conscious of who you are as a person and thought, "This is who I am"? What characteristics did you consider central to your identity?*

Follow-up Questions

- *Has your identity changed over time, and if so, how has it changed?*

- *If you were to give a snapshot of yourself when you were a child and another when you were a teenager, how would you describe yourself at those life stages?*

- *What aspect of your life has had the most influence on your identity (examples include the place where you were born, your family's level of income, your mother's or father's occupation, parenthood, etc.)?*
- *What did people tease you about when you were a child?*
- *Are there any family stories told about you when you were a child or teenager that you can share?*
- *What was your favorite activity when you were growing up?*
- *How do you think you take after your parents?*
- *How did you view your future prospects (future life and goals) when you were a teenager?*
- *Did having children change your identity, and if so, how?*
- *What made you decide to pursue the job you have?*
- *Have you had to adapt your identity to living in another culture?*
- *Did you ever feel oppressed because of your identity, and if so, can you give me an example?*
- *What groups do you consider yourself a part of?*
- *Do you have any unfulfilled ambitions?*

Some people have thought about questions of identity, and some haven't. As one grandparent said when asked about their identity, it was "a stupid question," since they were obviously a grandparent! Be prepared for some pushback if your parent or grandparent thinks you already know their identity very well. Identities are not stable, though, because the family changes, people age into different life stages, and everyone has multiple facets to their identity. Some parents and grandparents I interviewed were very thoughtful about this question and would start by saying something like "That's a big question." I knew then that their response would be interesting.

When one grandparent asked me what I meant by identity, I told her, "Attributes that would make you unique." She didn't think there was anything unique about her although she had just told me about how she never gave up on her dreams despite being discouraged by the people whose support she needed for ten years, until she finally prevailed. As your interviewee answers the questions in this book, you will see how singular they really are.

Identities are about singularity, as well as our relationships to other people and our environment. For example, if your parent or grandparent ever moved to a different town, region, or country, they'll know what you mean about changes in identity. My student Gabriel discovered that his grandmother, who moved from West Texas to California after she married, was discouraged to find that she didn't "meet the standard" for a respectworthy woman in the Californians' eyes because she was considered "just a housewife." She said, "It seemed like I didn't matter. I was so relieved to go back to [Texas] and just become a person again. Farmwives like my mother and me were essential and respectable. They were seen as part of the team, like girl athletes. It was refreshing to be out of the suffocating devaluation of the middle-class-housewife world. I think it has changed to some extent, but it still can be a thing."[1]

As this story shows, how we experience identity has a great deal to do with who's around us. As another grandparent, who grew up in Arkansas, said, "When country boys like me went to school in town, they were treated different. We were looked down on because we were country people. We were just little country urchins."

Deaf people have told me that they have a hard time getting beyond their identity as "the Deaf person" to hearing people. Deaf identity takes the forefront as soon as they start signing, eclipsing other identities like ethnicity or "top student." This is one reason why Deaf people feel most comfortable with other Deaf people, where being Deaf is not considered the sum total of who they are. If your family members grew up with the same group identity as society's elite, they may have little or no experience of prejudicial treatment because of their identity. But if they were members of a minority, for example, Black, Cajun, Deaf, or Yankee Catholic, they usually have stories like these to tell. And identities intersect so that categorizations including race, class, gender, and abilities overlap in an interdependent way.

Since 1963, when the term *baby boomer* was first published in a *Salt Lake Tribune* newspaper article, whole generations have been given identities, like Gen X, Gen Z, and millennial.[2] That's a lot of diversity for a single label, but generational identity is important in many cultures, including the Maasai in Kenya, who often ask what age group you belong to as soon as they meet you.

Everyone has multiple identities that can come into play in a single day. You might speak as a parent on one phone call, then as a son or daughter when you call your own parents, then exercise your authority as vice president of a company in one context, and then follow instructions as a trainee scuba diver in another. Some societies, however, consider your core identity to be stable—this identity could be related to your personality and character, or to the relationships you're born into. To Navajos, clan identity—specifically their mother's clan, father's clan, maternal grandfather's clan, and paternal grandfather's clan—is of primary importance. When a Navajo tribal member introduces themselves, they mention all four clans in that order because they define the person in the Navajo Nation, linking their past and present.[3]

Immigrant families have unique experiences with identity. The children of immigrants are socialized in a new cluster of identities, while their parents may worry that their children are losing touch with the cultural history and traditions that are a part of who they are. People living in a different country than where they grew up sometimes feel the tension of trying to keep "a consistent thread of me in two cultures," as one person put it. Traditional identities change in the new country. In the US, immigrants from South Asia often become close, which would have been less likely "back home" because of regional or ethnic differences that are more significant in the place they left behind.

Parents and grandparents construct identity through stories about what they liked to do as children. A grandmother who grew up in England told me that when she was ten, she helped the milkman deliver milk every Saturday: "Our milkman still had a horse and cart, and I loved horses and I used to go out on the cart to help him deliver milk. It was only so I could have a ride on the horse and cart, but he gave me a sixpence or something." We can also form identities around our complaints! Complaining entails taking a strong stance on something and can reveal how we interact with the world.

Some identities may have embarrassed your interviewee—for example, if their mother worked outside the home and wasn't a full-time homemaker like everyone else's mother in the neighborhood back then. The interviewee might remember how they loathed being different. Young children don't value uniqueness in identity and look to peers as their primary social reference group even at a very young age.[4]

While identity is usually thought of as a positive aspect of a person's self-concept, it can have a dark side, too, because identity is often used as a tool to discriminate.[5] Race is an obvious example. Although some consider race a natural category, a recent article in *Scientific American* described race as "a social construct without biological meaning," pointing out that there's more genetic variation *within* a single race than there is between groups designated as different races.[6] But the insistence that race is associated with biology makes it a significant part of a person's identity in many situations. My student Claire's grandmother was born in San Francisco and found that when she moved to Texas, people suddenly started asking her, "What's your heritage?" She realized that what they meant was "Since you're not white, what ethnicity are you?" It was a very disconcerting experience for her, and she now tries to preempt the question by mentioning early on in the conversation that she's Filipino.[7] For her, the question indicates that her sense of identity as an American isn't what other people see, and that's a shock she'd rather avoid. Identity can be seen from both the insider's perspective and the outsider's. The names that people choose for themselves are often different from the names that outsiders give to them.

One of the questions in this chapter asks your interviewee about how they would describe themselves when they were a child and a teenager. This can lead to some interesting answers because identities change over a person's lifetime, sometimes within a very short period. One grandparent talked about how sports gave him a new identity: "You know, junior high football saved my life. Once you become a football player and a good one, you're a hero all of a sudden; you're not a farm boy anymore. So, it literally changed everything in my life."

When asked how their identity has changed over time, your parent or grandparent may say that they are the same person they've always been, but with more wrinkles. They may still feel like that girl who grew up in a small town with unpaved streets and potholes. If that's the case, ask about that girl, what she was like back then and in what ways she's still the same.

A conversation about identity between older and younger generations can be a challenge, but it's ultimately a rewarding one. A student in one of my classes, Lilah, described her experience this way:

> With every question I asked, it was very easy to see how different my grandmother and I were and are from each other. For example, when she was my age, she was already pregnant with her first child and had only gone until sixth grade in school. Compared to me, attending

the University of Texas at Austin, pursuing a degree in neuroscience, living far away from home, it was almost night and day. Although we live very different lives, there are also several similarities between us. We value many of the same things—family and hard work. Although I haven't had to work my entire life, pursuing a degree at a highly ranked university is considered something taboo in my family. Meaning, not many people have pursued past a high school education.[8]

Learning about your parents and grandparents reveals how certain identities came to be a part of the language of your family–some remain across generations, while others may disappear. Who your parents and grandparents once were might surprise you, but that person, and who they came to be, not only resulted in the miracle of you, but a unique family.

NOTES FROM YOUR INTERVIEW

....

....

....

....

....

....

Questions on the Body and Adornment: An Expression of How You See Yourself and Others

No matter how you and your family members view clothing, whether you find it a chore or a pleasure, people the world over use the human body as a canvas for the creative play of ideas. And those canvases are heavily critiqued—disparaged or admired according to the location and decade. What people wear and how they look is used to judge not only their fashion sense but other aspects of their person, such as morality, gender, social class, identity, creativity, and desirability.

Opening Question

- *How have styles of dress and attitudes toward the body changed since you were a child?*

Follow-up Questions

- *Tell me about the clothes you wore when you were a child. Tell me about the clothes you wore as a teenager.*

- *Where did your parents buy your clothes?*

- What did you wear to school?

- Describe an outfit or item of clothing that you really loved.

- How did you wear your hair or have your hair cut when you were younger?

- What did your parents criticize you for in terms of how you presented yourself to the world?

- Did you have any battles with your parents about clothes, hair style, or the body, and if so, what did they object to?

- How have taboos in clothing changed over the course of your life?

- How have taboos concerning the body changed over the course of your life?

- If your parents or peers had an idea of what the perfect body type was, can you describe that?

- What did you teach your children about how people judged them for the way they looked?

Anthropologist Hilda Kuper described clothing as "visible cultural elements."[1] Whether dresses, breeches, veils, saris, kimonos, *kebayas, hanboks, shúkàs,* kilts, or agbadas, clothes convey meaning. From the moment a person is born, clothing is important. When anthropologist Justine Cordwell studied Yoruba culture, the people laughingly told her that dress was so important that they felt they must have been "born clothed."[2] Designer Kate Spade also described people's fascination with clothes when she said, "Playing dress-up begins at age five and never truly ends."[3] Even Charles Darwin believed people have an innate delight in and sensitivity for ornamentation.[4]

Dress, like all art, is supported by regimes and institutions. Just how each of us, as artists of our body, manages within these regimes and institutions is one of the most interesting aspects of anthropology, indicating how culture limits individuality, as well as how people embrace or reject dictates of class and society. Clothing is very stable in some places and highly changeable in others, although anthropologist Edward Sapir described modern fashion as merely tradition in the guise of departure from tradition. Anthropologist Alfred Kroeber disagreed, saying that changes in clothing could be used as a barometer of social and political upheavals; he compared the waist size and décolletage depth of evening gowns to show this.[5] A glance around the globe today reveals how far many elements of fashion have traveled and been remixed.

What we wear signals our group memberships, and our parents sometimes react to these signals and want to influence them. As one grandparent told me, "I remember going and buying a vest [sleeveless top]; it was burgundy and I put it on with a pair of jeans, and when I came down the stairs, my mother said, 'You're not going out in that.' She just didn't like the look of that on me." Another person I interviewed described a similar parental concern: "When you walk with me," her mother said, "wear something proper." These proper clothes "were so boring." They were like another type of uniform, "white trousers or skirt and a light-colored blouse, and of course you had to tuck the shirt in. I just wanted to wear something that my friends would wear."

The questions in this chapter are meant to elicit fascinating details about styles and dressing up, and how ideas about the body are so, well, revealing. You'll find from interviewing your older family members that attitudes toward clothing have changed a great deal—from suede loafers and white socks rolled down in the 1950s to cargo pants in the 1980s, from floor-length gowns in the eighteenth century to the shortest of skirts in the twentieth. Styles of dress have changed significantly over the course of recent generations and life-times. Take hats. In the US in the 1940s–50s, men and women didn't go out without a hat. I admired my grandmothers' hats, especially a pink one with a bow at the back and a delicate lacy net that covered her eyes. I remember the way my grandfather picked up his hat and put it on his head in a smooth two-part move as he was going out. Now hats are out. It surprised me to discover that it wasn't until the 1950s that future First Lady Jacqueline Kennedy made it acceptable across the country to own a sleeveless dress.

When I was at my grandmother's house in my twenties, she noticed me looking at an old photograph. In the photo was a child of about seven in a plain white cotton dress. "Is this you?" I asked her. "No, it's my father," she said. I was sur-prised to see a boy in a dress. But from the sixteenth century until World War I ended, young boys in Europe wore gowns or dresses until they were about eight years old. Irish boys wore dresses until they were twelve or thirteen years old, es-pecially in rural areas. If you look it up, you'll find that popu-lar historians give an economic reason for this—they say boys grew fast and cloth was expensive. When people are trying to understand something about behavior or culture, they're often satisfied with an explanation that doesn't take into account the native's point of view, assuming their own reasoning would apply to other decades and people. But as you interview your family, I hope you won't apply your own reasoning, but suspend your judgment in order to get your grandparent's or parent's point of view. I hope you'll notice that the ideas other generations grew up with—what attracts them, moves them, and seems worth fighting for—can be far more surprising than a simple calculation about thrift (cloth is expensive) or saving time on sewing alterations (boys grow fast). As a case in point, a little more research about boys in dresses reveals that in Ireland, people thought that evil fairies and spirits wandered around stealing small boys too young to protect themselves, so small boys were dressed as girls to deceive the demons, who weren't interested in girls. And it also turns out there was an important rite of passage that marked a boy's transition from child to young man centered on switching from dresses to pants. A "breeching" celebration was held when the boy put aside dresses at around age eight. Through this rite of passage, the boy crossed or was thrust into "the age of reason."

A grandfather I interviewed in the UK remembers undergoing a similar transition when he went from shorts to long pants at around age eight. Young boys in his part of Britain only wore shorts, even on the coldest days of winter. After switching to pants, they never again wore shorts, even on the hottest days of summer, except maybe if they were at the seaside, and even that was considered a bit eccentric. For women in the US and Europe, going from dresses to pants communicated their changing status in the 1950s. Similar to Kroeber's

ideas about changes in women's gowns, wearing pants signified important political change. Functionality alone didn't
drive the women's abandonment of dresses, since dresses are
still part of women's wardrobes. What drove this change for
women is a good subject to ask your parent or grandparent
about.

Some grandparents I interviewed said they didn't have the
"luxury," as they put it, of focusing on their clothes to create a
"look" because they got hand-me-downs, or their mother
sewed all the family's clothes with traditional patterns, or
their family had no money. Grandparents raised during the
Great Depression described having two shirts, two pairs of
pants or two dresses, a coat, and a pair of shoes. One grandparent told me, "You always had a good coat; money went on
a good coat. Mum used to knit, so we had wool jumpers and
cardigans, and we just layered up to keep warm." During war
years in Europe, fabric, like food, was scarce. Girls couldn't
get the uniforms they usually wore in the Brownies Club, the
younger girls' section of the Girl Guides and Girl Scouts: "I
can remember Mum dying a man's shirt brown to give me a
uniform," one grandmother told me, an example of how important the right clothing is to communicate group identity.

Interpreting what clothes are "saying" is a pastime people
enjoy. Clothing is judged before the wearer has even spoken a
word. It takes only a tenth of a second to form an impression,
and even after more time spent with someone, we often don't
alter our first impressions much (though we gain more confidence in our judgments).[6] Many people live by the belief
"People will stare. Make it worth their while."[7] You might

remember the commotion caused by the green silk dress that Jennifer Lopez wore to the 2000 Grammy Awards, when she broke new ground for what to wear at that venue. The former head of Google, Eric Schmidt, remembers the dress because it became the most popular query ever entered into Google's search engine. Moreover, with so many people searching for a glimpse of the dress, Google recognized a shortcoming: "We had no surefire way of getting users exactly what they wanted: JLo wearing that dress. Google Image Search was born."[8] She made it worth their while.

Gender has always been one of the most important messages "spoken" through clothing, especially if we take a look globally. Even in countries where there is little clothing, gender is marked. And in those places where both boys and girls wore dresses in the 1800s and 1900s? Boys' dresses were closed up to the neckline and buttoned at the front, and girls' dresses had a V at the waist. Your grandmother might also say she was held to "much higher standards" of dress compared to her brothers.

A daughter's clothing is often used as an emblem of her morality. Fiji made the news in 2015 for striking down a former law that had called for the whipping of village girls who wore shorts.[9] Changing the law wasn't uncontroversial, though, since exposing the upper parts of a woman's legs was considered a sign of questionable moral character or intent. And it wasn't only Fijians who considered shorts on women scandalous, but Americans, too. Honesdale, Pennsylvania, banned shorts in 1938, and Monahans, Texas, banned them on women in 1944. A woman in Texas was quoted as saying back then that wearing shorts was a disgrace to humanity, an "advertisement for adultery."[10] By the 1970s, though, clothing companies successfully introduced a fashion called "hot pants," made out of luxury fabrics and worn to parties. The attire celebrated the "traditional" link between shorts and a woman's sexuality, but with the confidence that, for some people at least, cultural ideas about the link between clothing and a woman's intention had changed. And pants sounded much less problematic than shorts anyway.

Men are fitted into norms of clothing, too. If you walk down a street in San Francisco, Berlin, Mexico City, or Tokyo at rush hour, you'll see business suits and ties, a nearly global form of attire that hides a man's body contours in what's been called by some anthropologists a "rigid, pre-shaped body veil."[11] Male sports celebrities sign contractual agreements to wear a type of uniform, "business casual," for public appearances, though they add certain accessories to communicate something more artistic and unique.[12]

Although the anthropologist Sapir wrote that new fashions are more traditional than people realize, every generation reads the "same" piece of cloth in new ways. When my sister and I were girls, my grandmother gave us her old flapper outfits from the 1920s to play our games of dress-up in. The filmy fabrics, sequins, beads, and colors set our imaginations alight. What delighted us, though, had been a shock for my grandmother's mother, who'd thought her daughter's skirt lengths too short and waistless style too boyish. Nana herself saw the dresses as an exuberant symbol of independence from her parents' conservative Victorian era, and for my sister and me, putting the dresses on transported us to a bygone era of splendor.

Another example of how the same bit of cloth can carry very different weight between generations was shared by my student Emily:

> There was one story my grandpa interrupted my grandma to tell. When he was younger, in early high school, he really wanted a pair of Levi jeans. He said he always got the cheap jeans for school when they went school shopping, but he really wanted a pair of nice Levi's for Christmas. He begged and mentioned he wanted them for Christmas, and that year he finally got them. He started laughing so hard. "I wore those jeans one glorious time and then put them in the wash. When my mom washed them, she cut off the little red Levi brand tag. I was so mad at the time because that little tag was the whole point!" His mom did not see what the big deal was and just thought it was a new jean tag like a price sticker, but Levi jeans were really in at the time and my grandpa was crushed. I thought this story was really funny when he was telling me because it is something so relatable. The idea that kids put so much work into their image and parents just don't understand ("You wouldn't get it, Mom") is timeless.[13]

Some grandparents told me that before World War II, teenage boys dressed just like their parents did. There wasn't a teenage style or teenage culture back then, but people who grew up in the 1960s, on the other hand, were mocked for their changes in style and were called "long-haired hippies" who listened to appalling music. People who were in their youth in the '60s remember what it was like to be the recipients of their grandparents' cold disapproval. Now grandparents themselves, they find plenty to mock about younger generations' styles, not without some irony. Your parents and grandparents will have a lot of thoughtful reflections on transformations in fashion, some of them quite humorous.

What's considered an ideal body type also varies across generations and cultures. Wallis Simpson, the Duchess of Windsor, famously said, "You can never be too rich or too thin," but in Pohnpei and many other places, thinness signifies weakness and poverty, while a big body symbolizes wealth, abundance, strength, and beauty. In Mauritania, where a slim girl would bring shame to her family, there's a tradition of force-feeding girls before their wedding day.[14]

Clothing affects the body and how it does or doesn't move. Victorian ladies went to their fainting rooms and swooned on their fainting couches, where they loosened their corsets to breathe. When I was living in Pohnpei, I wore a skirt, like the other women. I thought I knew how to manage this familiar garment, but getting into the back of a pickup truck revealed my ignorance. I saw some shocked looks and was immediately given instruction on concealing my knees, the proper etiquette in the culture.

Hair style is an important component of adornment as well. In the UK, girls' hair used to be kept short "because of nits," which were a focus of school health programs from the

1940s until the 1980s. Anthropologist Hilda Kuper described how changes in the hairstyles of Swazi women in Southern Africa weren't just about personal choice or peer group identity, but an announcement about other family members: "The cone [of hair] is deliberately 'torn down' if a grown son or daughter has died; if a husband dies a widow has her entire head shaved and covered with a cap of plaited grass. For the loss of a young child, or a distant relative, only the ringlets are shaved."[15] Mourning a loved one affects how the body encounters the world.

A trip around the globe shows a marvelous diversity of ideas concerning the adornment of the body, including scarification, tattoos, tooth filing, head binding, neck coils, makeup, face painting, jewelry, and lip plates, to name a few. Tattooing was first introduced to Europe after a voyage of Captain Cook's to the Pacific Islands in 1769, and body marking was practiced by indigenous groups in the US before that. Tattoos took a while to really catch on again though. While only 13 percent of baby boomers in the US have a tattoo, over a third of Gen Xers and nearly half of millennials have at least one.[16] In the Pacific, tattoos used to record a family's history or were for spiritual protection. The story goes that when the first European sailors arrived in Pohnpei, Pohnpeians saw their untattooed skin and asked how they kept track of their history. A sailor gave them a history book of Scottish chiefs. The women wove pages of the book into the garments they made because the sailors' histories now intersected with their own. When the rain washed out the print, the women weren't impressed that the history of the Europeans disappeared with the rain.[17] Most forms of traditional tattooing had disappeared by the time I did fieldwork there.

The body has always been a domain where both real and symbolic struggles are waged. It's difficult for anyone to see the body and clothing differently than the way in which they were socialized. Older people I interviewed expressed worries about what their grandchildren's clothing symbolized, yet they also mentioned the importance of freedom of expression. In short, grandparents felt conflicted about current fashions.

Learning details about your parents' and grandparents' dress might help you understand different experiences and sensibilities across generations, in addition to finding commonalities. You and you grandparent might even share some fashion favorites—what's considered vintage to you was once new to your grandparent. Asking parents or grandparents where they got their clothes when they were growing up and how clothing and the body were perceived offers a glimpse into how it felt to move, play, and enter a room back then.

NOTES FROM YOUR INTERVIEW

CHAPTER 10

Questions on Belief: The Ideas That Shaped You and Your Family

We rarely explicitly ask other people about their beliefs, yet beliefs are one of the defining elements of culture. What do you know about your ancestors' beliefs? The questions in this chapter offer an opportunity to learn more about the beliefs that have shaped your family's history.

Opening Question

- *How have your beliefs changed over the course of your lifetime, if they have? (These beliefs can relate to marriage, politics, men and women, wealth, education, work, etc.)*

Follow-up Questions

- *Who were the people who most influenced your beliefs?*

- *What has influenced you most in maintaining or changing your beliefs?*

- *How have your beliefs about human nature changed, if they have?*

- If your beliefs have changed, what was it like to reorient yourself to the world with a different set of beliefs?
- Did your family have any special customs tied to belief?
- How much did your family's beliefs affect your early decisions?
- As you began to recognize differences in wealth around you, how did seeing various levels of wealth shape your wants, desires, or ambitions, if they did?
- What social movements have impacted your thinking and beliefs?
- How have your beliefs about race or ethnicity changed over time, if they have?
- What would you think if your grandchild decided to go to university or not to go to university?
- What's the belief you would most want your children to share with you?
- Do you use any forms of nontraditional medicine or healing?

According to anthropologists Arthur and Joan Kleinman, belief is what's at stake for each of us in our everyday struggles with hopes, regrets, and losses. In my anthropology fieldwork, I have always found people interested in telling me about their beliefs, especially if I showed curiosity and a willingness to understand.

Anthropologists ask questions about belief not only to understand culture, but to reveal the invisible frameworks that people use to justify their actions. Belief provided me with an understanding of why the three-year-old in the family I lived with in Pohnpei reminded me to bring my flashlight when I went out at night. Yes, it's helpful to have a flashlight when jungle paths can be tricky to find a foothold on, but more importantly, she believed that a person needed a light to protect themselves from the spirits that roamed around in the dark. Belief explains why my grandfather stopped midsentence to touch wood or knock on wood, in order to attract some good luck for himself, after making a favorable prediction or describing something that hadn't happened and that he didn't want to happen, either.

Some anthropologists and philosophers differentiate between two types of belief: beliefs based on faith that can't be verified (belief-*in*) and beliefs based on human experiences that are constantly in flux (belief-*that*).[1] I find this a useful distinction, though it can be argued that trying to separate faith from other kinds of belief reflects a set of beliefs in itself. And there are significant differences around the world in terms of how much faith or religious practice influences how people make sense of human behavior, both their own and others', and how they're held accountable or grow into disciplined people, gaining a sense of what's forbidden and what's approved.[2] Although you might share the same religious faith as your parent or grandparent, I would be surprised if you shared the exact same beliefs on other aspects of daily life, like marriage, politics, education, and work. The questions in this chapter are designed to help you understand beliefs that are a product of your parents' or grandparents' experiences in life and their observations of human behavior. The questions focus on how their years of observations have led them to certain beliefs.

Although the focus of this chapter isn't on spiritual belief, it may come up when you start talking about belief in general, since spiritual and social worlds are connected, even for people who are just "twicers," as one person described her parents because they only attended church twice a year, at Christmas and Easter. Evolutionary anthropologists have suggested that the human capacity to believe in a spiritual dimension, whether acted on every day or twice a year, is found in all societies and springs from an innate capacity for awe.[3] And it's true that those who have "lost" their faith in organized religion can still tap into this sense of awe. As one grandmother told me, "I lost faith, but the sense of wonder at the universe is still with me, you know; when you look at the landing on Mars, you say there's got to be something bigger than this." And another grandmother, who no longer attended church and wasn't particularly religious anymore, told me, "You have to believe in something, a purpose, in the end, for a life I suppose."

When you hear about your parent's or grandparent's beliefs about issues such as marriage, wealth, politics, education, and gender roles, you'll be surprised by how diverse and unique they can be. People often think they can predict what their family members will believe based on experiences with similar types of people of the same generation, but don't rely on those assumptions. Political scientist Philip Converse compared the Amish and the Shakers, two groups that seem very similar on the surface, with their plain, old-fashioned dress, distaste for ornamentation, communal work ethic, shared property, and withdrawal from the world. But while the Amish are averse to modern technology, the Shakers fully embrace it and even develop innovative technologies of their own.[4] Prepare to be surprised by your parents and grandparents.

You're probably already aware of some of your parents' and grandparents' beliefs. And you will have already encountered some of these beliefs in their responses to the other questions in this book, since what a person believes intersects with other aspects of everyday life. But the questions in this chapter present a chance to ask more about this defining element of culture.

During this part of the interview, you may encounter beliefs that are so different from your own that they challenge your values. Conversations about belief have always been the greatest challenge of an anthropological approach. When anthropologist E. E. Evans-Pritchard lived with the Azande in North Central Africa and was trying to understand their point of view, their belief in magic was a sticking point for him. It seemed to him to be quite different from their other beliefs, which were empirically grounded or based on their observations of natural phenomena. When questioned further about their beliefs in magic, they explained that magic was the unseen force responsible for what couldn't be explained otherwise. Evans-Pritchard came to understand that belief in magic made it possible for the Azande to accept tragic losses, endure extreme hardships with dignity, and maintain a belief in justice.[5] Magic once played a role in American ideas of justice, too, during the Salem, Massachusetts, witch trials in 1692. Although your family members may not believe in magic or witches, this portion of the interview can mean accepting a different vocabulary for truth.

Belief isn't a simple matter of parents passing down a code to the next generation. Rather, belief comes from a lifetime of experience, where, as anthropologist Lucien Lévy-Bruhl put it, "to be is to participate."[6] The people with whom we participate affect our beliefs. This can include peers, teachers, parents, grandparents, mentors, children, and so on. Whether your parents or grandparents were once members of a youth group, or currently meet with neighbors to walk together in the morning, or get together with a motorcycle club for beers at the pub every Thursday night, they've been hanging out with people who are "vibrating sympathetically," as sociologist Émile Durkheim described it. Your parents and grandparents have been sharing beliefs through their stories and their commentaries on everyday life.

As you hear your family members describe their beliefs, you will discover what has influenced them, whether neighbors, clubs, civil unrest, increased affluence, unremitting poverty and oppression, education, natural disasters, or even science. As one person told me, "Yes, I suppose as a child, you wouldn't have ever thought parents should get divorced and split up, and now it's the norm, isn't it? It's called life, isn't it?"

When people from *different* groups first get together, each becomes aware of a lack of sympathetic vibration, as their different belief systems impact even the most ordinary things. When I studied engineers collaborating from different countries, I found that beliefs played a role in misunderstandings. One group of engineers told me about the anger they felt when they weren't greeted by name in emails "as a human being" should be. Other engineers felt that leaving off the greeting was showing respect by saving time and demonstrating an ongoing friendly relationship.[7] All the engineers believed showing respect and appreciation was a vital part of working together, but because they showed respect and appreciation in different ways, they experienced misunderstandings that made it harder to work together.

To use an example from the Deaf community, Deaf culture has a strong belief in the value of frank talk and directness, which sounds rude to hearing Americans, who equate indirectness with politeness. A hearing student might express their unhappiness with a grade I gave them by saying, "Excuse me, Professor, can I ask you a question about my grade?" I'm expected to know they're unhappy with their grade, since students who are happy about their grades never question them. A Deaf student, though, would be more direct in expressing dissatisfaction by saying something like "You gave me a B. Why?" Deaf people believe hearing people are annoyingly vague. In the case of grandparents and grandchildren, too, feelings of annoyance can arise from different ways of showing respect. The irritation is clear enough, but the underlying commonality in beliefs (that respect is important) is often invisible.

You may not have realized how the language we use—including metaphors, grammar, and even numbering systems—affects our beliefs in unconscious ways. For example, a Pohnpeian child learns around thirty different ways of counting. Choosing the right form of numbering requires learning to see the world in a certain way. It means noticing the shapes of things because shape affects the type of counting system you're supposed to use. Children learn what's important to differentiate, for example, whether something is edible or drinkable. I may perceive the same object in a different way because language includes an inherited belief system about what does or doesn't belong. Kava, which seems like a drink to me, is actually a food to them.

Metaphors also convey beliefs. For example, the idea that "Falsehood flies, and the truth comes limping after it" is credited to Jonathan Swift in 1710. Similarly, Mark Twain said, "A lie can travel around the world and back again while the truth is lacing up its boots." This belief that lies are spread much more readily than truth is widely held.

The metaphors our grandparents use can reveal something of the beliefs that shaped them as children. For example, one person I interviewed said, "We were probably poor white trash; I'm sure a lot of people looked down on us." This well-known American metaphor conveys the belief that some people are worthless, and "looking down" on someone who's believed to be less-than seems as natural as looking down from a greater physical height.

Leaving aside language and metaphors, beliefs are formed through sensory experiences, too. A colleague told me about a Deaf friend of his who got a cochlear implant, allowing him to hear. What the sounds he heard meant, though, had to be learned one by one. The first day after the implant operation, he heard a repetitive clinking noise and became curious about it. He followed the sound to the kitchen and discovered that it came from his father's fork hitting the plate while he was eating. Hopefully, as your family member describes their beliefs to you, they will convey some of the sensory experiences that influenced them.

I've been surprised to find that grandparents of different cultures share some similar beliefs. Grandparents who had grown up in places as different as Iceland and California expressed a belief in the importance of education. They valued not just the knowledge acquired in school but also greater access to jobs and other opportunities. Parents and grandparents from different countries had similar regrets about not having enough money for an education, or were proud of being the first in their family to go to college. The belief that too much leisure time should be avoided is also common. As one grandparent remembered, "Me and my brother would go every week to mow my grandfather's huge front yard. It was just what boys did; keep those boys busy and they won't get in trouble; my mother really believed that."

Beliefs reveal something about the workings of our minds, say, a fondness for cause-and-effect reasoning, for blaming, for finding ways to accept the unthinkable, for territorialism, for discipline, for channeling passionate emotion into action, or for disguising power dynamics. When talking about their beliefs, people show a surprising amount of emotion, even when they are being philosophical or abstract.

Most of the people I interviewed said their beliefs had changed over time. For example, one person told me that he had grown up in a small conservative mill town in the northeastern US, but later went to live in a city, where he was exposed to many different belief systems. Another person told me that his father's beliefs changed when he left home to go to the teachers' college. There, he was advised to shorten his Greek last name to make it easier for his future students to pronounce. He began to believe in the value of conforming: "He straightened his hair and he forgot how to write and read Greek—even though he'd been to Greek school in America until he was nine or ten. He worked at forgetting it; he believed it was the best way to be the all-American boy." A grandmother I interviewed told me her beliefs changed when she went away to school and saw that she was the only one kneeling down to say her prayers beside her bed at night. When she came home at vacation time, she told her mother, "I'm not going to kneel down and say my prayers because nobody else is doing that." Another person said, "Oh yes, my beliefs have changed. I used to go to Sunday school and want to be a Sunday school teacher, but now there's certain things you could question in religion and things which you wouldn't have dreamt of doing when you were growing up." One grandparent paused for a long time and breathed in before telling me that her beliefs had changed about how safe the world was. Some parents' beliefs changed when they watched their children struggle with old ideas in a new generation's world. For others, their beliefs changed after they were drafted into a war overseas, or after leaving another country for school in the US. Science and new knowledge can also change people's beliefs. If your parents' and grandparents' beliefs changed, ask what it was like for them to reorient themselves to new beliefs.

We act on our beliefs, often without realizing their impact.

By asking your parent or grandparent about their beliefs, they'll have a chance to self-reflect. One parent told me, "I've always lived by that old saying that it's better to regret a mistake than an opportunity missed." Others believed in the importance of finding a steady job and sticking to it, or fitting in to be successful. In these statements, you can see the older generation's beliefs about risk and loyalty.

NOTES FROM YOUR INTERVIEW

CHAPTER 11

Questions on Kinship and Marriage: The Making of a Family

Kinship was such an important focus in anthropology for many years that one scholar wrote that kinship is to anthropology "what logic is to philosophy and the nude is to art."[1] Kinship was also one of the most popular topics for people being interviewed.

Opening Question

- *What were dating and courtship practices like when you were young?*

Follow-up Questions

- *What were your expectations of marriage and romance?*
- *Tell me about your first and/or worst date or a memorable first meeting of a spouse/partner.*
- *About how many cousins, aunts, and uncles do you have?*
- *How would you compare mother-daughter, father-son, father-daughter, or mother-son relationships when you were growing up and now?*

- *What were your parents like when you were growing up?*
- *What were your grandparents like when you were growing up?*
- *Who were the dominant ones in your family?*
- *With which member of the family did you have your most treasured relationship?*
- *Who was your favorite relative, and what was special about them?*
- *Are there any secrets about relatives in your family that you found out later in life?*
- *Since friends are often almost like family, who have been some of your most treasured friends?*
- *How do you think marriage has changed over time?*
- *What family holidays do you remember, and who was there?*
- *Is there anything you wish you'd known about your family earlier in life?*
- *Is there anything you wish you'd asked your grandparents or parents?*

When early anthropologists like Malinowski went to live among the islanders of the South Seas, they realized there is a lot of variation in how people think about family and name various family members. The Sudanese kinship system is considered the most complicated because there's a different term for almost every family member. The Hawaiian kinship system is simpler because the same term is used for multiple people (*makua kāne* for both father and uncle, *makuahine* for mother and aunt), similar to how English speakers use the term *uncle* for both maternal and paternal uncles, who are differentiated in many other cultures.[2] Variation in kinship systems is also evidenced in the fact that the youngest person ever reported to become a grandparent was age twenty-three, while the oldest person reported to have become a grandparent was age ninety-five.[3]

In some societies, the biological father isn't the most important man in a child's life; rather, it's their uncle, specifically their mother's brother. Pohnpei is an example of one of these matrilineally organized societies. There, the chief's son doesn't become the next chief, but his sister's son does.

Anthropologists believe that kinship is fundamental to understanding the dawn of human community and the development of the human mind.[4] However, as often happens, what seems controlled by biology, in this case shared DNA, evolves into elaborate systems infused with symbolic meaning when humans, armed with the instrument of language, are involved. For example, people use kinship terms not just for blood relations, but to acknowledge what other people do or are compelled to do for them. For example, a boy may be sent to mow his mother's stepfather's acreage on Saturday afternoons. Kinship terms place the boy in a system that defines what he's obligated to do. Some companies use a family metaphor to foster long-term commitments among employees.

The ways people have adapted biological relationships make families even more interesting. Some societies refer to a concept called milk kinship, where a mother's milk creates a relationship between the mother and any infant she nurses, including those not biologically related, deeming marriage between adult "milk brothers and sisters" impossible.

Anthropologist David Schneider found that on Yap, a close neighbor to Pohnpei, people explained paternity not in terms of sexual intercourse, but spiritual intervention: "All of the older people and most of the younger people of Yap regard paternity as a purely social fact, not a biological relationship; coitus is believed irrelevant to conception," he wrote in 1953.[5] And nowadays new reproductive technologies allow for procreation without sex.

According to anthropologist Maurice Godelier, kinship is not just a family tree of relationships, but also a way for people to think of themselves, what it means to be a son, a father, a daughter, or a mother. The goal of the questions in this chapter is to find out what kinship has meant in your family. One person I interviewed described to me the system in her Texas family: "In my family, it's very Southern, and the women were kind of in control. They held everything together, so that was the skill that was passed down. I was told, 'It's your responsibility to maintain these social connections; you have to have these gatherings and make sure everyone stays connected.'"

You might already know that your grandfather remarried when your father was a teenager, but this interview gives you an opportunity to ask what it meant for your father to suddenly have a new, nearly grown stepbrother. According to one interviewee, "My father remarried, and I inherited a stepbrother six months younger than me, which meant we competed for girlfriends and jobs and things."

It's interesting to observe how familial relationships dictate behavior in different kinship systems around the world. For the Maasai, when someone passes away, you must avoid causing their relatives pain by never mentioning the name of the deceased. This means that those still living who have the same name as the deceased choose a new name, and the deceased's name is dropped from the repertoire of names for many years.[6] In Pohnpei and other parts of the Pacific, if you're in the company of a brother or sister, and a topic of an implied sexual nature comes up, one of you has to leave.

Even if you've only traveled across town to interview your relative, you'll find differences in how previous generations think of kinship. My grandmother was one of thirteen children, which made for a lot of aunts and uncles for my mother and her brother. But in just one generation, a lot changed. My grandmother had only two children, and one of her children didn't have any children, meaning I don't have any cousins on my mother's side of the family at all, versus the abundance of cousins my mother had.

Kinship is a sort of blueprint for collaboration. During World War II, relatives in Canada sent packages of food to family members in Britain. According to one interviewee, "The great-aunt in Canada would send something to the great-aunt up in the north [who lived in Kirkby Thore, a small village in Cumberland], and the great-aunt in the north would send us something from that, a tin of salmon or cream, a tin of fruit. The great-aunt up in the north also sent us a wild rabbit she shot for Christmas. It was a special treat because we didn't have the money to buy such things." In some cultures, patrilineal or matrilineal lineages are very much like corporations, with relatives holding assets in common and acting as a single entity in conflicts and acquisitions.[7]

Within kinship systems, there can be not only competition, collaboration, and attachments but also isolation and separation. Over time, families may be separated because of mobility and disconnected because of name changes. These disconnections gave rise to the professional role of heir hunter. One person I interviewed, Paula, had moved from the UK to Switzerland and got a call one day from an heir hunter. They asked if she remembered a cousin named Henry from the south of England. She did remember visiting him when she was a child. Henry had died without a spouse or children, and without any instructions about his estate. In conversation with the heir hunter, Paula learned for the first time that her grandmother had been illegitimate. "That was never mentioned in the family," she told me. "Certainly, when the children were around, it was never talked about. And you don't know those things. I mean I had never, it never occurred to me. It was really quite interesting. I suppose at that time having an illegitimate child was not acceptable, they kept it quiet, but they also didn't let them be turned out on the streets."

Families become disconnected by belief, too, as in the sad case of people who have been disowned after "coming out." For those rejected by their families, friendships become the primary relationships characterized by certainty, depth, and permanence.[8]

Marriage brings two family kinship systems together. But marriage also occurs between blood relations. One estimate suggests that 80 percent of all marriages in history have been between second cousins or closer.[9] In nineteen states in the US, first cousins can marry today. In societies like the Bedouin studied by anthropologist Lila Abu-Lughod, the paternal first cousin is the preferred marriage partner (for the first wife), and members of the royal families of Europe were known for marrying relatives, too.[10] In one famous case studied by anthropologist Jean Jackson, though, the Tucano of the Northwest Amazon preferred a marriage partner who spoke an entirely different language.

No one definition of marriage can be applied to all cultures. Monogamy is the favored system, but polygamy is found in about 2 percent of the world's families. Polyandry, a woman having more than one husband, is even rarer.

Arranged marriages make up 55 percent of marriages worldwide, perhaps including your parents or grandparents. People often prefer that their sons and daughters marry someone of the same caste or socioeconomic status. When one grandparent was telling me about her childhood home, she mentioned the bachelor who lived next door. He came from a wealthy family, and everyone in the neighborhood knew the story of his failed romance: "He once took a girl out—her family owned one of the big cigarette companies—but his parents gave him a good hiding when he got home for taking her out, because she was beneath him. They thought she wasn't good enough for him." Similar stories may lurk in your families, too. Hearing about dating and courtship from a parent's or grandparent's point of view evokes a sense of a time, place, and culture, which might be one reason why romance is a popular theme for novels and movies.

Grandparents told me about courting traditions I had only previously read about. For example, at county fairs and pie suppers in the US, men bid on pies made by women they were "sweet on." The bidding (with proceeds going to charity to avoid any hint of impropriety) could be quite competitive. According to *The Perkins Journal* in Oklahoma in 1934, "Our pie supper was well attended and had a nice program, plenty of pies. We made $16.97. Juanita George received the cake for the most popular young lady. Ted Tomlinson received a looking glass for the ugliest man, and Marvin Cruse and Stella Davidson got a jar of pickles for the most lovesick couple."[11]

Some of my students told me that when they asked their grandparents about dating or courtship, their grandparents looked at them like they must be joking, but then smiled and told them stories of adolescent crushes, sometimes musing aloud that they had never before talked to anyone about that time in their life. Some of this reticence around talking about romance dates back to a time when having a boyfriend or girlfriend was unthinkable to admit to anyone, and a girl who'd been seen with a boy would have been kicked out of her home and onto the streets. Silence between generations about courtship was prevalent. As one grandparent told me, "There were no sex talks. I was so naïve." Remarkably, these same grandparents have told their grandchildren that it doesn't bother them that couples nowadays live together without being married, showing the extent of changes over time and the ability of these grandparents to take new points of view.

In answering your questions about courtship, your grandmother may reveal herself to have been wilder than you expected! The bespectacled, gray-haired person talking to you may not seem like someone who once dated a different boy every week, or who can still name all the bad dates she had before meeting your grandfather. A grandfather might be more delicate about his wild side by saying he wasn't perfect and made a lot of mistakes.

In many places, relationships between husbands and wives have taken precedence over relationships with the extended family. A couple of generations ago, a newly married couple stayed close by to help the family, in addition to having their own children, but now, couples are much more mobile and independent. These changes led to a law introduced in Singapore in the 2000s, making it illegal to refuse to support one's elderly parents. Mobile phones make possible a certain closeness despite distance; you can be in touch with your family almost anywhere now.

Many parents and grandparents who my students and I interviewed said that their most treasured relationships today are with their family, and the questions in this chapter offer an opportunity to build even stronger bonds.

NOTES FROM YOUR INTERVIEW

CHAPTER 12

Questions on Material Culture: Your Family's Most Treasured Possessions

....

This chapter concerns what anthropologists refer to as material culture, those tangibles that pass from hand to hand, from generation to generation, and are vessels of that curious human cultural idea, value. Objects can accumulate or lose both sentimental and monetary value. They also help us accomplish practical and social purposes in our everyday lives.

Opening Question

- *What physical objects reminding you of your childhood have you kept?*

Follow-up Questions

- *Can you tell me the story of one or two things you've kept over the years?*

- *What is the most important object your parents passed down to you? Who does it remind you of?*

- *What do you wish you'd kept?*

- *Can you think of anything that you made yourself as a child or teenager that you've kept to this day?*

- *What photographs of your childhood do you have around you?*

- *Are there any letters or newspaper clippings from the past that you've kept?*

- *What was gift giving like in your family when you were growing up?*

- *Did you have an allowance or "pocket money" to spend on things as a child? If so, what did you spend it on?*

- *What would you say is your most valued possession?*

- *What is your favorite object in your home now? What makes it your favorite object?*

- *What object in your home now would be the hardest for you to do without?*

- *What differences do you see in the types of material possessions people have today compared to when you were a child?*

- *What gifts that you gave to others are particularly memorable to you?*

- *If you were to choose one object for people to remember you by, what would it be and why?*

While hiking on the Isle of Man, my husband and I came across a Viking burial ground. Small stones marked the outline of the site. There was a plaque that read:

> The stones mark the position of a ship in which beneath a low cairn of stones, the richly adorned body of a Viking settler was buried. Sacrificed and buried with him were

a woman, his horse and other livestock. This pagan
burial of the late 8th century directly overlay Christian
burials in stone lined graves of the same period.

What struck me about these words were first, the sacrifice
of the woman, and the many questions that raised, and second, what material culture was considered essential to take
into the afterlife. This gravesite revealed that Vikings of the
eighth century thought they needed a ship, the right clothes,
livestock, and a female partner—perhaps the widow or a
slave—for the afterlife.[1] Even if we're not staring at the con-
tents of a grave, there's plenty to think about in terms of the
material things we value, although we're more likely these
days to believe that "you can't take it with you."

According to philosophers, humans need material culture
because we are quite helpless at birth and even for an extended period afterward, compared to other species. But what
an inventive bunch humans have proven to be, continually ex-
tending our capacity, even to travel into space in capsules of
our own design. People have not only created advanced life-
support systems for environments more hostile than Earth
but also continually create whimsical items like the odd stuff
you find in a kitchen catalog: an implement that's a spoon and
fork on one end and chopsticks on the other, or a pancake
pen, which my grandfather would have found handy, since he
used to make pancakes in the shape of the letters of my mother's name.

Archaeologists have always been fascinated by the material culture they find buried and left behind. James Deetz,

who taught the first archaeology class I took as an undergraduate, spoke of "small things forgotten," the objects that play a big part in helping us understand the past.[2] You have an advantage over archaeologists when you interview your elders because they are human witnesses to the past. By asking them about material culture, you're inviting your parents and grandparents to explain small things not forgotten.

The grandparents I interviewed had fewer material possessions in childhood than their grandchildren have today. Even at a young age, the idea of scarcity increases the value of material culture. As one grandparent said, "We didn't have very much money, but nobody did; we didn't expect things. I can remember going to a birthday party, and we always used to get a pencil at a birthday party, and that was absolutely wonderful to actually have your own pencil—a completely different ball game than these days, you know; we were just thrilled to have that pencil to come home with."

When some of our grandparents were younger, it was unusual to own expensive items like a washing machine, TV, or car. As one grandparent told me, "A friend of my mother got a washing machine, and that was unheard of; we had to wash clothes either in a sink or in a dolly tub [an iron tub with an implement called a dolly-stick that was 'dollied up and down' to mash the clothes]." Another grandparent told me that the first time she watched television was when she was eleven, on the day of the coronation of Queen Elizabeth II: "When there were important things to watch like the coronation, all the neighbors would gather and watch, to be able to see it."

One reason why people had fewer material things back then was the absence of credit. It wasn't until General Motors started the installment plan for buying cars (35 percent down payment) in 1919 that more people could afford a purchase like that. But it took some time for credit to catch on, since the idea of borrowing was considered morally tainted. Many people I interviewed still felt this aversion to borrowing and had a fear of being in debt. Debtors' prisons were a part of life in Western Europe through the mid-nineteenth century. These memories lingered, and it wasn't until the 1950s that credit cards became widely used.[3]

Anthropologists have found that people have a hard time talking about the meaning of material things, even though these items play an important role in our lives.[4] It may be that when we're asked about our relationship with our possessions, we fail to see that these things really represent relationships to people. If someone doesn't seem to have a lot to say about their material things, we can ask about the relationships those things bring to mind. When I asked one person to tell me about an object that she'd kept that reminded her of her childhood, she described a stool. The stool had a practical value, certainly, but more importantly, it symbolized special time with her mother:

> Mum used to say to me that the best part of the day was me coming home from school, coming in the back door, and sitting on the stool in the kitchen and just talking, a mother-daughter thing. I've still got that stool from the

kitchen. My father built it in evening classes. My children remember sitting on the stool in the kitchen, too, while Grandma was baking, passing time, drinking cups of tea, and eating shortbread.

Gift giving is one obvious way in which an object can represent a relationship and is one of the most significant cultural practices anywhere; every society has rules, both spoken and unspoken, around giving and receiving. It's not just that you have to take care to give an odd number of flowers for happy occasions and an even number for sad occasions in Latvia, but you also have to keep track of what you've received because according to anthropologist Marcel Mauss, gifts are never really free—they compel the recipient to return something of similar value.[5] More than that, a person gives something of themselves, which makes it difficult to throw away a gift without feeling like you're denigrating the giver.

In Pohnpei, gift giving is a public event with important consequences for the whole society. There, giving to the point of completely emptying your land of its produce is a way to gain status in the community at giving celebrations called *kamadipw*, which literally means "to beat the bushes" or to harvest everything. Historian Dorothy Johansen described a similar road to status—not through beating, but through burning. In the potlaches of the indigenous Northwest coast, a host chief challenges a guest chief to see who can destroy the most in a huge bonfire. If the guest burns up more wealth (a larger fire) than the host, the host and his people lose power and status.[6] Where I grew up, the reverse was true: Burning through wealth was shameful, while acquiring wealth brought status. If you think about it, the Pohnpeian system is a shrewd way of sharing wealth, which is redistributed to the community.[7]

By asking your parents or grandparents about items they've kept over the years, you'll learn about memories of people and places that have stuck with them. For instance, your grandparent might mention a platter they've kept that their mother used when fishermen came around selling fish in the neighborhood. And that memory might remind them of how the butcher and the grocer came around every week and sat at the kitchen table to get their order. Your grandmother might still have the pitcher she took out to the milkman with his horse and cart so he could dip his measure into his container to fill hers. What a different kind of home shopping this must have been!

Material culture can be a celebration of excellence in artistry, too. A Texas grandmother remembered fondly how her mother "made such lovely things," and she wished she'd kept "some of the things she made for me." One eighty-year-old man I interviewed went to his closet and brought out two beautiful sweaters hand-knit for him by his mother sixty-five years ago that he still wears.

Material goods have impacts on the environment and the ways we live today. For example, a nanoscientist colleague once remarked to me about the costs of cars. He asked, with some irony, "Who would have intentionally designed a transport system where thin steel containers filled with highly combustible liquid race at high speeds towards each other, separated by a narrow line on the road?" Although traffic accidents kill more than a million people and hurt 20 million more each year, we are so enchanted by this form of transportation and have a hard time imagining an alternative.[8]

When interviewing grandparents, I found that the list of material things they kept from their forebears was a short one. They included items like an embroidered sampler, a gold ring from their father's high school graduation, "the odd vase," a silver bowl, a shaving mug, their grandmother's wedding dishes, small figurines, a letter, and photographs. These grandparents said they would never give these things away—"someone else will have to get rid of them." These objects are sparse in number but rich in relational meaning.

NOTES FROM YOUR INTERVIEW

CHAPTER 13

Questions on Fear:
Learning Courage Through Fear

F ear is a universal human feeling that arises, as part of our evolutionary inheritance, when we recognize some threat or risk of harm or pain. Although fear is a shared human experience, not everyone is afraid of the same things. This chapter will give you an opportunity to learn about the fears of your family members.

Opening Question

- *What were you most fearful of as a child?*

Follow-up Questions

- *Can you remember a scary story from your childhood?*

- *If there were any places you were fearful of as a child, what were they?*

- *What strategies or rituals did you use to cope with fear as a child?*

- *What gave you confidence when you were a child?*

- *Is there something in your life that's been hard or even impossible to do because of fears?*

- *What were your own children fearful of when they were young?*

- *What are you fearful of today?*

- *Who in your life has helped you most in dealing with fears?*

- *What has given you the most personal autonomy or efficacy over the years?*

- *What has been your bravest act?*

Charles Darwin noticed that people and animals expressed fear and other emotions in similar ways. Today, neuroscientists have identified two distinct pathways in the brain for threat responses: a "low road" (fast and direct) and a "high road" (slow and more accurate). People feel a fast response of fear at a sudden movement in the grass or a stick that *looks* like a snake. The slower response comes when they realize that it's the wind or a twig in their path. A 2014 YouGov poll found that more American adults are afraid of snakes than anything else. Heights come second, and speaking in front of an audience, third.[1] Although speaking in front of an audience isn't life-threatening, the way your pulse races makes it seem so. The fear comes not from the danger of being rushed to the hospital, but of dying a kind of social death if you are judged incompetent and humiliated.

Everyone knows fear: Suddenly your pulse accelerates, you feel a flash of adrenaline, it's hard to breathe, you can't swallow, you start to sweat. One grandparent remembered well the fear she experienced during the war years in London:

> I was very frightened that there was a war on and one might be killed. The war started when I was eight and didn't end until I was thirteen. Even when it ended, there were those buzz bombs coming over, which were horrible. When a bomb was about to drop, the motors of the missile would cut out, so you would first hear them zooming over and then if they went quiet, you thought, "Oh God, not on me surely."

For children especially, the precipice between security and fear always seems nearby. Children may be afraid of losing teeth, of TV characters, of certain foods, among many other things. One summer when I was a child, I was preoccupied with the possibility of getting lockjaw from stepping on a rusty nail because all the kids went barefoot in the summer. No doubt my parents used fear to keep us in our shoes, but all I could think about was how to eat through a straw for the rest of my life. Several grandparents shared with me their childhood fear of drowning that resulted from falling or being pushed into water. One grandparent told me that as a child, he learned to be afraid of "probably the same thing that bothers kids today: the way that other people treat you."

Every anthropologist doing fieldwork has observed manifestations of fear in the stories people tell them and the warnings they receive about dangers lurking around them. In

Pohnpei, I was taught to approach the dark as a serious threat, but the islanders laughed heartily at my fear of rats and cockroaches. Fears are doggedly persistent, though, and mine resisted mockery and even new information.

Getting back to snakes, I've heard many firsthand accounts of them through the interviews I've conducted. One person said, "Everything you did on the farm, you looked for snakes." When someone else killed a snake, "as big around as half of my leg," the snake was shown around. I learned that buttonwood bushes leaning over the creek hid water moccasins, "old, stubby-tailed, mean ones." Eastern diamondback rattlesnakes, endemic to the southeastern United States, could be a death sentence if you got bitten. I learned from one grandfather why some snakes are so dangerous—their hollow fangs fill with venom, so when they bite you, the venom goes through tiny holes in the fangs directly into your bloodstream. In the movie *Indiana Jones and the Raiders of The Lost Ark*, Indiana Jones groans, "Snakes, why did it have to be snakes?" after his torch illuminates hundreds of snakes in the archaeological site into which he's about to climb.

Many grandparents remember how they overcame their fears. For example, one seventy-year-old recounted that after he'd been hit by a wave at the beach, "My father would say, 'Get back out there and take the next wave. That's how you're going to get over it.'"

Although some grandparents I interviewed said they couldn't remember being afraid as a child, now they likely worry a lot! Parents and grandparents have fears about health, violence, pandemics, the state of their country, outliving their savings, and the possibility that the world could be a harsher place for their children and grandchildren than it was for them.

One grandfather said he most fears the advance of technology. Although he's in favor of innovation, he has a hard time keeping up. This was a common concern I heard among grandparents: that technology is great for younger people, but thorny for older ones. Their lingering apprehension of the digital world is a result of actually being around when the first personal computers became available and were quite unreliable at the time because of incompatible software and frequent crashes that were difficult to recover from. Though computers are reliable now, the fears remain. And since socialization takes place through participation, most older people are at a disadvantage because they don't interact much with younger people who are more adept with digital tools.

Culture influences our perceptions of what's dangerous and how we deal with risk. In many places, famine and undernourishment are less of a concern than the health consequences of eating too much. Child abduction is considered more of a risk now than sixty years ago, when many grandparents remember leaving their house or apartment doors unlocked and playing on their own. Today doors are always locked and children playing alone outside might be reported to the police. Some grandmothers remember being told to "always choose a train compartment with other women" or "find another compartment if a man enters" when they were traveling alone. Fear is often used to affect behaviors, for example, to persuade people to wear safety gear.

Fear can obviously be protective, for example, to avoid getting bitten by a venomous snakes, but it can also be destructive, in the case of fear based on others' appearance, heritage, politics, or health if they have a stigmatized illness. Author Rebecca Makkai described the heartbreaks of the AIDS epidemic in the 1980s: "Everyone that spring just wandered. You'd find a friend in a cafe, and even if you'd hardly known them you'd run and kiss them, and you'd exchange news about who was dead."[2]

Despite the pervasiveness of fear, some people heartily consume scary television shows, movies, and books, as if they'd like to experience fear for its physical and psychological thrill. Favorite villains include evil clowns, destructive ghosts, possessed dolls, and the ever-popular vampires. Parents put children to sleep reading fairy tales where evil beings lurk in dark forests with the intention of capturing or deceiving children like them. On the popular television show *Fear Factor*, contestants line up to have snakes, spiders, and insects poured on their bodies or are buried alive or risk drowning. Go figure.

Some of the grandparents I interviewed mentioned that hardship and fear had eroded the self-confidence they'd had as young children, while others weren't afraid of anything because they felt that age had granted them a certain confidence. Perhaps you'll be encouraged to find that your grandparent is not fearful or anxious because they have faith in the goodness of most people.

Fear is what makes courage possible, though. Acts of courage when unemployed and searching for a job, or caring for another person, often go unnoticed. I recommend asking your family member, "What has been your bravest act?" You may hear your parents or grandparents share about making difficult decisions that weren't supported by their family or culture, or about taking on new responsibilities despite risk of failure. Each culture and family celebrates overcoming fear with acts of bravery.

NOTES FROM YOUR INTERVIEW

CHAPTER 14

Questions on Memory: The Things You'll Never Forget

The topic of this chapter—special memories—builds on everything your family member has told you so far but zooms in on particularly memorable moments. This part of the interview gives your parent or grandparent space to describe memories that didn't already come up in the previous chapters.

Opening Question

- *What is the strongest memory of your childhood?*

Follow-up Questions

- *What's your earliest memory?*
- *What do you remember about holiday gatherings during your childhood?*
- *What food triggers childhood memories?*
- *Do you have a favorite or cherished memory?*

- What are some of your strongest memories from when you were a teenager?
- What are some special anniversaries in your life?
- Is there a certain song that triggers your memory about a specific time or something that happened?
- What does memory mean to you?
- Do you have a memory of what you were doing during a famous historic event (like the moon landing, for example)?
- What's your favorite family story?
- What is something your parent or grandparent told you that's stayed with you?

If you were interviewing actress Marilu Henner about her childhood, she would be able to tell you with great clarity what she was doing on any given day, what day of the week it was, and even the color and fabric of what she was wearing.[1] Henner has an autobiographical memory, the kind that's so rare that it's only found in about a hundred people around the world. Your grandparents and parents might not have a spectacular memory or be ready for the World Memory Championships, but as you've likely already discovered while asking them the questions in this book, they can talk easily about the past. While specific dates and details might be hard to remember, everyday routines can be recalled even from a vast distance in time.[2] I vividly remember summer weekends at the beach in Long Island when I was eight years old, exploring tide pools or building sandcastles with my cousins and my sister. This memory is especially precious to me because we moved away the next summer, and I lost the easy companionship of my cousins and the delighted attention of our grandmother. Luckily, my grandmother decided I should be her pen pal, and when she wrote to me, she always enclosed an envelope with a stamp and her address on it. She instilled in me a curiosity I still have about writing and what a good story is.

Culture affects how we describe our memories. As children, we learn what other people want to hear, what fits in with their memories, and what's believable to them. One grandmother told her grandson, David, a student at UT Austin, about her memory of seeing a white person for the first time when she was a girl in China. She was on an errand to buy rice for her mother, a job she'd done many times, when she saw a tall man with yellow hair, green eyes, and "ghostly skin." When she told her mother, her mother thought she'd made it up.[3]

Who is entitled to tell a certain memory also varies across communities. In the US, it's widely accepted that anyone who's participated in an event has the authority to describe what happened there, but among the Australian Aborigines of Darwin, it's not those who have suffered illness or accident who have the right to describe that experience, but the people who nurse the sick back to health.[4]

Anthropologists have always been collectors of memories (and sometimes they've tread on the rights of others to tell their stories), but it's only recently that anthropologists have thought much about the nature of memory itself, as psychologists have. For example, Canadian psychologist Endel Tulving described 256 types of memory, including flashbulb memory, which a person experiences after a particularly vivid and emotional event, especially one that dramatically changed history in a public or more personal way.[5] Some well-known flashbulb memories are the first moon landing and the fall of the Berlin Wall. People can recall with precision where they were and what they were doing when these events took place. One of the best examples of this was told to me by a grandmother describing the day Britain entered World War II:

> I remember being driven from Portsmouth to Brighton that night, sitting in the back of the car and looking at the moon. We were abandoning our house, our toys, our books, everything. In the flick of an eye, my parents got us in the car with just our immediate clothing. Yes, my biggest memory is that one of driving along in the car at night, a very vivid memory. A full moon. And thinking how strange life was.

People can remember when they were lost, or when their children or siblings were lost. I remember being in the car in Chicago, after a day at the beach on Lake Michigan, when my mother hit the brakes hard and said, "Where's Paul?" We had forgotten one brother back at the beach. It was a moment of real alarm for us, but he was playing with some other little boys in the sand when we returned. Hearing these kinds of memories is a reminder of the fragility of normal, everyday life.

It turns out that we remember quite well things that happened between the ages of ten and thirty, a concept called the reminiscence bump.[6] A lot is going on in those years, including growth, education, work, living independently, and potentially marriage and the birth of a child. What happens during those years is recorded in our memories with all the intensity of youth. One grandmother recalled this memory from when she was ten years old: "I can remember when my father would come home on leave from the Air Force, and I'd get into bed with him in the morning, and my mother would bring up eggs and bacon and fried bread, and we'd have breakfast in bed, my father and I. You know, I've never forgotten that." Research shows the reminiscence bump only affects happy memories, and for better or worse, the ability to recall sad events stays stable for most people, no matter their age.[7]

Winners of the Memory Olympics know that visual material is remembered more easily and with more detail than most other kinds of material. They take advantage of this by converting abstract symbols like numbers into visual images. Autobiographical memory is mainly encoded in the form of visual images, too. This is one reason why chapter 4 on space, centered on your parent's or grandparent's childhood home, works well to start the interview.

We tend to think of memory as a purely mental phenomenon, but memories are also externalized in material culture and stories. According to anthropologist Pierre Bourdieu, our bodies are unconscious repositories of memories, too, not only of skills such as bike riding or skating but also of cultural prescriptions, like how our bodies remember and enact what our culture tells us about how we should move and carry ourselves according to our gender.

The idea of a photographic memory has long fascinated people (especially those studying for exams) but may not really exist.[8] Nonetheless, it's clear that some people do have extraordinary memories, and I've heard more than one grandparent express surprise at how much they could remember during an interview.

A special memory can suddenly flood into the present through food. The taste or aroma of food triggers memories at an earlier age than other memory cues. And even memories of food can be triggers. Like other anthropologists doing fieldwork far from home, I was able to recall foods I missed, like coffee, all too well. In the mornings at the chief's house, there were often ten to twelve people to cook for, and only a single kerosene burner. No one else even thought about hot beverages in the steamy equatorial surroundings. To get a cup of coffee, I would sometimes walk a few miles to a Catholic school, where they made coffee for the teachers and priests. Today, with coffee close at hand, it's the scent of a ripe papaya that will instantly remind me of Pohnpei; I'm quite certain I would walk several miles for a breadfruit baked in an earth oven (if only you could buy breadfruit in Texas!). I have vivid memories of food in India, too, where my colleague and I went to interview engineers.

When I asked people for their strongest memories of childhood, one person remembered in detail her favorite pickle shop in Japan. It was a traditional cedar wood building "with kimono cloth smells everywhere" and tasty delicacies, including what looked to her twelve-year-old eyes like a cricket. "It looked awful," she told me. "I just didn't get why these could be so tasty and why they were the most expensive and sold out every day." One of her strongest memories was the day she finally decided to buy one of these locusts and try it. Another interviewee told me about V-E day (Victory in Europe Day), when her uncle was "home from the war, home from sea, and taking the wooden doors off the air raid shelter and putting them on the bonfire that we had, a street bonfire." Another person recalled the unfortunate experience of her father having to drown a sheep that had been fatally injured by another car on a road in Wales: "My father said, 'We have to kill it.' There was a pool of water nearby, so he dragged it over to the water and drowned it. And he cried all the way home. But he made himself do it."

Not all memories are possible or desirable to access. Your interviewee may decide not to talk about a part of their past, and do as my father used to, hold his hands together in his lap and look away without saying a word. Françoise Zonabend, a French anthropologist who collected memories of World War II, found that just mentioning the war was too painful for some people, even after forty years. Filmmaker Peter Jackson also described some veterans of World War I who were reluctant to talk about that period in their lives. Researchers interviewing Russian descendants of those killed in Stalin's Purge found that they didn't want to revisit those times, either. If your older relative is a veteran of the Vietnam War or Afghanistan or another conflict, they might resist saying anything about this part of their past. They might even ask, "Can we move on?" But then again, your parent or grandparent is more likely to share memories and perspectives with you than they would a stranger. Still, their silence may be related to post-traumatic stress disorder, and it's best not to press in these cases.

Your family member may want to suppress less savory aspects of the past for other reasons, because they want to shield you, or to serve as a responsible role model, or to preserve family myths. If they were part of some activity now stigmatized or disapproved of, they might be inclined to maintain silence. Some of the families I interviewed tested my reactions before starting to talk about their experiences with mental hospitals or family members who went to prison. Some families are open about telling their children and grandchildren about their difficulties, while others choose to tell only the morally exemplary stories.

NOTES FROM YOUR INTERVIEW

CHAPTER 15

What Do You Wish People Knew About You?

....

What do you wish people knew about you?" became one of my favorite questions in my research with families, as it always revealed interesting and sometimes surprising answers.

············ **Opening Question**

- *What do you wish people knew about you?*

············ **Follow-up Questions**

- *Do you have a skill, experience, or passion that most people don't know about?*

- *Were you especially good at something as a child or teenager?*

- *What qualities do you have that you're especially proud of?*

- *If people knew you better, what would they see?*

- *What do you wish the younger generations knew about you?*

- *Is there anything that you would have liked to do, but you feel like you've missed the opportunity?*

- *Is there anything you would still like to do that you haven't done?*

In response to this chapter's Opening Question, one ninety-three-year-old told me she wished people knew that she had realized late in life that it's not necessary to go it all alone: "Life as a whole is hard, especially if you have to fend for yourself. Many times, I think I was so stupid to do that, but I didn't know better." She also wanted people to know that she dreamed of inventing something to make people's lives easier. Other grandparents told me they wished the younger generations understood what they had done. The questions in this book can help them fulfill this wish, as my student Vy found when she learned that her grandmother, who grew up in Vietnam, was the only daughter among five who had learned to read and write. At a young age, she had to work long days to help support her parents and younger sisters. After the interview, Vy said, "I am able to understand my grandmother more than I ever have."[1] Other grandparents wished that young people knew that family "is a big deal" because they are the ones who help through difficult times.

What people want others to know about them takes many forms. It's probably not surprising that some grandparents and parents want the younger generation to know "how hard it was." Elder generations don't often get to mention the hard work and privation they knew well. A now-wealthy grandfather who grew up poor because his father moved from place to place looking for work wished younger people knew what it was like for him. His grim, unstable childhood made it difficult for him to connect with the day-to-day complaints of his grandchildren, who have a comfortable lifestyle and a wealth of opportunities, even as he would not wish his own experience on them. One of the students, Henry, wrote of his grandmother:

> In terms of things that she wishes my generation knew about her generation or about life in general, my grandmother wishes that we would realize that one can have fun doing lots of different things. They don't have to involve phones and computers but can simply involve people and exploring nature. She wants us to climb trees and maybe fall out of a few while we're at it to understand that failure isn't always fun, but we often gain a lot from it.[2]

Grandparents wish that their grandchildren would ask them more about their past, so the grandchildren can gain a better understanding of who they are and how they and their families were shaped. As one person told me, her family had lost everything so many times in the war through repeated bombings of their homes, so they "struggled, really struggled." And they struggled not only with finding shelter but obtaining equal rights and fighting the social stigma that came with taking in boarders to make ends meet.

Another person answered the question "What do you wish the younger generations knew about you?" with "Hmm, that

I'm way hipper, cooler, and smarter than they are." The interviewee then laughed and added,

> That I lived a life that they could never imagine, that I
> partied in nightclubs with Andy Warhol, and you know,
> went to Paris alone, and, you know, did all these cool
> amazing things that are now legendary in the '80s in
> New York, and I was like the coolest person around, and
> they just see me now and think, "Oh, there's some old
> person who's boring, who's never done anything and
> doesn't know anything," and I was way cooler than
> they'll ever be.[3]

This response expresses very well what often remains hidden as people age outwardly into the role of "older person."

Elder generations are aware of negative stereotypes that
young people have about them. One grandmother saw this as
rather unfair and wished for more open-mindedness toward
older people. She said that she knew where these attitudes
came from, that she, too, had had encounters with older people that made her question their rationality but nonetheless
she learned a lot about life from them. One grandmother
wished people knew her background in digital technology.
She was "fed up with people asking me, 'Do you have access
to a computer?'" "Yes," she always told them, "I've had access
to computers since before you were born."

Grandparents are often judged harshly for not keeping up
but wish that the younger generation would be less rushed
and have more respect and appreciation for their way of life.

They hope the younger generation won't forget them, re-membering not only their quiet retirement years but also their hope and ambition. Some grandparents wanted people to know that at the end of their lives, they'd made peace with their past and what they'd endured. The loneliness they feel now is ameliorated by thinking of their family.

Grandparents are painfully aware that they aren't the "go-to" people for advice or expertise. Yet they are experienced observers of people after a lifetime of interacting with thou-sands of individuals, and they've had a great depth and breadth of experience. One grandparent said she wished the younger generation could know how much her generation loved them. Another mentioned that she wished the younger generation knew that people can change. My student David's grandmother wished that young people would remember that "the sun comes up in the morning, and joy follows."[4]

NOTES FROM YOUR INTERVIEW

CHAPTER 16

Conclusion: How to Avoid Genealogical Amnesia

....

When I started researching what people knew about their older family members, I found out that people were missing essential clues to their lives. I was struck by what people didn't know or the secrets they found out only after their parent or grandparent had died. Often, the secrets weren't even intentional. Maybe your grandfather thought everyone knew that his mother had died when he was four years old. These were more secrets of omission than secrets buried in hearts. But if the secrets are only discovered after your parents' or grandparents' deaths, questions can emerge when it's too late to get answers. You might feel regret that you couldn't show admiration for your parent's and grand-parent's courage, or new knowledge about your elders might have given you strength for past challenges. Personal family stories have more power to move us than does statistical data about economic turbulence, divorce, inequality, or disability. But sometimes the stories remain secrets.

One student, Sloan, said of their grandfather, "I've known

him all of my life, but I didn't know half of the stories he mentioned. He is an avid storyteller at family gatherings, but when prompted with questions, he really started to remember things that were very important to him and reflected aspects of himself that he didn't realize were there."[1]

As people age to a grandparently patina, we have a hard time seeing past their physical appearance. The questions in this book are designed to help you discover their youthful spirit, which is alive and well. Though an *abundance* of youthful optimism and daring might be the younger generation's privilege at this point, asking your parent or grandparent to remember a special memory or two from when they were a child can get at some of your shared experiences of life. Given that one in nine people over the age of sixty-five experiences some form of cognitive impairment, there's no time to lose.

Your interview is an exploration of how place, time, memory, people, identity, socialization, and beliefs intersected in your parents' or grandparents' lives while they were seeking what Kenneth Burke called equipment for living.[2] Despite characterizations in the media, or perhaps because the media doesn't often talk about elderly people, you may be surprised to hear your parent or grandparent speak about the changing world with grace and hope. I've heard grandparents express support for young people, saying, "It's their time now."

I wish I could have included more of the wonderful words of people I interviewed in this book. I'll always treasure their stories and be grateful for how they shared parts of their lives with me. When you seize the opportunity to interview older family members, you'll not only learn more about their lives and who they are as people but you'll create a chain of knowledge to pass down to future generations. As my former student William wrote, "Thank you for this assignment. I have not said that very often over the course of my college career. It has been more meaningful than I could have imagined when I started. I am lucky enough to have 4 living grandparents, and this inspired me to record some of their thoughts and lives so my family can have them long after they are gone."[3]

If you're anything like me and my students, you'll be thrilled to hear more about your family in your parent's or grandparent's own words. You'll be surprised at the connection you can make across generations.

Acknowledgments

This book would not have been possible without the generosity of the exceptional people who allowed me to interview them, nor would it have been possible without my students at the University of Texas at Austin, who showed me how much could be gained by listening, if you have the right questions.

I thoroughly enjoyed talking with each person I interviewed. I heard unforgettable stories about childhoods not only in the US but also in Germany, Switzerland, the UK, Iceland, the Isle of Man, Japan, Kenya, Hong Kong, Ireland, and Norway. American rules about anonymity for research on human subjects preclude my thanking each person here, unfortunately. I hope you will each know how much you contributed to this book. I wish I could have included more of the interesting things I learned while researching this book, but readers will be intent on gathering many fascinating stories of their own.

I want to thank my anthropology colleagues around the world whose inspiring research has provided a background for the anthropologically framed questions in this book, the very questions that drew me into the study of anthropology. And very special thanks to all the colleagues at the University of Texas at Austin who have contributed in many ways, not the least of which is by creating a space for students to flourish. And to those students, my gratitude for always showing what energy, commitment, and kindness can accomplish together with excitement for learning.

While writing the book, I've had crucial support from others, too, especially from my husband, Allan, whose belief in the book has sustained me from the earliest kernel of the idea, and whose support is crucial to all things, and other members of my family who tolerated my disappearances from weekends and gatherings while I was researching and writing, especially Roy, Lesley, and Juan, whose ideas of family have been a real source of inspiration to me.

Special thanks to my wonderful editor, Joanna Ng, for expertly steering the publishing process and for her careful attention to the beauty of a well-crafted phrase. And to Tisse Takagi for her constant enthusiasm and guidance.

Notes

Chapter 1: Introduction: The Anthropology of Family

1. Pierre Bourdieu, *Outline of a Theory of Practice* (Durham: Duke University Press, 2007).

2. Cole, "Final Project Interview" (unpublished manuscript, December 1, 2020), typescript.

3. Sydney, "Fieldnotes from Interview with AL" (unpublished manuscript, December 2019), typescript.

4. Bronislaw Malinowski, *Coral Gardens and Their Magic: A Study of the Methods of Tilling the Soil and of Agricultural Rites in the Trobriand Islands* (Oxfordshire: Routledge, 2013).

5. Henry, "Final Assignment" (unpublished manuscript, May 2019), typescript.

6. A quote by Simone Schwarz-Bart, theysaidso.com, https://theysaidso.com/quote /simone-schwarz-bart-when-an-old-person-dies-a-whole-library-disappears; accessed March 4, 2021.

7. Diane Wilson, *Spirit Car: Journey to a Dakota Past* (Minnesota Historical Society, 2008), Kindle edition.

8. Thomas Charlton, *Oral History for Texans* (Texas Historical Commission, 1985). See also James Hoopes, *Oral History: An Introduction for Students* (Chapel Hill: UNC Press Books, 2014).

9. Jerome Bruner, *Actual Minds, Possible Worlds* (Cambridge: Harvard University Press, 2020).

Chapter 2: Tips on Interviewing Your Family

1. "AAUW Oral History Interview Tips," https://ww3.aauw.org/files/2014/05/ AAUW-Oral-History-Interview-Questions-and-Tips_NSA.docx; accessed October 31, 2020.

2. William, "Anthropology Final Assignment" (unpublished manuscript, May 13, 2019), typescript.

3. Willow Smith, "Loneliness in Canadian Seniors an Epidemic, Says Psychologist," *CBC Radio*, last updated September 20, 2016, https://www.cbc.ca/radio/the current/the-current-for-september-20-2016-1.3770103/loneliness-in-canadian -seniors-an-epidemic-says-psychologist-1.3770208.

4. Sam Fardghassemi and Helene Joffe, "Young Adults' Experience of Loneliness in London's Most Deprived Areas," *Frontiers in Psychology* (2021): 1750.

5. Taylor, "Final Project" (unpublished manuscript, December 2020), typescript.

6. "Great Depression History," History.com, https://www.history.com/topics/great -depression/great-depression-history; accessed October 14, 2020.

7. See Keith Basso, *Portraits of 'the Whiteman': Linguistic Play and Cultural Symbols Among the Western Apache* (Cambridge: Cambridge University Press, 1979).

8. Edward Sapir, "The Status of Linguistics as a Science," *Language* (1929): 207–14.

9. Tanya Stivers, "Stance, Alignment, and Affiliation During Storytelling: When Nodding Is a Token of Affiliation," *Research on Language and Social Interaction* 41, no. 1 (2008): 31–57.

10. Sean, "Assignment 2 CAC" (unpublished manuscript, December 2019), typescript.

11. Henry, "Culture and Communication" (unpublished manuscript, December 2019), typescript.

12. William, "Assignment 1" (unpublished manuscript, February 2019).

13. Madeline, "What Does Grandma Think?" (unpublished manuscript, December 10, 2018), typescript.

14. Carl Sagan, *Pale Blue Dot* (New York: Random House USA Inc., 1994), 6–7.

15. Alex, "Final Assignment: Semi-Structured Interview, Investigating Culture, Narrative Knowing" (unpublished manuscript, December 1 2019), typescript.

Chapter 4: Questions Space: Learning About Where Your Elders Grow Up

1. Jigyasa, "A Narrative in My Grandma's Life" (unpublished manuscript, December 9, 2019), typescript.

2. This is mentioned, too, in the book by Christopher Paul Curtis, *Bud, Not Buddy* (London: Laurel Leaf, 2004).

3. See also Sascha Cohen, "No Unescorted Ladies Will Be Served," *JStor Daily*, March 20, 2019, https://daily.jstor.org/no-unescorted-ladies-will-be-served/.

4. Julie Cruikshank, *Do Glaciers Listen?: Local Knowledge, Colonial Encounters, and Social Imagination* (Vancouver: University of British Columbia Press, 2007), 25.

Chapter 5: Questions on Time: Connecting with the History of Your Family

1. "The Popularity of 'Time' Unveiled," BBC, June 22, 2006. http://news.bbc.co.uk /2/hi/5104778.stm#:~:text=The%20word%20%22time%22%20is %20the,snapshot%20of%20our%20everyday%20language.

2. William Edward Hanley Stanner, *White Man Got No Dreaming: Essays 1938–1973* (Canberra: Australian National University Press, 1979).

3. Nancy Munn, "The Transformation of Subjects into Objects in Walbiri and Pitjantjatjara" (Perth: University of Western Australia Press, 1970).

4. Rafael E. Núñez and Eve Sweetser, "With the Future Behind Them: Convergent Evidence from Aymara Language and Gesture in the Crosslinguistic Comparison of Spatial Construals of Time," *Cognitive Science* 30, no. 3 (2006): 401–50.

5. Staffan Burenstam Linder, *The Harried Leisure Class* (New York: Columbia University Press, 1970) and Marshall Sahlins, "Hunter-gatherers: Insights from a Golden Affluent Age," *Pacific Ecologist* 18 (2009): 3–8.

6. Edward P. Thompson, "Time, Work-Discipline, and Industrial Capitalism," *Class: The Anthology* (2017): 27–40, 87, and Nancy D. Munn, "The Cultural Anthropology of Time: A Critical Essay," *Annual Review of Anthropology* 21, no. 1 (1992): 93–123.

7. E. E. Evans-Pritchard, "Nuer Time Reckoning," *Africa* 12 (1940): 189–216.

Chapter 6: Questions on Social Interactions: The Importance of Everyday Encounters

1. "40 Ways to Say 'Hello' in English and the Right Way to Respond," Lingoloop Blog, https://www.lingoloop.com/learn-english-online/40-ways-to-say-hello-in-english-and-the-right-way-to-respond/; accessed February 20, 2021.

2. Elizabeth Keating, "Technologically Mediated Sociality: Negotiating Culture, Communication, and Access," in *Linguistic and Material Intimacies of Cell Phones*, eds. Joshua A. Bell and Joel C. Kuipers (New York: Routledge, 2018), 148–66.

3. Erving Goffman, *Relations in Public: Microstudies of the Public Order* (New York: Basic Books, 1971).

Chapter 7: Questions on Becoming: Rites of Passage and How Your Elders Were Raised

1. Jacob, "Culture and Communication Assignment 2" (unpublished manuscript, December 2018), typescript.

2. Margaret Mead, *Growing Up in New Guinea* (New York: Blue Ribbon Books, 1930), 259–60.

3. Margaret Mead, *From the South Seas: Studies of Adolescence and Sex in Primitive Societies* (New York: William Morrow & Company, 1939), x. The word *primitive* is an unfortunate choice by Mead in the book title. It was a common word choice among anthropologists of the time, now criticized, see e.g., the statement by the Association of Social Anthropologists in Britain: "All anthropologists would agree that the negative use of the terms 'primitive' and 'Stone Age' to describe [tribal peoples] has serious implications for their welfare. Governments and other social groups . . . have long used these ideas as a pretext for depriving such peoples of land and other resources." https://www.antropologi.info/blog/anthropology/2007/anthropologists_condemn_the_use_of_terms.

4. Margaret Mead, *Culture and Commitment: A Study of the Generation Gap* (New York: Doubleday, 1970), 72.

5. Eleanor E. Maccoby, "Gender and Group Process: A Developmental Perspective." *Current Directions in Psychological Science* 11, no. 2 (2002): 54–58.

6. Emily Lodish, "Global Parenting Habits That Haven't Caught on in the U.S.," *NPR*, August 12, 2014, https://www.npr.org/sections/parallels/2014/08/12/339825261/global-parenting-habits-that-havent-caught-on-in-the-u-s?t=1557219836577.

7. "Sleep and Settling Help for Babies and Toddlers," raisingchildren.net.au, https://raisingchildren.net.au/babies/sleep/solving-sleep-problems/help-with-sleep-settling; accessed November 1, 2021.

8. Charles L. Briggs, *Learning How to Ask: A Sociolinguistic Appraisal of the Role of the Interview in Social Science Research*, no. 1 (Cambridge: Cambridge University Press, 1986), 69.

Chapter 8: Questions on Identity: The Factors That Made You Who You Are

1. Gabriel, "Final Project Notes and Commentary" (unpublished manuscript, December 10, 2019), typescript.

2. Nicole Spector, " 'OK boomer' Is Dividing Generations. What Does It Mean?" November 6, 2019, https://www.nbcnews.com/better/lifestyle/ok-boomer-diving-generation-what-does-it-mean-ncna1077261. Generation X are those born between the mid-1960s and the early 1980s, millennials are those born between 1981 and 1997, and baby boomers, those born between 1946 and 1964.

3. daybreakwarrior's vlog, https://www.youtube.com/watch?v=VYAd9KuScoc; accessed November 1, 2021.

4. Daniel Haun, Yvonne Rekers, and Michael Tomasello, "Children Conform to the Behavior of Peers; Other Great Apes Stick with What They Know," *Psychological Science* 25, no. 12 (2014): 2160–67.

5. Identity became a symbol of menace to those living near so-called sundown towns in the US, where there were signs that no Mexicans or Negroes were allowed after dark, https://en.wikipedia.org/wiki/Sundown_town.

6. "Race Is a Social Construct, Scientists Argue," https://www.scientificamerican.com/article/race-is-a-social-construct-scientists-argue/; accessed October 15, 2021.

7. Claire, "Assignment #2" (unpublished manuscript, December 2018), typescript.

8. Lilah, "Anthropology Assignment 2" (unpublished manuscript, December 2018), typescript.

Chapter 9: Questions on the Body and Adornment: An Expression of How You See Yourself and Others

1. Hilda Kuper, "Costume and Identity," *Comparative Studies in Society and History* 15, no. 3 (1973): 348–367.

2. Justine Cordwell, "The Art and Aesthetics of the Yoruba," *African Arts* 16, no. 2 (1983): 56–100.

3. https://www.azquotes.com/author/36635-Kate_Spade.

4. Winfried Menninghaus and Alex Skinner, "Biology à la Mode: Charles Darwin's Aesthetics of 'Ornament,'" *History and Philosophy of the Life Sciences* (2009): 263–78.

5. Joanne B. Eicher, "The Anthropology of Dress," *Dress* 27, no. 1 (2000): 59–70.

6. Janine Willis and Alexander Todorov, "First Impressions: Making Up Your Mind After a 100-Ms Exposure to a Face," *Psychological Science* 17, no. 7 (2006): 592–98.

7. Harry Winston, an American jeweler who donated the Hope Diamond to the Smithsonian Institution in 1958 after owning it for a decade.

8. Eric Schmidt, "The Tinkerer's Apprentice," *Project Syndicate*, January 19, 2015, https://www.project-syndicate.org/onpoint/google-european-commission-and -disruptive-technological-change-by-eric-schmidt-2015-01#yMSC5IlY7s HATDCO.99.

9. Jonathan Pearlman, "Fiji to Ban Public Floggings After Girls Whipped for Wearing Shorts," June 15, 2015, https://www.telegraph.co.uk/news/worldnews /australiaandthepacific/fiji/11674949/Fiji-to-ban-public-floggings-after-girls -whipped-for-wearing-shorts.html.

10. Linton Weeks, "When Wearing Shorts Was Taboo," *NPR*, April 7, 2015, https:// www.npr.org/sections/npr-history-dept/2015/04/07/397804245/when-wearing -shorts-was-taboo?t=1614689319874.

11. Mary Ellen Roach-Higgins and Joanne B. Eicher, "Dress and Identity," *Clothing and Textiles Research Journal* 10, no. 4 (1992): 1–8.

12. Oscar Moralde, "The NBA Dandy Plays the Fashion Game: *NBA All-Star All-Style* and Dress Codes of Black Masculinity," *Journal of Popular Culture* (Boston) 52, no. 1 (2019): 53–74.

13. Emily, "Assignment #2" (unpublished manuscript, December 9, 2019), typescript.

14. Mohamed Yahya Abdel Wedoud, "Women Fight Mauritania's Fattening Tradition," CNN, October 12, 2010, http://www.cnn.com/2010/WORLD/africa/10 /12/mauritania.force.feed/index.html.

15. Hilda Kuper, "Costume and identity," *Comparative Studies in Society and History* 15, no. 3 (1973): 348–67.

16. "Tattoo Takeover: Three in Ten Americans Have Tattoos, and Most Don't Stop at Just One," Harris Poll, https://theharrispoll.com/tattoos-can-take-any-number -of-forms-from-animals-to-quotes-to-cryptic-symbols-and-appear-in-all-sorts -of-spots-on-our-bodies-some-visible-in-everyday-life-others-not-so-much-but -one-thi/.

17. David L. Hanlon, *Upon a Stone Altar: A History of the Island of Pohnpei to 1890*, vol. 5 (Honolulu: University of Hawaii Press, 1988).

Chapter 10: Questions on Belief: The Ideas That Shaped You and Your Family

1. See Joel Robbins, "Continuity Thinking and the Problem of Christian Culture: Belief, Time, and the Anthropology of Christianity," *Current Anthropology* 48, no. 1 (2007): 5–38; and Henry H. Price, "Belief 'In'and Belief 'That'." *Religious Studies* 1, no. 1 (1965): 5–27.

2. See e.g., Talal Asad, "Anthropological Conceptions of Religion: Reflections on Geertz," *Man* (1983): 237–59.

3. Alberto de Mingo Kaminouchi and Agustín Fuentes, "Why We Believe: Evolution and the Human Way of Being," *Studia Moralia* 59, no. 1 (2021): 224–27; Agustín Fuentes, *Why We Believe* (New Haven: Yale University Press, 2019).

4. Philip Converse, "The Nature of Belief Systems in Mass Publics," *Critical Review* 18, nos. 1–3 (1964).

5. E.E. Evans-Pritchard, *Witchcraft, Oracles and Magic Among the Azande*, vol. 12 (Oxford: Clarendon Press, 1937), 73; E.E. Evans-Pritchard, "Sorcery and Native Opinion." *Africa* 4, no. 1 (1931): 22–55, 30.

6. Emmanuel Levinas, "Lévy-Bruhl and Contemporary Philosophy," *Entre Nous: On Thinking-of-the-Other* (New York: Columbia University Press, 1998), 39–51.

7. Elizabeth Keating and Sirkka Jarvenpaa, *Words Matter: Communicating Effectively in the New Global Office* (Oakland: University of California Press, 2016).

Chapter 11: Questions on Kinship and Marriage: The Making of a Family

1. Robin Fox, *Kinship and Marriage* (New York: Penguin Books, 1967), 10.

2. In Hawaiian, though, whether the speaker is a male or female affects which kinship term is used. A female uses *kaikunāne* or *kunāne* for brother or male cousin, while a male calls his brother or male cousin *kaikua'ana* or *kua'ana*.

3. "Rifca Stanescu Became World's Youngest Grandmother at Age 23," *Huffington Post*, https://www.huffpost.com/entry/rifca-stanescu-became-wor_n_833108, updated May 25, 2011; "Oldest First-time Grandmother," Guinness World Records, 2008. https://www.guinnessworldrecords.com/world-records/oldest-first-time-grandmother.

4. Claude Lévi-Strauss, *The Elementary Structures of Kinship* (Boston: Beacon Press, 1969).

5. David M. Schneider, "Yap Kinship Terminology and Kin Groups," *American Anthropologist* 55, no. 2 (1953): 215–36.

6. Eti Dayan, *One of Them: My Life Among the Maasai of Kenya* (ebook Pro, 2020).

7. This is how kinship groups of some Native American societies have been described.

8. Kath Weston, *Families We Choose: Lesbians, Gays, Kinship* (New York: Columbia University Press, 1997).

9. Justin E. H. Smith, "Seriously, What About Cousin Marriage?", *3quarksdaily*. "The eminent kinship scholar Robin Fox [Rutgers University] estimates that fully 80% of marriages in human history have been between either first or second cousins." July 19, 2010, https://3quarksdaily.com/3quarksdaily/2010/07/seriously-what-about-cousin-marriage.html. Richard Coniff, "Go Ahead, Kiss Your Cousin: Heck, Marry Her If You Want To," *Discover Magazine*, August 1, 2003, https://www.discovermagazine.com/health/go-ahead-kiss-your-cousin.

10. Lila Abu-Lughod, *Veiled Sentiments* (Oakland: University of California Press, 2016).

11. Sarah Baird, "Looking for Pie in All the Wrong Places," *Modern Farmer*, November 21, 2014, https://modernfarmer.com/2014/11/pie-supper-culture/.

Chapter 12: Questions on Material Culture: Your Family's Most Treasured Possessions

1. David Wilson, *The Vikings in the Isle of Man* (Aarhus Municipality, Denmark: Aarhus Universitetsforlag, 2008).

2. James Deetz, *In Small Things Forgotten: An Archaeology of Early American Life* (New York: Anchor, 2010).

3. Jeff Desjardins, "The History of Consumer Credit in One Giant Infographic," *Visual Capitalist*, August 29, 2017, https://www.visualcapitalist.com/history -consumer-credit-one-infographic/.

4. Pierre Lemonnier, "The Study of Material Culture Today: Toward an Anthropology of Technical Systems," *Journal of Anthropological Archaeology* 5, no. 2 (1986): 147–86.

5. Marcel Mauss, *The Gift: The Form and Reason for Exchange in Archaic Societies* (London and New York: Routledge, 2002), 4.

6. Dorothy O. Johansen and Charles Marvin Gates, *Empire of the Columbia: A History of the Pacific Northwest* (New York: Harper & Row, 1967), 7–8.

7. See also Matthew Engelke, *How to Think like an Anthropologist* (Princeton: Princeton University Press, 2018).

8. "Road Traffic Injuries," World Health Organization, June 21, 2021, https://www .who.int/news-room/fact-sheets/detail/road-traffic-injuries.

Chapter 13: Questions on Fear: Learning Courage Through Fear

1. Peter Moore, "Argh! Snakes! Americas Top Phobias Revealed," YouGovAmerica, https:// today.yougov.com/ topics/ lifestyle/articles-reports/2014/03/27 /argh-snakes.

2. Rebecca Makkai, *The Great Believers* (New York: Penguin Books, 2019).

Chapter 14: Questions on Memory: The Things You'll Never Forget

1. "Marilu Henner's Exceptional Memory Spurs Interest in Brain Health," *Brain and Life Magazine*, "Celebrity Profiles,", February/March 2019, https://www.brain-andlife.org/articles/actress-marilu-henner-has-a-highly-superior -autobiographical-memory-a/.

2. Paul R. Thompson, *The Edwardians* (New York: Routledge, 2002).

3. David, "Assignment 2" (unpublished manuscript, December 2018), typescript.

4. Basil Sansom, "The Sick Who Do Not Speak," in *Semantic Anthropology*, ed. David Parkin (New York: Academic Press, 1982): 183–95.

5. Endel Tulving, "Are There 256 Different Kinds of Memory?" in *The Foundations of Remembering: Essays in Honor of Henry L. Roediger, III*, ed. James S. Nairne (New York: Psychology Press, 2007): 39–52.

6. Jonathan Koppel and David Rubin, "Recent Advances in Understanding the Reminiscence Bump: The Importance of Cues in Guiding Recall from Autobiographical Memory," *Current Directions in Psychological Science* 25, no. 2 (2016): 135–40.

7. Ashok Jansari and Alan Parkin, "Things That Go Bump in Your Life: Explaining the Reminiscence Bump in Autobiographical Memory," *Psychology and Aging* 11, no. 1 (1996): 85–91.

8. "Does Photographic Memory Exist?" *Scientific American*, January 1, 2013, https://www.scientificamerican.com/article/i-developed-what-appears-to-be-a-ph/.

Chapter 15: What Do You Wish People Knew About You?

1. Vy, "Semi-Structured Interview, Investigating Culture" (unpublished manuscript, December 2018), typescript.

2. Henry, "Final Assignment" (unpublished manuscript, May 2019), typescript.

3. Thanks to the student who gave permission to share this (and wishes to be anonymous).

4. David, "The Story of the Granddaughter of a Polish Migrant" (unpublished manuscript, December 10, 2018), typescript.

Chapter 16: Conclusion: How to Avoid Genealogical Amnesia

1. Sloan, "Interview with a Member of the Greatest Generation" (unpublished manuscript, December 10, 2018), typescript.

2. Roger C. Aden, *Childhood Memory Spaces: How Enduring Memories of Childhood Places Shape Our Lives* (New York: Peter Lang Incorporated, International Academic Publishers, 2018).

3. William, personal communication to author, April 2019.

About the Author

Elizabeth Keating, PhD, is a professor of anthropology at the University of Texas at Austin. A linguistic anthropologist who studies culture and communication, she has been a Fulbright Scholar in Ireland and a visiting scholar at the Freiburg Institute for Advanced Studies in Germany and the Max Planck Institute for Psycholinguistics in the Netherlands.